THE
TERMS OF
RELEASE

BA Tortuga

Dreamspinner Press

Published by
Dreamspinner Press
5032 Capital Circle SW
Suite 2, PMB# 279
Tallahassee, FL 32305-7886
USA
http://www.dreamspinnerpress.com/

The Terms of Release
© 2014 BA Tortuga.

Cover Art
© 2014 Leah Kaye Suttle.
www.leahsuttle.com
Cover content is for illustrative purposes only and any person depicted on the cover is a model.

ISBN: 978-1-62798-613-7
Digital ISBN: 978-1-62798-614-4

Printed in the United States of America
First Edition
March 2014

To my J, who gave me a home.

Chapter One

"SON, I need to talk to you."

Sage sighed but kept it soft enough that no one could possibly hear. Momma didn't call often—once a week—and she talked to him for exactly fifteen minutes. Hell, he wasn't sure if the calls were habit for him or for her, but it was what it was, and it kept the costs on his pay-as-you-go phone low. If she called on a Saturday morning, when she knew he'd been working on the docks all night, it had to be important.

"Sure, Momma. What you need?"

He leaned back on his bed, looking out the little window. His eyes followed the hairline crack that climbed through the glass. Some days he thought maybe that weird, crookedy little line wanted to be a word or something. A picture. Not today. Today it was only a place for a tiny spider to climb. God, he was tired. The trucks had been filled with hundreds of small heavy boxes, and his muscles were screaming for rest. Not sleep, not yet. That wouldn't come 'til eleven or so. It wasn't like he came home and crashed once his feet found their way back through the mess in the streets and the little pockets of nighttime assholes on the corners, waiting for the bolder daytime assholes to spell them. This was his primetime, after all. He had a cup of coffee and a Louis L'Amour book he hadn't read, which he'd found in a dumpster on his way to work a couple of days ago. It was all good.

"Are you listening to me, Sage Marlowe Redding?"

"What? Sorry, Momma. I must've dozed some. Long night. Say again?"

"I need you to come home."

He sat up and frowned, his heart doing that sickening little hiccup and roll that meant something shitty was going down. "What happened?"

"Well, nothing that you'd think was an emergency, really. Your daddy, though, his hands…. He can't work the horses as much."

Sage closed his eyes. Fucking Parkinson's. Daddy'd been fighting it for damn near eight years, but it was a losing battle. "Momma, I…."

"Son, that Teddy Dale, he's going to take the land. You know he will. He's waiting. I need you to cowboy up and come on. Now."

"Teddy Dale's the reason I ain't come home, Momma. That man hates the sound of my name." Not that Sage blamed the crusty old bastard. Angelo, the man's only son and the apple of his momma's eye, had died in Sage's company ten years ago. Leastways that was the story and what was taken as God's honest truth.

Ten years, ten months, fifteen days and… fourteen and a half hours ago.

"Well, we need to be able to train these horses. Your daddy has a contract. If he can fill it on time, we can pay for six months of bills. Sister's took pregnant on me, Son. Her and that ass hat she's married to caught like a pair of hounds."

"I don't even have a car, Momma, and I sure don't have the cash to bus it right now. I get paid in two weeks." A baby? Rosie? Christ, when had he gotten old? He looked at the calendar. "I can get on a Greyhound then, if I clear it with my parole officer."

They had rules for men like him, and he followed them because he wasn't going back in.

He couldn't.

"I can wire you the money." She sighed, lowering her voice. "It would kill your daddy to lose this place."

"I know. I'll come. I have to make arrangements, Momma. You know that."

"I know that you paid your debt to society already, baby, for something that shouldn't have all been on your shoulders."

"I paid my stupid tax, for sure." He smiled a little. "Let me see what my parole officer says, and I'll call."

"Okay. They… they'll let you come home, right?"

"I'll have to go in front of a judge. You know that." It sucked, but it was what it was.

"I know, Son. Maybe you'll get Judge Shannon. He's not in anyone's pocket, leastways in my memory."

"Maybe. You'll need to send me doctor's information so I can start everything."

"I can send it overnight unless you have one of those Kinko's places. I can fax there."

"I'll have to call you, Momma. I don't know. There should be a phone book down in the management office."

"Okay. I-I'm sorry, Son." He could hear the tears, right there in her throat. He hated for his momma to cry.

"Shit, what for? You didn't make me a fuck-up, you didn't make Daddy sick, and you didn't make Rosemary decide to have children that her crazy fuck of a husband can't feed. Seems to me like we should be apologizing to you."

She sniffled, but the chuckle was just as strong now.

"I'll call you with the Kinko's number. Later. I got to work all weekend, but I'll get in to see Jack on Monday." If he could.

"Thanks, baby. I'm sorry. I know it's borrowing more trouble for you, but I need your help."

"I got your back, Momma. I won't let you down." The *again* was there, unsaid and implied.

"I love you, Son."

"I love you, Momma. Talk to you later on." He hung up and sat there, his head pounding, feeling swole as a rotting melon. Much as he hated California, he hated the thought of begging some Texas judge to let him come home even more.

God, what a mess.

"Damn you, Angel. You and me, we fucked everything up, and you had to up and die and get out of everything."

Angel never answered back, which was good, since the man was dead. Would make it awkward if he hung around.

Sage chuckled, rubbed his forehead, and set his alarm. He'd get a couple of hours of sleep, then get to work.

He had a feeling he was fixin' to have a lot to do.

CHAPTER TWO

SAGE GOT off the bus, as tired as he'd ever been. The scent of red dirt and mold and cow shit hit him, at once horrifying and comforting as all get-out.

He'd gone before the judge in L.A. He'd said his piece about Daddy and the ranch, and Momma and Cousin Rich had stood for him too. He'd laid out his life for all those folks to study and sneer at, and his head felt stuffed with cotton wool. He just wanted to rest his body a minute.

A sheriff's vehicle was there, with Sheriff Jim Dale staring at him. Sage ignored it. He wasn't looking to find trouble, wasn't looking to get into trouble. He was not in the trouble business. He was here to work and make sure Daddy kept the ranch. That was it, damn it.

His momma pulled up, and the familiar rumble of her old truck sunk deep inside him.

She parked between him and the sheriff, and he put his duffel in the back before climbing in. "Momma."

"Son. Welcome home."

Sage's gaze cut across the parking lot to where Jim glared. Dead Angel Dale's favorite uncle lifted his hand and pointed his index finger at Sage, thumb raised like a pistol. *Right. Welcome home.*

"Thank you, Momma."

Momma glared at Jim, then leaned over to kiss Sage's cheek. "You don't let him get to you."

"I don't want any trouble. I'll lie low, like I promised."

He wasn't going to cause anyone any stress. No way. He would work and he would sleep.

"I think he ought to be the one who has to."

Sage shrugged. "Don't you worry on it, Momma. I'll take care of sh—things."

"Good. You're a good boy." She started up the truck and got them moving. "I made a pork loin."

"Rosie and her man coming over?" Rosie's husband Greg hated Sage with a fiery burning passion.

Momma ducked her head. "Not tonight. Rosie said she'd come soon and to tell you she loves you. You know how that little fuck she's married to is. He invented some bullshit reason not to show."

"It's no big thing." He reached over and patted her hand. "I know, huh? It sucks to have the shitty son."

"You hush. You're my son, no matter what you did or didn't do, and I love you." His momma, she could be fierce.

"Yes, ma'am." His heart didn't want to look at things as she drove off, see how much had changed and how much hadn't. His eyes, though, they were curious and determined to look at everything. McCallum's pharmacy was still there, and the Ridgeway Cinema was too, even though it was a dollar theater now, showing shit that was on TV for those who could get satellite. The roller rink was a Dollar General now, and they'd thrown up one of the Mexican convenience stores, and somewhere that looked like it'd been a movie store, about five years ago. Thank God the Dairy Queen was still the same. "They still let you smoke in there?"

"They do. The city made a fuss, but the place sits five yards outside the limits." Glaring some, she looked over at him. "You ain't smokin', are you?"

"No, ma'am. I quit." Not because he wanted to, but because he couldn't afford it. He couldn't afford any vices these days, so he was a fucking paragon of clean living.

"Well, good on you." She sighed and looked back in the rearview at the near empty street, her hands relaxing on the steering wheel, and Sage got it. No one was following them, thank God.

The farther they got out of town, the less change Sage saw. The Shields' house still stood in the center of the gnarliest grove of pecan trees on earth, the Pecinas still hung out their shingle for leatherwork, and the world's biggest pothole was still there—Momma not even noticing as she drove around it.

"Still haven't fixed that, huh?"

"Nope. I don't reckon they ever will, Son. Ain't but four families on this road and ain't none of us that have a pot to piss in or a window to throw it out of. County don't care about old folks."

"You're not old, Momma." Although he knew she had to be as ancient as his body felt these days.

"I ain't young." She laughed, but it was strained.

"I'll make it right, Momma. I won't let you down." Once more, Sage didn't say the *again*. He didn't have to. They both knew it was there.

"I know you'll do fine." She turned off onto their road and bumped down the dirt track.

He needed to grade the drive after he got finished riding fence. The gate looked solid enough, and the cattle guards were still whole, rattling under the tires as the big dually trundled over them.

The house looked so familiar it made his belly ache, and when the truck stopped, he felt frozen.

"This is your home, Sage Redding. Your place. Nothing will change that." Momma sounded like she was fixin' to lose her shit, and he couldn't deal with it. "We put a single-wide back behind the barns, so you have your own spot."

"Y'all didn't have to...."

"You hush. A grown man needs something not his childhood bedroom. It's real nice. Your daddy traded for it—that old tractor that no one was gonna use no more."

He leaned over and kissed her cheek. "Thank you. Is Daddy out to the barn or in the house?"

"Should be in the barn. Supper in half an hour."

"Yes, ma'am." He'd take his duffel to the trailer afterward. First, he'd get to work. "I'll help him out, and we'll be in to eat."

"I'll see you then." She gave him a ghost of a smile and headed for the house, leaving him on his own.

Sage hopped down and walked to the barn, whistling loud enough that the critters and Daddy could hear him and not be surprised. He looked out over the pasture as he went; the grass was browning, proving it was just on the other end of vicious Texas summer. Late

September could be deadly—hot and humid, with air that felt like syrup in your lungs.

Daddy was singing, the words stuttering a bit but sounding loud and clear. Sage joined in, singing old Bob Wills songs like he had just come home from the store a half hour ago, not damn near eleven years ago.

Daddy's head whipped up, but Sage saw no censure, no disappointment, nothing there but a huge grin, and they rolled into the big finish together, yodeling like fools.

The horses tossed their heads and snorted like they were singing right along. Silly things.

Daddy came and pounded on Sage's back when they were done. "Son!"

"I'm home." For what it was worth, he was home.

"You are, and it's about damned time."

"Yes, sir." It was. "Momma says supper's in thirty. What you need me to do?"

"I need that bale moved, and I've got about a thousand little things."

"I'll get on it." He set to working, the motions and rhythm of this so deep in his bones that no time could rust it. Out of the corner of his eyes, he watched his father, those gnarled hands shaking now, the tremors obvious. God was a mean, vicious scorekeeper, and Sage thought He cheated more often than not.

They finished up the work in time for supper and made for the house, the wind picking up.

"Sounds like it's fixin' to storm."

Daddy nodded. "You ain't got one of them fancy-assed phones to tell you what the weather's going to do?"

"No, sir." He couldn't afford one, and he didn't have no credit. He had a pay as you go from the Walmart.

"Good." Daddy spit into the dry ground. "Rosie's asshole husband has one attached to his fucking palm. Worthless piece of shit."

Sage shrugged. His knees told him when it was going to be really bad. That was his one truly painful souvenir from prison. At least he'd been given a choice—teeth or knees. He'd reckoned no one could do worse than what a horse could, and he'd been right. He could cowboy up.

His teeth had cost his momma and daddy too much money to let someone knock them clean out....

Momma opened the front door, and he forced himself to simply walk in and pretend like he belonged. Christ on a crutch, not a goddamn thing had changed, at least at first glance. The floors were still wood, and the walls in the mudroom still frog green. Pairs of rubber boots still sat in the old wood milk crate that Momma had bought at the First Baptist Christmas Yard Sale and Craft Show when he was eight.

Somehow it smelled the same too—like salt pork and beans, cornbread and chili.

As they walked in, he noticed the little things that were different—there were pictures of cousins' babies where his and Rosie's school pictures used to be, and the console TV cabinet had a little flat screen on it.

It made him breathe, finally, and made him smile. Time did march on.

"Come in and sit. You want milk or tea, Son?" Momma had already given Daddy his water and milk, and she had a cup of coffee by her plate.

"Tea, please." It occurred to him, a little distantly, that he'd never sat at this table and had a beer. Not once, and he was fairly sure he never would.

"Here you go." She handed him a glass, and he wanted to scream all of a sudden, wanted to break up the normalcy of the little scene.

He sat instead.

Daddy prayed and they ate, the food good, familiar, filling. He was going to crack like a dropped pie plate, right down the middle.

When the meal was finally over, he hauled his bones up, refusing the offer to sit and watch the evening news. His soul felt brittle, and he didn't think he could bear it a bit, Momma crocheting and Daddy napping through one pointless show after another.

"Here's the keys to the trailer, Son. There's plumbing, gas, lights. I set it up for you."

"Thank you, Momma. Daddy." He took the keys and the wrapped-up plate of leftovers. "I'll see y'all first thing."

"We'll be here." Momma smiled for him and Daddy nodded, though that could have been the Parkinson's.

Sage walked out to the truck and grabbed his duffel, thankful the storm hadn't found them yet. He carried the bag to the trailer, standing and staring at it for a long time. Damn. It was plumb nice, really, even had a wee baby porch on it.

He didn't see the pit bull sitting there, not until he climbed the stair. Little and blue, the whipcord tail set to wagging, *thump, thump,* and he frowned. "Copper?"

It couldn't be. She'd been an old dog when he'd gone to California. She had to be long buried. Still, the pup was her spitting image and had a collar on her with a tag. He put the bag down and the plate on the porch rail, then bent down. "Who the hell are you, pup?"

Her tag said "Penny," and he couldn't help but grin. Momma did have a wicked sense of humor.

She licked his face, tail just thumping. Lord, lord. Looked like he'd have some company.

"Come on in, then, but you'd best not piss on my floor." He liked a clean house. He'd never live in filth. Never again.

She trotted in next to him, and she didn't jump on nothin', just settled on a dog bed in the corner of the little front room.

The place was spotless and simple, with a TV, a little DVD player, and a sofa. The kitchen had the basics, and Sage knew if he looked, the pantry would have Corn Flakes, cans of Wolf Brand Chili, and quick grits.

Hell, there was even a mason jar filled with green apple Jolly Ranchers.

Oh sweet Jesus. He was home.

His knees buckled, and if that sweet pup came and licked tears off his cheeks, well shit, there wasn't a living soul to tell on him.

For the first time in ten years, no one was watching.

CHAPTER THREE

ADAM DALE Winchester, aka Win, walked into the sheriff's department and checked the board to see where everyone was. The sheriff was in his office, which was good, because Win thought they needed to talk.

"Hey. Where were you last night?" he asked his uncle when he stepped in and closed the door. "I thought you were on call."

"How is this your business, boy?" Jim snarled, not even looking up.

"Because I got called in for a traffic collision when I was off duty, that's why." People thought he'd gotten his job because Jim Dale was his uncle. Shit, it had all been in spite of that. The man was a petty tyrant.

"You could have called Barb."

Right, because Barb as a single mom with one disabled boy and one under four needed to do a 10:00 p.m. call. *Ass hat.*

"Or, you could have been on call. What the hell was so fucking important that you just disappeared?"

"Watch your fucking mouth, or I'll beat you to within an inch of your life."

Win sneered. "You'll try." He hadn't spent all that time in the Army for nothing. Neither of his uncles could even think about raising a hand to him these days like they had after his daddy died.

"Look, I was following a lead, huh? We got a murderer just moved into town. I was making sure the guy didn't cause no issues."

Win raised a brow. "A murderer?"

Jim nodded. "That fucker that killed your cousin Angel. You know, your Uncle Teddy's boy."

Sarcastic asshole. No. No, he didn't remember Angel.

Oh. Oh man. Talk about a cluster fuck. Win shook his head, wondering what he'd missed about the Redding family. What emergency had brought Sage Redding home? "You really think the man needed to be watched?"

"He killed five people."

Win rolled his eyes. "He got manslaughter for being the one not killed when the meth lab went up, and you know it." He'd read the reports when he'd gotten home from overseas, trying to help his family make sense of it all. The way he saw it, Sage had gotten a raw deal, but that was a fairly unpopular opinion. Hell, Win barely remembered the guy from school.

"He's a fucking fag, a drug addict, and he corrupted your cousin, and you'd do well to remember that. The neighbors on either side of that ranch have kids."

"Corrupted Angel?" He clamped his mouth shut. It did no good to talk ill of the dead, and it would only make it worse for Sage Redding if Win kept on defending him. "Well, I hope this ain't gonna be so much of a pet project that you forget where you work."

"I'll make sure he knows we're watching. He'll screw up. They always do."

In general, Jim was right. Lifelong criminals messed up over and over. He hoped for Sage's momma's sake that this man honestly had been in the wrong place at the wrong time. "You know the law, though. You can't harass him."

Somehow, saying that felt important.

"Uh-huh. Don't you have work to do?"

Jesus, he wanted to beat the living fuck out of the man. He sighed, handing over a sheaf of papers. "Here's last night's report. I'll take off at three today. Comp time."

"That works. You need to remember to go out to the school, give the prehomecoming text and drive lecture."

"Lord." He grinned a little, though. He didn't mind that at all. Kids were, as a rule, decent little shits and way more ready to listen than adults.

He waved, heading back out to the bullpen, wanting to get on with his day.

Grace was at the front desk, her coffee cup steaming. Win kissed her cheek, laughing. "Hey, lady. You ready for a crazy day?"

"Am I ever?" She winked at him. "I have news. My Leanne caught pregnant. I'm gonna be a granny."

"You know it's not me, right?" He ducked when she swatted at him. "Seriously, that's great news, honey."

"It is. They've been trying so long, you know?"

"I know." He gave her a hug, making a mental note to get her something for her daughter.

Grace squeezed him. "How's the bear this morning?"

"Prickly. I pissed him off already."

"Go you. Shit, Win, you've been in here for, what? Eighteen seconds?"

"Maybe twenty-five." He grinned some more, feeling better already.

"Oh, honey. You're off your game." Look at that evil smile.

"You think?" He grabbed the dailies and rifled through to see if he had any routine calls to make.

Everything had been quiet, which was par for the course. They'd have issues come Friday night, between the Rail and Buddy's, depending on who started shit—cowboys or bikers. Today, it looked like the biggest thing was a warning not to let Sage Redding breathe hard on anyone.

"Lord, he has a hard-on for this guy."

"Yeah. Redding's daddy's sick and...." Grace stopped, lips pursing. "Damn shame, that."

"Yeah." Well, at least Grace agreed with him.

Grace didn't say another word about it, which meant she had more to say and wasn't about to say it in front of the sheriff. He'd have to take her out for coffee. The woman loved a diner.

Win did too. He never turned down pie.

"I'll be at the high school this afternoon. One 'til two thirty. Tell all the bad guys no emergencies."

Grace nodded. "Will do, Win."

He headed to his desk. E-mails. Then coffee. Then he could get the hell out of the office and pretend to do something.

He had a good bit of time to kill, after all. That was the best thing about being the law in a small town.

The ancient computer that wheezed and groaned, he liked that less. He crossed his fingers and sat, hoping it would boot up.

"You should get you one of them tablet deals. All the youngsters have them now."

"Shit, lady. I still haven't figured out my new phone."

"Well, you'd best get with it," Grace said. "The newest version just came out."

"Newest version of what?"

"That phone. You'll be replacing it in no time." She waved at him and went to get more coffee.

Right. His phone did more than was reasonable, and really, he just wanted to make phone calls. Though he had to admit, texting could be nice.

His phone went off about then, and he sighed at the notification he was being called out for a breaking and entering. He wasn't going to have that slow morning.

Damn it.

"I'll be back. Someone's busted into Dick Walker's tool shed again."

"Lord. Don't let him shoot you."

"I'll do my best, honey. See you this afternoon."

"Later." Grace waved, and he headed out, glad he'd just missed Jim, who was coming into the bullpen looking like a thundercloud. Whatever bee Jim had in his bonnet, Win didn't want any part of it.

He'd have to keep an eye on what Jim was up to with Sage Redding, though. Man didn't deserve any more shit.

Whatever happened years ago, the evidence didn't show that anyone was a cold-blooded murderer—more like a stupid shit who got lucky and didn't burn to death. All eighteen year olds were stupid. Look at Win. He'd joined the Army....

Shitty as it was, it was better than the pen.

The food might be worse.

He was grinning as he headed out, hat brim down to shade against the brutal late-September sun. Time to go see who had violated Dick's stuff.

CHAPTER FOUR

SAGE FINISHED hammering shingles onto the barn roof, the sun beating down on him, the heat like a living thing. Lord have mercy, it was like breathing in a swimming pool out here.

He shook his head and sighed, shooing the gnats and moving his bundle of shingles and tar paper to the edge of the barn. "Daddy? You down there? I'm fixin' to drop the shingles."

"Yep. I'm out of the way, Son."

"Good deal." The bundle went down, and then he gathered the tools and nails and shimmied down the ladder, his knees screaming.

"All patched up. Looks good up there." Better than he'd feared, honestly.

"Good deal. Come on and have a sandwich."

"Pimento cheese or ham?" Momma only made two kinds.

"Ham. Though she makes me turkey now. Says it's better for my cholesterol."

"Ah. Well…." What was he supposed to say about that, exactly?

"Yep. Now you're here, I might get me a pimento cheese."

"I bet you do." They shared a conspiratorial little grin. Momma did love feeding people. All he'd have to do was ask once, and Momma would make a shit-ton of pimento cheese.

"Tell her to ease off on the pepper this time, Son? Last time my tongue damn near burned off."

"Well, if it's been that long since you had it." He winked, unwrapping his sandwich and his chips.

"I think she's bored. Not enough people to cook for. She applied for a job at the diner. Your momma, working in that place." Daddy spit on the ground. "I won't have it. I'll provide for her."

"You will. She'll see." He'd get profit back into this place if it killed him.

"She will." Daddy nodded and leaned back against the barn, his hands shaking.

Sage bit back the instinctive "are you all right" that wanted to come out. Daddy didn't need him pointing things out. Getting old sucked, and Parkinson's sucked harder. It was what it was.

The crunch of boots on the track made them both look up, but it was only Momma, smiling, carrying a little covered dish. "I decided you two needed cobbler."

"Apple?" he asked.

"Peach?" That was Daddy.

"Blackberry. June brought me a huge load."

June was Momma's best friend—a weird, hippy-dippy old woman with about a dozen cats, a huge garden, and an art studio where she sold scary dolls to witchy people in Austin and Houston.

Sage had always been a little in awe of June, but she was good to his Momma.

"Did you give her all that wood I picked up for her?"

Momma shook her head. "No, sir. She looked like she'd been beat. The MS crawls all up in her. I thought Sage could drop it off on his way to the feedstore."

He fought the immediate urge to say no. He didn't want to leave the ranch, not yet. He bit back the no. He needed to cowboy up. They needed him strong.

"Sure, Momma. Whatever you need."

"Tomorrow. Today, you're Daddy's. I'm cooking chicken and dumplings for supper."

"That sounds good, honey," Daddy said, smiling.

Momma beamed, then headed off, all the dogs following her—pit bulls and hounds, collies and mutts wagging like she was magic.

"Lord have mercy. Look at that."

Daddy hooted. "Them beasts love her."

"They do." He chuckled. "She's the crazy dog lady."

"That's it. Woman will send us all to the poor house, feeding them." Daddy watched her walk, all the way back to the house. "Did she threaten you to make you come back here?"

"No." No, and his reasons were his own. He hoped Daddy took the flat response for what it was.

"Good. Let's get the stalls cleaned up. I want to introduce you to all the new girls."

Sage asked the question he didn't want to. "Did you sell Sugarbaby?"

He hadn't seen hide nor hair of the mare. Daddy'd given her to Sage for his fourteenth birthday, and she'd just been getting to her prime when he'd gone.

"Nope. She's out in the pasture with the rest of 'em. She dropped her fourth foal this spring. I hadn't worked her for a while."

"She still bite before she decides to be nice?" He was glad she was still there. He'd missed that silly horse.

"Yep. She throws a pretty foal, though."

"She's a good girl." They ate, working through the cobbler and a couple-three Cokes. He patted his belly. Damn. He was going to gain fifty pounds in a month.

"I know, but you'll work it off. Come on." Daddy gave his hand a pointed look before he grabbed a pitchfork. "Let's get on it."

"Yes, sir." Sage started gathering up shingles and nails, knowing he had to get it all up or the animals would end up with injuries.

"Maybe this afternoon we'll take the four wheelers down and look at the horses."

He grinned, looking forward to that. "I'd like that a lot."

Daddy nodded, and that was that. "Then we'd best get to work."

He could breathe, really breathe, and the hot, humid air tasted damn good in his throat. Sage got back to work, his muscles aching because he was doing real labor instead of slinging weights in the exercise yard or chunking boxes. Good work.

Something in him still waited for the bells to ring, for the sounds of steel doors clanging together. For the random acts of violence. He still spent most of his time waiting to duck. His shoulders spent most of their time up around his damned ears.

Still, worried and out here with the horses was better than in. Any day. The dark place inside him might only be about 10 percent filled with sunlight and home, but that was better than it had been.

Whatever he got, Sage thought he'd better take it. A man never knew when his life was gonna change.

CHAPTER FIVE

"CHRIST, I need a day off." Win's neck felt like someone had frozen it with that liquid nitrogen stuff. The whole fucking county had lost their minds in the last few days, and if it wasn't for the dog food he needed to pick up for Mrs. Simpson and that old mean basset mix she'd rescued, he'd be home letting his new showerhead work out the kinks.

"Me too." Grace winked. "Don't forget you need dog food for Lucy Simpson, and lightbulbs."

"Lightbulbs. Right." He'd stop by the feedstore. They had a little section of hardware.

"You're not on the schedule tomorrow. I'd keep your phone off, if I was you."

"Thanks, lady." He could so do that. Or at least he could pretend to keep it off unless Grace or one of the other ladies sent a real distress signal.

He wandered out to his truck, whistling tunelessly, sighing at the weather. Fucking September. Fucking heat.

Everyone all over the country was going on about fall. Not in Texas. No, it was hot as the hinges of Hell.

He slipped into his truck and turned on the AC and the radio in damn near the same motion. The cab was so hot his skin prickled up with goose bumps, a cold sweat breaking out on his upper lip.

Okay. Okay, what the fuck had he been heading out to do? Feedstore. Dog food. They were expensive beasts, neighbors.

He pulled out onto the frontage road, whistling along to Alan Jackson, wishing he'd brought a bottle of water from the station fridge. At least when he looked in the rearview, his lips were coming back from that blue tone they'd taken on. Thank heavens for air conditioning.

He pulled into the feedstore lot and parked beside Carrie Walter's little pink pickup. Lord, that woman's husband was something else. She was a harpy when she drank, but she was hilarious on coffee and doughnuts.

The place was busy but weirdly quiet, with a little group up by the counter all huddled and whispering.

He had to fight the urge to sneak up on them and yell, "Boo!"

"Win. Evening." Johnny Barnette nodded to him. "How you doing?"

"Just fine. How are y'all?"

Carrie looked at him and whispered, "Is that Sage Redding in the back? The one that murdered Angel? Why's he back in town?"

Win glanced around, wondering why everyone was talking about that now. "Well now, Miss Carrie, I do hear Sage Redding is back. I would be careful calling him a murderer, though."

"It's what he is. A goddamn convict." Bill Waters spit on the floor. "Why didn't they keep him in California?"

God, there were times small towns were vicious. "I need some dog food, Johnny."

"Surely. You picking up the Simpson bag?"

"Yep. There was something else." Damn it, something hardware? Shit.

A little pocket cowboy came up to the counter, a bottle of Vetericyn wound spray, a currycomb, and a dog collar in his hand. Win gave the man a sideways once-over, and the guy looked familiar, but not so much that Win could say hi.

Everyone stared at the man, no one saying a word. Finally, he sighed softly and placed the items on the counter. "I need two hundred pounds of sweet feed, fifty pounds of whatever dog food Ellen Redding uses, please, along with these things."

"How you gonna pay for it, son?" Johnny's lip actually curled.

"My daddy, Sam Redding, called you earlier today, Mr. Barnette, and told you to put it on his account. He also paid his account down, so there is room to charge it." The words were soft, gentle.

"Well, your daddy's money is fine here, but I ain't sure you're welcome."

Lord. Win shook his head. "Johnny."

"What? I don't have to serve him, I don't want to. That's in the law. I don't serve convicts. Murderers."

"Your prerogative." The items were left there in a little pile as Redding turned and walked out.

Win raised a brow at Johnny. "You gonna make his old man come get the order? You know how it is with him, John. You gonna make Mrs. Redding do it?"

"I… I don't want his type in here, Win. It ain't safe."

"He's done his duty to society, Johnny." Win believed that. After seeing Sage in person, he believed it even more.

"You tell that to your Uncle Teddy." Carrie Walter's voice was low, hurt. "There's never been a man that came out of prison better than he went in."

"I've told that to my uncle, both of them—Teddy and Jim—but then, I don't think Sage Redding was all that bad when he went to prison in the first place." He snapped his hat against his thigh, so damned frustrated he could stomp a bit. God, he was sick of the whole Angel was a saint bullshit, even after all these years.

"Win!" His name snapped out so fast he couldn't quite tell which one got it out first. They all stared at him, and he shook his head and sighed.

"I need Mrs. Simpson's dog food, y'all."

Johnny tried to stare him down, but Win was used to dealing with way worse, and he tried to be patient. Finally Johnny grunted and gathered up the dog food and the lightbulbs when Win remembered that was what he was there for.

He headed out about the time Ellen Redding came slamming through the door like a short round redheaded avenging angel.

"John Barnette, you lousy motherfucker! I covered your ass when you were shitfaced and drove your truck into my fence, I went to the doctor with SueAnn when Billy Cooper knocked her up, and I have never once bad-mouthed you, and you refuse to serve my son?"

Carrie opened her mouth, and Ellen pointed a finger at her. "Don't you say a word, you sanctimonious whore. You think I won't go to Brother Howard's wife and tell her that you're the feet sticking out from underneath the pulpit, you got another thing coming. You stuck-up pieces of shit, so scared of the goddamn sheriff and his brother that you treat a decent man like a pariah?"

Then she turned on Win. "And you!"

He held up his hands. "Hey. I defended him. Ask them. They'd be happy to rat me out."

"Give me my goddamn order, and I'll be going into Greenville for my business from now on." She looked at each and every one of them in turn, staring them down. "And you'd best pray I don't decide to start singing your secrets to everyone who'll listen. This is a tiny town, and my family's had its skeletons pranced around this place like prize ponies. Y'all so much as breathe hard on my son and there will be hell to pay, you mark my words."

Johnny stood there like he was frozen, but his cashier, Dan, started loading up the order, never saying a word. Only Win knew that Dan had a couple of misdemeanor drug charges on his record. Maybe Dan knew how Sage felt.

She handed over a credit card and paid the bill. "I have my truck. Are any of you assholes going to help me load three hundred pounds of feed, or are you going to sit there with your teeth in your mouths?"

"Just let me put these lightbulbs in my truck, ma'am. I'll help out." Win thought Sage's momma was something else.

"Fine. I'll be outside." She turned on her heel and headed out, leaving a bunch of gasping people behind her.

Win ducked his head, hiding his grin. "Dan, if you get it outside, I'll help load."

"I got it." Dan started moving the bags on the dolly, whistling as he went.

Ellen stood by her truck, lips tight, arms crossed.

"Mrs. Redding. I'm sorry about this." Not that Win had done it, but it was only right to let her know he felt bad.

"I am too. He's a good man and we're good customers."

"They only know what they're told. My uncles...." Win trailed off. Why state the obvious?

"Have their heads so far up their asses they fart and think it's flowers?"

Damn, she was good at that. He grinned a little. "Yes, ma'am. That's exactly what I was thinking."

"Thank you for your help."

"Mrs. Redding?" Dan put the dog food in her truck. "If you need an order, you can call me direct and I'll take care of getting it to you."

"I'm not sure, Danny. I don't know if I want to spend my money with John." She reached out and touched Dan's shoulder. "I won't put you out of a job, though, don't worry."

"Thank you, ma'am. You be careful going home."

"I will." Ellen glanced back at Win. "You're nicer than your family."

He snorted, the sound surprised right out of him and resembling nothing more than a buffalo with a nose cold. "Uh, thanks."

"Anytime. Thank you for your help and your service in the military. If I catch anyone you work with harassing my son, I'm holding you personally responsible."

"Sure. Just call me." He handed her a card before she could slip away, then watched her drive off. "Wow, Dan. That lady is something else."

"She is. She's pissed. I don't envy any of those guys in there."

"Nope." Win gave Dan a smile and a nod. "Thanks for all your help, Dan. They give you any trouble, you holler."

"They won't. I'm twenty years too young to be on their radar."

"Yeah. No shit." Win clapped the man on the back and hopped in his truck. He had dogs to feed, and he was off duty, damn it.

This whole thing... shit, it sucked, because Sage Redding was going to get pushed into fucking up. It was inevitable, and then Sage's ass would be back in jail, and there wouldn't be anything his momma could do about it.

Maybe he'd stop by the Redding ranch later on and have a little chat with Sage, just to let him know someone was on his side.

Or maybe he'd just… sit in his front room with his phone off and his feet up.

It was his fucking Friday night.

He'd better enjoy it before someone did something stupid and he had to go play cop.

"HEARD YOU got into a fight at the feedstore."

Sage didn't bother to answer his piece-of-shit brother-in-law. Hell, what the fuck was he supposed to say? He didn't fight with anyone. He kept his peace and got on with life.

"It's a matter of time, you know, before you fuck up again. You fucking faggots always do." Greg spit at his feet, and Sage kept unloading Momma's Chevy. "I went with the sheriff, warned both sets of neighbors to keep their kids inside, you know. Don't want you sticking your dick in them."

"Greg! Sage isn't a… a… sex maniac." Sage's sister Rosie stood at the door, looking pale as milk, the dark eyeliner making her look a little like a raccoon. "He's a good man."

"He's a pervert and an abomination in the eyes of God. You think he'll be back in the slammer where he belongs before you pop that baby out? I pray he does."

"He belongs here. This is his home. He's my brother, damn it, and I love him."

Sage didn't have a chance to wallow in the words, because Greg turned on her, one hand fisted up. "Get your ass in the house, woman. Don't you dare talk back to me."

Sage didn't like how she flinched and stepped back, hand on her belly. Didn't like it at all, and he reckoned he'd have to nudge Momma on it.

Speaking of Momma, she hollered for Rosie, and as soon as Rosie disappeared inside the screen door, Greg grabbed at Sage's arm, only getting shirtsleeve. Sage stared the evil fucker down, calm as deep water as Greg hissed, "I'll never let you see my babies, ever. You'll get your ass thrown back in jail, and I'll—"

"Teddy Dale won't get this land, Greg, no matter what you think, so you'd best let it go." No matter what. He knew Rosie, he knew Momma, and it wasn't going to leave the family. Their blood was sunk into the black land itself. "This is Redding land."

Greg snorted. "Rosie's not a Redding."

"Sister will always be a Redding. You can't rinse that stain off in hot water like she can from your tin wedding ring."

Taking advantage of the sudden, shocked silence, Sage grabbed the currycomb and the spray and headed toward the barn, telling himself that he was right, that he knew his sister, his own strength.

Walking away from a fight wasn't a natural thing, it was learned, but God help him, he knew how to do it and he would, for Daddy.

For the land.

CHAPTER SIX

SAGE SAT in the back of the Red Wagon, his gimme cap pulled down low and eyes on his book. He found if he came in at 8:00 p.m., right before closing, he could have a cup of coffee and a piece of pie and read without anyone giving him shit.

It wasn't the most convenient time, but Daddy came up at six in the morning, and the older cowboys stared and sucked their teeth. At lunchtime there were the cops and the coffee klatch, and supper time was when the rednecks were looking to impress their women by protecting them from the big bad convict.

Wilma didn't take any shit, though, and she didn't give any, making sure his cup was full, his pie was fresh, and no one fucked with him, so he came out every night. He sat for an hour until Bulldog, Wilma's husband, came to take her home.

Bulldog understood, and the man didn't seem to worry that Sage was molesting anyone, so it all worked out.

Today he was eating cherry pie, carefully making sure he got a bite of cherry in each mouthful, and he was still on his first cup of coffee. The second cup was the one he waited on—the perfect balance of sugar and bitter. The little things were both the best and the scariest about being out of prison. They were so easy to take away.

Bulldog came in—long gray hair tied back in a braid, riding leathers on. "Hey, baby."

"Hey, love. You want tea?"

"And pie, yeah. Howdy, Sage."

"Evenin', sir." He nodded at Bulldog, who had an air of calm around him that was completely infectious.

The door opened again a few seconds later, the bell jingling. "Hey, Wilma," said the man who walked in wearing a county deputy uniform. "Am I too late for pie? I heard it was cherry today."

"Howdy, Win. Never too late. Have a sit. Coffee?"

God, police. Please, just let me sit here.

"Thanks. I can take it to go if you're ready to go." The cop shook Bulldog's hand and glanced at Sage curiously.

"Nah, have a sit. We're solid."

Sage nodded once, focusing on his book.

The cop sat at the counter, which put his back to Sage. *Hallelujah.*

Sage kept his head down, but he couldn't focus, couldn't actually read even a single word, because his brain was filled with worrying. If he was smart, he'd leave, but then the damned cop might think he'd done something wrong, and he didn't want that.

God, his head hurt.

Soon it would be 9:00 p.m., and then he'd head home so he could have the door locked for lights out and.... *No. No, there wasn't a lights out anymore.* He could go home and wait for Dan Henry to lie to him about the weather on KDFW.

"Sage? You need anything else, honey?"

"Can I have my second cup, please? Then I'll get out of your hair."

"Of course, darlin'." Wilma smiled at him, her gold tooth flashing. "How's the pie?"

"Delicious, thank you, ma'am."

"So polite. I tell my man, I never worry at night now, because Sage is here 'til he comes for me."

His cheeks heated, and he ducked his head when the cop glanced back at him, brows raised. "I reckon there are some who'd not say that."

"There are a lot of assholes in this fucking town, kid." Bulldog growled the words, the sound vibrating in the huge man's chest. "Don't let them get to you."

Wilma hooted. "Preach it, stud. No offense, Win."

"Why would I be offended?" the cop said easily, swiveling to grin at them. "I am not an asshole."

"Nope. You just wear asshole clothing." Bulldog gave Win a wicked smile.

Win, the cop, laughed out loud, the sound strong, like a hooty owl. "Yep. An ex-military guy like me has two choices. Become a tattooed weirdo like you or be a cop."

"Poor, poor stupid cop." Bulldog flexed, the wild ink shifting in the florescent lights. "When you could have been one of my enforcers."

"I'm not your type, Bull." Win winked at Wilma. "I could never compete."

Wilma laughed, and Sage ducked his head again, fighting the smile that wanted out. They had an easy way together that told him maybe he didn't need to worry so much. He didn't even freeze when he glanced back up to see Win smiling at him.

He couldn't find a smile, but he could nod. That worked well enough.

Win nodded back before turning to face the counter again and digging in to his food.

Sage finished his cup of coffee and managed another ten pages on his book before he handed Wilma a ten spot. "I'll see you tomorrow, ma'am. Mr. Bulldog. Sir."

"Night, Sage," Bulldog said.

"Night." Wilma smiled at him.

"Night," Win the cop murmured, surprising him.

"Good night." He headed out to his truck, parked under the light where he could see it.

Time to go home and feed his dog. Maybe read something more adult. That was one of the best things about having a private place. No one confiscated his books. Singing with Luke Bryan on KSCS out of DFW, he headed to the house, keeping the truck at three miles under the speed limit. When the lights came on behind him, his heart stopped.

He hadn't been doing anything wrong. Nothing.

Sage pulled over, keeping his hands visible on the damned steering wheel, and told himself to breathe. He hadn't done anything wrong. Nothing.

"Good evening, sir," the deputy said when Sage rolled the window down. "License and registration?"

He got his registration and proof of insurance out of the glove box, then handed everything over, not even asking what they were pulling him over for. He knew. They were pulling him over for daring to be alive. Go him.

"Have you been drinking, sir?" The guy was all business, but Sage knew that tone of voice—embarrassment mixed with anger. Prison guards who had been told to rough up a prisoner used that same tone.

"Just coffee, Officer." Just like last night. And the night before.

"Step out of the vehicle, please."

"Yes, sir." He counted backward from one hundred as he got out. God, he was tired of this shit.

"Step away from the door for a sobriety test, please."

He gritted his teeth, his feet moving even if he didn't want them to. The second set of lights going off behind the first made him want to scream. It was going to happen, one day there'd be something, no matter how hard he'd try, and he'd be back in jail again. It was inevitable. *But please God, don't let it be today.*

"What's going on here, Bill?" a new voice asked, and Sage knew it, which surprised him—the cop from the diner.

"Just making a routine stop. DUI."

"Yeah?" Win walked into the circle of light, peering at him. "Funny, I just saw him leave Wilma's, and you know she doesn't serve booze."

The cop shrugged. "I got…. Sheriff said to."

"Well, you've done your part. Now, move on." Win's voice cracked like a whip.

"Yes, sir. Win." The kid handed Sage his driver's license back.

Sage stood there. Was this where the man was going to start whaling on him?

"Go on, Bill. You get any flack, you tell the sheriff to talk to me."

"Night, Win." The lights went off, and the black-and-white headed away, leaving Sage standing there.

Waiting.

"You okay, then?" Win stood five feet away, almost as still as Sage was.

"Yes, Officer. I don't drink." Ever.

"No, I don't imagine you do." Win stepped closer, and Sage tensed, his muscles pulling in, ready for the blow he expected. So long as he could get home, that was all he needed.

"I'm not out to hurt you, Sage. Believe it or not, I'm on your side."

"I doubt your uncle or your boss would approve of that." *Oh Christ, Sage. Shut. Up.*

"Teddy and Jim are both my uncles, believe it or not. They don't much approve of me." The sudden grin Win gave him made Sage want to smile, almost.

"No? They're not my biggest fans either."

"I know." Win shook his head, lips pressing tight. "Look, I'll do my best to keep the department off your back."

"I'd appreciate that. I am keeping my nose clean. I see my parole officer. I do my piss tests. I'm good."

"Yeah. Yeah." Win sighed. "Look, I'm sorry, okay? Just, from someone who knows better about Angel and all."

Sage's eyes went wide so fast they pulled on the corners. No one but Momma had said that, ever. He wondered for a moment if it was some kind of trap, trying to get him to say something stupid, but Win just grimaced.

"I know it's shitty to talk ill of the dead, but he never did live up to his name." Win pulled out a card. "You call me if you need help. Okay?"

He took the card, surprised to see his hand shaking. "Thank you."

"No problem. I mean it." Win's grimace turned into a warm and genuine smile. "It took guts to come back here."

"My folks need me. I owe them."

"Well, remember there's more than them in your corner."

"I appreciate it." He just didn't believe it. "Have a good evening, Officer."

"You too, Sage." Win stood there, though, staring.

He didn't know quite what to do. "You... you done with me?"

"I—Yeah. Yeah, I'm sorry."

"No apologies necessary. I... I'm sorry your cousin died."

"Thanks." Win stepped forward, thrusting a hand at him. "I— Thanks. It's been good to meet you."

"Shit, man." He shook. "I'm just glad you didn't shoot me."

Win laughed, a short, surprised sound. "Not me. I'd be aware of how tall a hat I wore, though, if I were you."

"I know. Thanks for the warning." Sage backed off, feeling about ten thousand years old and almost like he'd never left the joint. It was time to get home. He should have asked Wilma for an extra piece of pie to have tomorrow. "My dog's waiting for me, Officer. Have a safe night."

He didn't wait for Win's response. He got in his truck and headed home.

CHAPTER SEVEN

WIN THOUGHT about calling in. Things at the office had been fucking tense, and he wanted to go fishing or something. He could plead the plague. Maybe tuberculosis.

His phone rang and he grabbed it. "'lo?"

"Win? Win, this is Wilma from the diner, honey. I need a favor."

"Anything, lady." He got up, figuring he'd have to head to the diner.

"Can you pop over to the Reddings' and check on everybody? Sage hasn't been in for four days, and he never missed once, not since he came home. Me and Bulldog, we're worried, but my stubborn shit of a husband says he ain't got reason to stop in." Her voice rose, heading toward shrill. "He's a bit of a pansyass, my old man."

Right. Pansyass. Bulldog. Still, it might stress Mr. Redding right the fuck out to see Bulldog on his big hog pulling down the drive. Old cowboys and bikers weren't the most natural of bedfellows. Shit. He sure hoped nothing had happened to Sage. "Sure thing, Wilma. I'll stop by." Hell, he'd even do it in street clothes.

"Thanks, honey. We miss him."

"I'll tell him." He'd make sure Sage's momma didn't need anything too.

Win phoned in, let Grace know he was on a call, and got dressed in jeans and a T-shirt. He'd take his truck too. No reason to stress folks out. Win tried hard not to worry that his family had gone and done something incredibly stupid, but it was tough to get out of his head. The whole thing sucked—Sage Redding seemed to be a decent guy. Scared, at best. PTSD at worst, but decent.

He headed across town, out into BFE, and stopped at the gate, and gave the main house a ring to warn them he was coming.

"'lo?" Ellen sounded out of breath.

"Um, Mrs. Redding? This is Adam Winchester. Win. Doing a welfare check."

"Pardon me? A what?"

"A welfare check, ma'am. Wilma down to the diner called, worried about your son."

"Sage? Sage is at the barn, working the colts."

"Would you mind if I went on down? I'm not harassing him, I promise."

"Sure. I got biscuits and gravy and sausage. Y'all want some after, come up to the house."

"Thank you." Win felt absurdly pleased that she trusted him enough not to tell him to go to hell. He opened the gate, then made sure it closed after he went through.

The main house looked better than the last time he'd seen it, when someone had vandalized the horse barn—the sagging front porch was put back to rights and the carport freshly painted. That was a damned good sign. He'd have to put in a good word with Sage's parole officer.

He headed down to the barn, strangely eager to see Sage.

The pocket cowboy was in the ring training a beautiful little filly, encouraging her to move around and around. Every time she tossed her head and pranced sideways, Sage stopped, murmuring to her and stroking her nose when she turned to him for encouragement.

Finally, Sage chuckled and whistled, and a fine mare trotted up to the fence. "Come on, you. Go run with your momma and rest. You did good work." He opened the little gate and out she danced, shaking out her mane.

"Those are some pretty girls you've got there," Win said.

Sage started and looked at him with wide hazel eyes. "Officer. Howdy. Yessir. What's wrong?"

"Nothing. Nothing. My name is Win." Okay, that was stupid, but he was caught in Sage's gaze, those eyes a fascinating mix of green and gold and gray.

Said eyes stayed on Win a long moment before Sage blinked. "Now I remember you. Your name is Adam. We were in Ms. Daughtry's Spanish class together."

Was that a smile?

"We were." Win hoped that was a good sign. "Went military, after school."

"Good deal. You like it?"

Whoa. A smile and now small talk. Win was floored. That was kind of amazing.

"It was okay. I saw the world, you know?" He'd been lucky enough to pull the Med his first tour. "Turkey, Italy." Combat on his second tour hadn't been so fun.

"Wow. I don't have a passport. Folks seem to like it. Going, I mean." Sage looked at him. "Why are you here?"

"Wilma called. Says you haven't been in to see her. Four days. I figured I'd make sure no one was giving you a hard time or anything." Neighborly. That was him.

"No. No." Sage blushed and shook his head. "You said to keep my head down. I took your advice."

"Oh shit, man. I didn't mean to stay home forever." Win grinned. "I just wanted you to know folks were out to make it hard for you."

"I know. I figured maybe I shouldn't make it easy."

Win could see that. Really. Still…. "Well, Wilma and Bulldog miss you."

"That's nice of them. Maybe I'll stop by and say hi." Sage shrugged. "You got horses at your place?"

"Me? No. No, I grew up with them, but I'm not home enough." He felt weird admitting it.

"They need attention."

"Sage? Sage, your momma says you boys need to come and eat biscuits!" Mr. Redding was standing on the porch, just bellaring.

"Lord."

Win's ears went hot. "I don't have to come up. I would understand if you wanted me to fuck off."

"Momma makes good biscuits. Come on up. There's coffee."

"Thank you." He meant it too. For someone who knew everyone in town, Win had precious few people who would invite him in for coffee and biscuits.

Sage climbed the fence, then carefully worked his way down. "Let's go up."

"Sure." He followed Sage to the house, trying hard not to stare at the man's back.

A shitload of dogs came running up, wagging and slobbering, and they each got love from Sage, one at a time. Win grinned, waiting to wade through, but they paid him no mind at all, every one of them wagging and trailing Sage. Oh, someone was well-loved. That as much as anything told Win he was probably right about Sage being in the wrong place back during the Angel thing. Anyone dogs loved that much couldn't be bad.

"Go on, y'all. Food's done been poured." Sage stomped his boots off and wiped his neck with a kerchief that he dug out of his jeans.

Win checked to make sure his boots were clean before following Sage inside. God, it smelled good.

"Hey, boys. Breakfast is ready. Deputy, how do you like your coffee?" Mrs. Redding was wearing a T-shirt that said, "Give Me My Chocolate and No One Gets Hurt."

"Morning, ma'am. Just black is fine."

"Boys and their black coffee." She poured out four cups, adding generous milk and sugar to one. "Give me my nummy brew."

He grinned. "I bet you like them fancy things from Starbucks."

"You know it. I love the caramel ones." She handed him a mug. "Have a seat, y'all. I'll dish up. Who wants gravy?"

Mr. Redding grunted, nodded, and sat.

"Please." Win sat too, feeling oddly at home.

"No gravy for me, Momma. I'll grab the honey."

Four plates hit the table—*bang, bang, bang, bang*. Then Mrs. Redding sat. "Eat up."

Win waited to dig in, wondering if the Reddings said grace. It was strange how little he knew about them.

Mr. Redding bowed his head quickly. "Good food, good meat. Good God, let's eat."

"Sam Redding!" Ellen almost managed to look horrified. Almost. Sage cracked up, laughing hard, and Win loved to see it. He even let himself chuckle, then dug in happily. He'd opened a lot of cans since he'd left the Army, and this was a treat.

They didn't eat in silence. He wasn't sure the Redding men had ever known a single solitary moment of silence in their entire lives. Bless her, Mrs. Redding talked about chickens and horses, about neighbors and church.

Mr. Redding grunted and clicked, but Sage, that man talked back, voice surprisingly deep and weirdly musical.

Win found himself sitting back, listening, soaking it in. No one who heard this could believe that these people raised a killer, that Sage was trouble. The whole vendetta Win's family had against this man was so ridiculous it made him ashamed.

They all finished eating, and then Sam Redding stood and nodded. "I got a doctor appointment in Greenville. You gonna be able to handle things this afternoon, Son?"

"Well, I don't know, Daddy. I might blow the whole county to kingdom come while I'm mowing the backyard and cleaning out the old garage so Momma can make me set rat traps."

Mr. Redding actually grinned. "Don't be an ass, Son."

"It's genetic, Sam." Ellen winked at Win, her hazel eyes twinkling. "He gets it from his daddy, you know."

Sam swatted her ample backside playfully. "Woman, go get your shoes and purse. Son, you're on your own for supper. I'm taking Momma to Red Lobster and a movie."

"And Starbucks!"

"And Starbucks. Spoiled girl."

Win waited until the folks were up and moving before blurting out what he wanted to say, "Hey, I could bring supper by."

"I…." Sage looked utterly gobsmacked. "Yeah? Why?"

"Sage!"

"Sorry, Momma. Adam. Shit, you surprised me." Sage blushed dark, managing to meet his eyes. "I haven't had pizza in a dog's age."

"Well, I can sure do that. What do you like on it?"

"I'm easy."

"Pepperoni and mushrooms okay?" How weird was this whole situation? Still, Win wanted to spend more time with Sage. Something about the man drew him in.

"Sure. That's cool." Sage was as wild-eyed as one of the colts in the pasture.

"Cool. I'll come on by around five thirty." He sopped up the rest of his gravy with one last biscuit. "Anything y'all need from the store, Mrs. Redding?"

"Nope. We'll shop at the big Brookshire's in town. Thanks, though."

"Yes, ma'am. Thank you so much for breakfast. I got the day off, if you need any help, Sage." Win didn't, to be honest, but he could sure use one. Go riding. Get some air.

"Oh, I'm going to mow and clean out the garage."

So, was that a no? Win had to think it was, so he bowed out gracefully. "Okay. Well, I'll be back in time for supper, huh?"

"Yeah. That'd be cool."

"Okay." He stuck a hand out impulsively, letting Sage decide whether to shake or not. Sage's hand was callused and warm, and the shake was normal, not too tight, not too loose. When Sage let go, Win did too, reluctant as he was. "Well, I'll see you tonight."

"Yes, sir. I'll be about. You got my phone number?"

"I don't." He could get that too. That was a fine thing. He tapped it into his phone when Sage told him, smiling at Mr. Redding, who was waiting for him to leave, he thought.

Sam Redding nodded at him, once. "You ain't looking to get my boy in trouble, are you?"

"No, sir." He wasn't sure what he was looking for, save letting Sage know not everyone was against him. "I just think he needs a friend."

"I can see that. Momma, come on, girl."

"Coming!" Mrs. Redding walked Win out. "He always liked pepperoni. He liked those pepper rings too."

"Like banana peppers?"

"Uh-huh. I'll call on our way back home, if you want a fancy coffee, boys."

Sage looked like he wanted the floor to swallow him. Win gave the man a smile and took pity on him. "Thanks again for breakfast. I'll see you later, Sage."

He headed to his truck and waited until he was out of sight of the house to call Wilma back.

"Red Wagon Diner."

"Hey, honey. It's Win. I checked in on Sage. He's fine. Just tired of getting pulled over on the way home."

"Oh. Well, that's good, I guess. Tell him we miss him here, though."

"I will. I bet you see him soon."

"I hope so. Have a good day, Win. There's coconut cream pie tonight. I know that's your favorite."

"I'm having pizza…." He pondered that. "Hey, can I pick up a couple of pieces about 5:00 p.m.?"

"Surely can. I'll set two back for you."

"Thank you, ma'am." Time to go put his uniform on and play cop for a few hours.

Then he'd go get to know this town's biggest news story in years.

Chapter Eight

God, where did Momma get all this shit?

The yard was mowed and looked pretty good too, and Sage was organizing the workshop, sweat pouring down him like rain. He'd moved about ten thousand boxes of random crap, a million jars of old nails and screws, and killed a spider the size of Godzilla.

Hell, he'd even gone through the old trunk that was like a rat colony on steroids.

Still, it was starting to look like something reasonable, finally, something that he could make workable and keep shit safe in.

He heard the crunch of tires on gravel and glanced outside, surprised it was so late. Well, damn.

Actually, he hadn't expected Adam to come back, and this tiny little voice whispered low that they were alone and Office Winchester had a pistol. Officer Winchester, who was Angel's cousin.

Sure enough, though, Adam stepped out of the truck, wearing jeans and a T-shirt and carrying a bag and a pizza box.

"Hey. Hey, man. Sorry, I got busy in this trap."

He got a grin, Adam's teeth white in his tanned leather face. The man looked like one of those Indians in the schoolbooks—maybe Geronimo or Crazy Horse. Angel used to say that their folks came from some tribe over by Louisiana.

Angel had been a stubborn ass about not being Mexican. Hell, half of Texas was part Mexican, but whatever.

Adam nodded. "Time gets away. Wilma called me again, asking when I was gonna come get pie. I was buried in paperwork."

"Come on, then. I got to feed real quick and clean up. I won't be long."

"Sure. Pizza's good and hot."

Sage grinned. Yeah, he could smell it, all garlic and spice.

"My trailer's over there, past the barn. I…." Sage paused. Should he send Adam over without him, have the man come with him to feed?

"I can leave the food in the truck and help you feed."

Bless him, Win was pretty sensitive to the mood.

"That don't seem fair…." Sage had to feed, though. Had to.

"What? That way we can both go in together." Adam went and stashed the food right in the truck, then came back, hands in the back pockets of his jeans.

"Okay. Did you have a good day?" God, he didn't know what the fuck to say.

"It was fine. I mean, I ended up getting work done." Adam shrugged. "Show me what to do."

"Oh, you don't have to. You can just…." He looked around, trying to search out something, anything for Win to do. *Oh. Oh.* "You want to fill that old tub with water for the pups?"

"Sure." Adam chuckled, getting the hose. "I'm sorry I'm not more familiar with what you're doing."

"It's not your job." Sage poured out sweet feed and kibbles, the rhythm like a good country song or a train on the tracks. Right and solid and written on his DNA.

"I guess not. I like to be useful, though."

"I can understand that." He got everything settled, easy as pie. Life was starting to work the way he needed it to, now.

Adam ran the water for the dogs and filled a bucket for the donkey and all. It made everything go faster.

"Thanks for the help." It took two more shakes to get things done, and then he nodded. "Come on, then. We'll grab the pizza and head to my trailer." He stopped. "Unless you'd rather go to the main house. It's not as small."

"If you don't mind, we'll go to your place. Your folks' house is weird if they're not there." He got a grin, Adam's dimples carved deep.

"Yeah. Yeah, it is."

They stopped at Adam's truck again, then headed out. His Penny was on the porch, her tail thumping as she stared the stranger down.

Adam waited, letting Sage introduce them. 'Course it helped that the man held a pizza.

"This is my little girl, Penny. Penny, this is Adam."

She sniffed, licked, then dropped her head on her paws, soaking up the last of the sun.

"She's a good girl." They walked inside and Adam held up the bag. "This is pie. There's an ice pack in there, but you might want it in the fridge."

"Pie?" Sage couldn't help his grin. He'd missed his dessert, and he was stupidly pleased that he could have it again tonight. "Can you put it in there, please? I got to clean myself up some."

"You bet. Wilma says hey."

"I'll have to tell her thank you." He headed to his little bedroom and stripped off his work shirt, found a clean T-shirt, and gave himself a spit bath in the sink with a washrag and a bit of soap. It would work.

When he got back, Adam was digging out plates and paper towels, looking natural in Sage's kitchen.

"There's Cokes in the fridge, iff'n you want. I got Sprite and Dr Pepper both."

"Oh, I like the good Doctor. Which do you want?"

"I'll take a Dr Pepper too. It cuts the grease." Sage had himself a wee wooden cafe table, with two tall chairs. He'd made them for Momma when he was a teenager in woodshop, and she'd kept them.

"Sure." Adam finally came to the table and laid everything out. The pizza wasn't as hot as it had probably been when Adam had shown up, but it was cheesy and spicy and good. Sage ate, not sure what to do, focusing on the food, on not bumping into Adam, not spilling.

He didn't have cable. He had a DVD player and a copy of *Tombstone* and one of *8 Seconds*. Neither of them were really pizza movies.

"That was good." Adam sat back, patting his belly, which was nice and flat.

"It was. Thank you. I haven't had pizza since...." Since he was a teenager. "...a long time."

"Well, you're welcome." Adam leaned his elbows on the table, looking right at him. "Look, I'm sorry if I'm being pushy. I just— somehow, I want to get to know you."

"Why?" Why on earth would a cop be interested in learning about him? He was an ex-con, totally out of place here, and he'd have kept his shame in California if he could have. He couldn't figure out how to not help Daddy, though, and he owed his folks, big time, so here his happy ass stayed. "It'll get you in trouble, won't it?"

"Oh, I reckon it will make some folks mad." Shrugging, Adam sat back and held up his hands. "I do that anyway."

"So, uh. You were in the Army? Everyone says you're a hero." Sage felt about as stupid as anything.

"I did one tour in the Med, one in, uh, someplace a lot less pleasant." Adam picked up the plates and went to wash up. "I'm not sure a stint in the Green Zone in Baghdad makes me a hero."

"You should take the compliment. There's nothing wrong with being a hero." Right? Heroes were... heroes. The alternative was whatever he was. Or a supervillain.

He wasn't a supervillain, right? He was a cowboy.

"I try to. I saw a lot of shit going on over there." Adam chuckled. "Want some pie? Or is it too soon?"

"I'll probably wait a bit. Do you want a cup of coffee?"

"Sure. I'd love one."

Sage made a pot of Folgers, fed Penny, wiped out the sink, and poured two cups. "Black, right?"

"Yep." Adam watched him in the most unnerving way. There was no speculation, no maliciousness. Just pure, intense interest. It was like being caught—a butterfly on a pin.

He handed the coffee over, then sat, about as wigged as he could be.

"Do you need me to head out, Sage?" Those dark brown eyes were too damned knowing. "I don't want to make you uncomfortable. Really."

"No. No, I just... I don't know what to do." Everything was new. Everything. He had a place of his own, sort of. He had someone there.

He had things that were his. He'd been so young when he went in that he didn't know how to process any of it.

"Okay. Cool. I mean, cool that you don't want me to leave." Cheeks heating, Adam glanced away, then back.

"We're a pair, huh? I got a deck of cards. You play cribbage?"

"I do. I used to play with my aunt."

"Wanna play?" That was friendly, right, but not gambling, like poker.

"Sure I do." Adam rubbed his hands together. "I'm way better at cribbage than Boggle."

"Boggle is okay. My mom likes it." He found the board and the cards, then handed them to Adam to shuffle. "I'm more of a math person."

"Me too." Having the cribbage board to focus on helped, and it seemed to help Adam too.

They discarded and started playing, and Sage found himself relaxing, actually chuckling as he stole a point from Adam. Adam seemed easy in his skin, laughing with him, grumbling about mulligans.

His knees started screaming at him after about three hands, and he shifted, searching for an easy position.

"You okay, man?" Adam asked after Sage had moved around for the third or fourth time.

"Yeah. I got...." He tried to figure out the best way to put it. "...bad knees."

"Oh hey, if you want to move to the couch or something, I'm not picky."

"Yeah, if you don't mind. Penny won't be evil."

"Oh, I may not know feeding and ranch work too much, but dogs I get." Adam moved the cribbage board to the coffee table and helped Sage get settled. The warm touch of those big hands shocked him—not a static electricity kind of shock, but something deeper, more like the buzz after you'd peed on a live fence.

"Thanks." Sage sat down, his knees hating him.

"Do you need something? An ibuprofen or whatever?"

"No. I don't take stuff." He never took anything.

"Okay." Chewing his lip, Adam stared at his legs. "Do you have any Bengay?"

"Yeah. I'll be okay. I just get sore. I'll bet there's rain coming. I'm like one of those bobbing birds."

Adam laughed. "I have an ankle like that. Popped it coming out of a troop carrier on a drill."

"Oh damn. That sounds like it hurt." He was kneecapped his second night in maximum security. He guessed he knew pain, but it wasn't something he shared.

"It did. I reckon we've all got stuff to deal with, huh?"

"Yes, sir. We all do." He dealt the cards again. He was at least six pegs ahead, and he was about to have the best hand of the night. He had all tens and fives. "Were you and Angel close?"

"As kids? I guess as close as any cousins. I mean, we saw each other a lot up until middle school. Then we started drifting, I suppose."

"Ah." Sage could remember the first time he saw Angel. He'd fallen in love—fallen hard too, even though he hadn't known what that meant at the time.

"You were, uh, real close, huh?" Those dark eyes carefully looked away from him, but he thought Adam was more embarrassed than judgmental.

"We were lovers." He wasn't going to lie about that either, damn it.

"Yeah. I mean, I figured." Adam shrugged a little. "He was wild, but he did care about people."

"He was a stupid kid, but so was I. I guess lots of folks are, at eighteen." Maybe not as stupid as Sage.

That got him a blinding smile, direct and honest. "Hell, Sage, eighteen only comes in stupid."

"No shit on that." He grinned back, and it actually felt like he could breathe.

"There was this night, right after graduation. I reckon you and Angel had already left town. I was about to leave for basic. Anyway, I got jacked up with Robbie Marton. You remember him?"

"I do." Robbie had been the only openly queer boy Sage had known, back then. There'd been a handful of them who had been into guys, but it had been quiet as all fuck. Robbie, though, that boy had been on his knees for all of them, any of them.

Adam shook his head. "We were trying to impress each other, I guess, and I was in my dad's old truck. Let me tell you, I never even saw that tree coming. I was glad I didn't smoosh Robbie's head."

Sage blinked, then he caught on, and he hooted, laughing hard. "Lord, lord, man. Ain't no one told you it's bad to get blown while you're driving?"

"Shit, if someone had told me that then, I wouldn't have believed it. Getting blown was all I thought about." Adam started laughing too, and before he knew it, they were cackling together, slapping their thighs with it.

Idiots. They were both idiots.

He guessed that was okay. It was good to be able to let loose with someone, and Adam was easier to be with than anyone he'd met in a long time.

Adam beat him on the first game, he took the second, and he looked over. "You want to play again? There's the pie."

"I'd love to, but we can break for dessert." Waving him back down, Adam grinned. "Mind your knees. I'll get it."

"You sure?" Sage nodded in thanks. "Appreciate it."

"No worries. I know where stuff is now."

Like there was a lot of space. Or stuff. But his kitchen had what he needed. Adam found a couple of plates and brought back pie and forks, along with the coffeepot for refills.

"Thanks. I feel lazy." Oh man. Look at that pie. Creamy and sweet, the scent of coconut making his mouth water. It looked like heaven, and he missed Wilma and Bulldog sharply.

"You should come back to the cafe. I can follow you home."

"I couldn't ask you to do that."

"You don't have to. I'm offering. I mean I can't do it every night, but I'd be happy to."

"Maybe. We'll see how it goes. I might stop in tomorrow."

"Well, let me know." Adam reached across the table and touched Sage's wrist. "You should be able to go and do."

"I know, but that's it, isn't it? You pay and pay. I'll always be an ex-con." He knew that. He got it. He would never get to be more than that. It was how it worked, and, he figured, why it was so hard to stay out. Shit, if you had to work this hard, at least in the joint there were understandable rules.

Adam's mouth flattened into an unhappy line. "Doesn't mean it doesn't suck."

"You know it. Shuffle the cards. Let's play."

Adam nodded, his tanned fingers working the cards. He shuffled, and they played, and that was that. Looked like he had himself a friend.

Weird.

He'd take it, though. Friends were important, no matter where you got hold of them.

CHAPTER NINE

WIN HEADED into the office, whistling under his breath. It had been a good night with Sage, playing games and eating pizza and cream pie. Hell, he'd gotten along with Sage as well as he had anyone in years. Sage Redding was funny, surprisingly smart, and incredibly quick and charming. It fascinated him. Oh, he knew he ought to back the hell off, but he couldn't. God knew, Sage needed a friend.

Grace made a face at him as he came in. "Sheriff is gunning for you."

"What now, for god's sake?"

She rolled her eyes. "Someone said you took pizza to the Redding place."

Win wanted to snarl, but this was Grace. "What I do in my off time is my business."

"You think I don't know that?" She dropped her voice. "Shit, Win, Ellen Redding is my sister June's best friend."

"I know." He sighed. "Sorry, lady. I know this whole thing is weird." Win gave her a smile, weak as it probably was.

"It's not my problem. Not yours, if you don't let it be." Grace winked, eyes crinkling around the edges. "Just watch your butt."

"I will." Maybe he'd let someone else watch it for him. Oh, now. That was a new thought. He hadn't been thinking those sorts of thoughts in a long time. Sighing, he headed in for his daily meeting with the boss.

The sheriff sat at his desk, face gone all thundercloud and lightning.

"What's up, Jim?"

"What are you doing, boy? Spending the evening at that murdering fag's trailer?"

Win counted to ten, not letting anything show on his face. He hoped. "You got any business to discuss, or can we skip the check-in this morning?"

"Answer my goddamn question."

Raising a brow, Win crossed his arms. "I played cards with the man, yeah. How is this your business?"

"He killed your cousin, man. That's not enough?"

"If Angel had survived that explosion, he would have been the one to go to jail." Win kept his voice steady.

"He didn't. He got corrupted by that little fuck, and he got killed. Your Uncle Teddy is beside himself."

Privately Win thought that Uncle Teddy was beside himself about not having the Reddings' land. That was what it came down to. Sage was just an excuse.

Thank God the women in his family were more reasonable.

"Anything else? Because we're done with this conversation."

"Stay away from him. This is your last warning, kid. He doesn't need protection." Jim looked serious as hell, eyes glittering like a snake's. Too bad Win wasn't scared of critters.

He just shrugged. "You watch yourself, not me. State police would be mighty interested in how you're harassing folks like Wilma and Bulldog."

Jim arched one eyebrow. "So now you're protecting the head of a biker gang and his bitch? What are you, the Robin Hood of Hunt County?"

"No, I just think honest folks deserve a chance." This was getting them nowhere, and it hurt his soul to be at odds with a man who'd been his hero once upon a time. "I'm on patrol today, so I'll see you later."

He didn't wait to hear any more, and he didn't even stop to say good-bye to Grace. Not now. He needed outside and in the heavy weight of the September sunshine. This shit sucked hairy donkey balls. It was only going to get worse, and while he knew he could take it, he sure wished he didn't have to.

Hell, he wished none of them did, but if wishes were fishes.... Win stopped in the garage to get a mobile unit, and he checked all the systems before pulling out of the garage.

Lord, what a fucking mess.

Why on earth had he come back here to work?

His phone rang as he got himself headed down the highway. His momma's name popped up on the hands free. Win pushed the button. "Hey, Momma."

"Hey, baby. How's it going?"

"Oh, you know, been a heck of a morning already. Everything okay?"

"Yes, I had a need to hear your voice. You've been on my mind." Uh-huh. He'd bet Uncle Teddy had been pushing.

"Anything I need to know, Momma?"

"Yes. Don't you let those ass hats get to you."

He grinned. Yeah, that was the more reasonable side of the family. "Thanks. I appreciate it. Want to do lunch tomorrow? We could go into Rockwall and go to El Chico."

"I would love that. We can share that amazing apple pie on the hot skillet." She actually sounded excited, and Win loved that. He loved making her happy with simple things.

"Cool. And I can tell you what all I'm doing wrong."

"You know I live for that. Make a list."

Evil woman. "I love you, lady. I'll pick you up at eleven thirty tomorrow."

"I'll be ready. You be careful out there, and remember your momma loves you."

"I will." Bless her heart, she'd put a smile on his face. He'd so needed that.

He headed into town, checking things out. It was a hard thing—trying to decide whether to be happy all was well or to wish shit would happen so time would pass. He figured he should be grateful for a quiet day. Maybe he could stop and get a coffee. He'd missed his bullpen sludge, thanks to Jim.

He pulled into the diner's parking lot and headed in, waving to Kelly and Heidi at the counter. Heidi grinned and nodded.

"Just coffee or breakfast, Win?"

"I think coffee and a cinnamon scone, honey." They teased him unmercifully about his carb intake, but he only drank beer once in a while, so he needed his empty sugar from somewhere.

"You got it."

He slid into a stool at the counter, nodding to Mike McBride and Terry Mann. The old cowboys nodded back, Mike giving him a crooked grin. "You hear 'bout Nate and them, Win? His woman done had triplets this morning."

"No shit? I thought twins, but triplets is scary."

"Two girls and a boy. Babies are going to be in Presbyterian for a bit, but they're doing good. Nate's fixin' to drop his teeth, though. They wasn't thinking there was a son hiding in the mess."

"No kidding? Well, I'll say a prayer for them." This was how Win got most of his information about the town—chatting.

"Pastor Brown is putting a collection together for them at First Baptist." Kelly put his coffee and sweet down in front of him. "I know they need clothes and another crib for sure."

"I'll stop by, then." He sniffed the scone. Mmm. Cinnamon. He wondered suddenly if Sage liked scones.

Hell, had Sage ever even had one?

"Can I get another scone to go, hon?" he asked. He wouldn't be able to deliver it until late in the evening, but he'd bet Sage wouldn't mind.

"Surely can." She refilled him. "Man, I'm ready for this summer to be over."

"Too hot for you?" She'd tell him if it was something else.

"God, yes. And then there's the TV—everyone's going on and on about fall. It's not going to be fall here 'til Thanksgiving."

"I hear that. Maybe not even that, if it stays like it has." He grinned, always happy to jaw about nothing.

"Don't say that, now." She sighed. "I'm thinking about packing up, moving somewhere with snow."

Right. Like Kelly was going up north. That girl was Texas, born and bred. She had the helmet hair and sparkly tank tops to prove it. He grinned, shaking his head. "Uh-huh."

"Don't you laugh at me, now... you butthead."

The bell above the door jangled, and Ellen Redding came in, tote bag dangling off one arm, and nodded at the girls and him. "I'm meeting June, honey."

"Of course you are, it's Tuesday. You want iced tea?"

"I do, thank you."

Win smiled. "Morning, ma'am."

"Morning, Win." She grinned and gave him a wave. "Mike. Terry."

The old cowboys nodded as one, both of them sipping their coffees. Win wasn't sure if it would give her problems if he asked how Sage was....

"How's Sam doing, honey?" Kelly brought Ellen her tea.

"Better now that Sage is home helping. It's a lot of work for an old man."

"I'm sure Sam is glad of it." Kelly patted Ellen's shoulder.

"He is. I am too, you know? I missed his face."

"Well, of course you did. He's your son."

Win hid a grin, his relief probably completely out of proportion. He'd known there had to be other people who didn't think Sage was a demon. Hell, the entire town knew what happened, or at least a version of what happened.

There were times when it was better to let folks believe what they believed. Then there were times to fight it.

Mike sighed softly. "Poor gal. That boy of hers broke her heart. I was glad to hear that he came to make things easier on her."

"He seems like a decent sort, actually," Win murmured, putting a bug in the guys' ears.

"He cowboys up. Rode fence and fed for me last week when I was down in the back." Terry shrugged. "Shit happens. He did his time."

Well, good. If the old cowboys approved of Sage, he'd have some allies when he needed them.

Of course, old cowboys tended to fall on the other side of the law, if the shit hit the fan. There was a little... moral flexibility there. They would call it the cowboy code or some such.

"You want a warm up, guys?"

Two coffee cups were held out, and Win grinned, pushing his over too. Might as well have one more while his radio was quiet.

For the first time all day, he felt like he was home.

CHAPTER TEN

GOOD LORD and butter, Sage was sweating like a whore in church. Daddy'd set him to digging out some pipe running out from the house to the meter so Rick Martin could come lay copper in the morning. That damned black gumbo soil, though, had dried up to pure stone, fighting his shovel but good. He'd lost his button-down around noon, and his T-shirt by three. Now it was running toward five thirty and he was one ball of wore-out cowboy.

He stopped, leaned against a fence post, and panted like he was one of the dogs.

The crunch of tires on gravel made him cringe. He wasn't expecting his folks to be back around until seven. *Please don't let it be the sheriff or some other fool.* He was doing everything right, damn it all to hell. Every fucking thing.

The truck that pulled up was familiar, but in a good way. Adam Winchester. His momma called Adam "Win," but that seemed so weird.

He grabbed his T-shirt, intending to put it on, but oh Lord. No way.

There was no way.

"Hey." Win climbed out of the truck, eyes hidden by sunglasses. "I, uh, brought tacos. And a scone. Tacos for us. Scone for you."

"A what?"

"It's almost like a cross between a muffin and a biscuit. Cinnamon."

"Oh yum. Thank you. I...." He motioned to himself, his gross, sweaty nakedness. "It's vicious hot out here."

"Uh-huh." Adam just stood there.

"You want to come in?" He wasn't sure what the fuck to do.

"Sure. If you're done, I mean. I know it's a little early, but I had this damned scone."

Sage stepped over. "I got about another nine inches to pull out and I'll be done."

"Did you need some help?" Win grinned over the sunglasses. "I can put the food in your place. This I understand better than animals."

"Ain't no sense in both of us getting nasty. You can keep me company, if you want." He grabbed the shovel and got back to it, digging in.

"You make me feel lazy." Adam settled, though, planting his butt on a little camp chair Daddy had put out earlier.

"You been working, I'm sure." He started sweating again, in seconds, as he put his back and mind to his job.

"Yeah. It was a quiet day, though."

"That's good, right?"

"Yeah. It is." Adam chuckled. "Worst thing today was the fire department got called out because Mr. Lopez fell again and was all naked and stuff in the backyard."

"Oh, Lord. That man's been old since I was a kid. Now he's a thousand." Maybe more. Hopefully that wouldn't be Daddy one day.

"Yeah. Well, he wouldn't fall, he didn't drink so much. I think he's pickled."

"He comes from drinkers. He don't have a choice in it, I reckon." God, this dirt was a stone-cold bitch.

"Here, man. I feel like an idiot sitting here." Adam hopped up and came to help, standing close.

"This fucking dirt is killing me. Plumber's coming tomorrow, though." Lord, Adam smelled good. Damn good. Like a memory of something right.

"Yeah, well, let me take a turn, huh?" Before he could argue, Adam was in there working, grunting, and sweating.

It took Adam a few minutes to get the dirt moving, and then Sage finished off, his hands feeling like hamburger.

"There we go."

They grinned at each other like fools, Adam's face covered with grit.

"You're all dirty now. What would your momma say?" Sage was damn near drunk on it, on that goofy smile.

"That I'd best wash up before I meet her for lunch tomorrow. Other than that, she wouldn't care." Adam's shoulder rubbed against his. "Supper?"

His belly jerked, tightened, and he hoped Adam didn't see. "Hell, yeah. And the biggest glass of tea on earth."

"Sounds good." For a moment Adam leaned against him, and Sage thought he might melt, and not from the extra body heat.

His mouth was lacquer dry and *shit, shit,* what was he fucking thinking? He was outside and getting hard with a cop.

Adam cleared his throat, and damned if a glance down didn't show the cop getting hard for him.

Okay, whoa. "Come on. I need to get off. The dirt, I mean. Clean it."

Damn it.

"And eat. Tacos." Adam nodded, heading to the house, hobbling a little.

"Tacos are the perfect food, you know?" *Stop looking at Adam's ass. Stop looking at Adam's ass. Stop looking at that tight, perfect round ass.* The man had to wear Wranglers, didn't he? Why couldn't he come in his uniform? That would have killed Sage's interest.

The jeans, though? Fuck him raw.

Sage half grinned, half grimaced. Most fellers didn't know what a bad reference that phrase was.

Still, it was enough to calm him down as he climbed the steps to his trailer. "Have a drink and a sit. I got to wipe down."

"Thanks. I'll pour you some tea." Adam took the sunglasses off and set them aside, and the man was... staring. Looking hungry.

"You're a good man." A fine, hard, good man.

"I try." Those eye lines crinkled, and Sage's knees went weak.

Okay. Okay. Bathroom. He got in there and started the water going, loud enough that no one would hear if he jacked off, fast and hard and brutal, pulling himself and shooting into the toilet, his balls aching. His knees sagged, and he breathed deeply, trying hard to keep himself upright.

Fuck, fuck, he was out of his mind, doing this. He didn't even know what he was doing, exactly. The cop and the ex-con? That sounded like a bad porn movie.

Hell, it probably *was* a bad porn movie.

When he came back out, Adam had laid out food and poured drinks and was standing in the front room, hands in his pockets.

"Hey. Sorry, I had to...." *Get my rocks off.* "...clean up."

"No worries. Uh, you thinking about a shirt?"

"Oh God. Yes. Yes, sorry. Sorry." He hurried back to his bedroom and found a T-shirt from the closet. Adam made him stupid.

Adam waited for him, right where he'd left the man. "Hey, I was enjoying the view, but I thought you might be uncomfortable with me staring."

"I just.... Uh.... Tea?" What? Staring? At who? Him? Lord almighty.

"Here." Adam thrust a glass of tea at him.

"Thanks." He gulped it down, hoping to douse the fire in his chest. It didn't, but at least he didn't choke.

"No problem. I—sorry, man. I don't want to freak you out or anything. I'll try to keep my eyes to myself."

"Ain't got nothing you don't, and you know I ain't into boobs." What was he supposed to do?

"I know." Adam sighed and scrubbed a hand over his face. That smile went all crookedy and wry. "I want you."

"Me?" Well, now. That was an interesting thought. "Honey, I'm messed up. There ain't no good queer men here?"

"I'm sure there are." Spreading his hands, Adam shrugged. "I mean, there have to be. I know it would be smarter to want someone else, for sure."

Sage heard that, and as bad as it stung to admit, he had to agree with it. "No shit on that. Your boss would cut your nuts off. You want chips and salsa with the tacos?"

"That sounds good." Smiling a little, Adam moved a little closer. Maybe too damn close. "No one ever said I was smart, Sage."

"No?" He looked up—and up and up—this close, Adam was tall.

"Nope." Adam touched him, hand on his arm, sliding up over his shoulder to his cheek, thumb rubbing along Sage's jaw.

Well, he'd be goddamned.

"You're touching me." He ducked his chin, sort of wallowing in the sensation.

"Is that bad? I think it feels good."

That big body rubbed against his in the smallest ways. A brush of shoulder, their thighs sliding together with a scratch of denim.

"It does." He felt like every muscle was tightening, responding to Adam. "God, it so does."

"Oh, excellent." He'd never seen a smile like that, up close and personal, lighting up Adam's face just before the man kissed him.

He gasped, lips parting in pure-D shock. *Kissing him.* No one had kissed him in so long. God, what if his breath was nasty? What if his teeth didn't feel good to Adam's tongue?

Adam didn't seem to be so worried. The man didn't hurry, tasting him deep. One square hand came up, cradled the back of his head and supported his neck, and damn, but that felt fine as frog hair. He leaned into the touch, letting Adam guide him, letting the feel of that hot mouth on his flow through his whole body.

His spent cock woke right up again, like it was going to shake hands with Adam's, give a hello and howdy. He almost pulled away to stare down at it, but Adam wouldn't let him. No, sir, the man clung to him, hips starting to rock against his. Adam's prick was heavy, unmistakable, and the promise of it made Sage's mouth water.

He wanted, but he had no idea what to do. Eight years in, and he'd never, ever been the one to initiate any kind of contact.

The kiss eased up, then came back, like a wave on the edge of the water. He didn't want to think of the beach, of California. He didn't want to remember anything. He wanted to be right here, right now.

So he reached up, grabbed Adam's wide shoulders, and held on, letting that big body support him when his knees sagged.

"You're okay. Fuck, you're so fine." Adam's kisses went on and on, driving him crazy.

Sage couldn't think, couldn't reply. When Adam's thigh slid between his legs, all he could do was hump.

Adam was talking—encouraging him, urging him on—all the while one hand on his hip stroked him, like the man was stoking a fire. So strong. Lord, Adam was strong. That big old body never wavered, just held him up.

Sage was diamond-hard, as randy as he'd ever been—maybe more. He didn't know. He wanted Adam to keep on.

Moaning, Adam changed the angle a little, giving him more friction.

Oh, sweet Jesus. Yes.

Sage was fixin' to blow his load, just lose it. It was fucking heaven, right here in his kitchen. He'd never even dreamed about such a thing, and when Adam unzipped his jeans, he stared at the man in amazement.

"Shit, honey. Look at you. So fine." Adam's voice had gone all husky and deep, and Sage waited, held his breath to see what happened next. When he didn't answer, Adam stared him right in the eye and pushed that hand in Sage's jeans to grab his cock.

"Adam. Oh goddamn."

That touch made him buck, push right into Adam's palm like something had been let loose in him.

"That's it, Sage. You're on fire for me." Adam kissed him again, tongue pushing into his mouth. Sage grunted, the sound echoing inside his chest, and he went up on tiptoes, driving into the kiss.

He never wanted it to end, but he had to breathe at some point, so he had to pull back and pant, his body rocking back and forth.

Adam's eyes were on him, eating him up, and that fucking hand, it kept moving, working him like there was no tomorrow. Maybe there wasn't a tomorrow. Maybe he'd just explode and die happy.

"Gonna." Even though he had already. Christ.

"Good. Want to watch that." Adam tugged harder, thumb sliding against Sage's slit.

"Adam!" He jerked up on tiptoe and came, just like that.

"Oh God." That long body jerked against him, and he swore he could smell Adam, too, strong and musky. Did Adam just come in his pants? Oh, Lord above.

He reached up, touched Adam's cheek, about as stunned as he could be.

Adam smiled at him, cheek curving under his fingers. They stood there for the longest time, touching each other.

He didn't say a word, because he didn't want to fuck it up. Not yet.

Adam finally leaned in and kissed him before clearing his throat. "We should clean up before supper, huh?"

"Uh-huh. I…. Come on, I'll get you a rag and a pair of shorts." There was no way his sweats would fit Adam. Ever. "I got a washer and a dryer."

"Thanks." Adam laughed, then went to wash up, and it wasn't weird. It was cool, like two guys hanging out.

He changed into shorts, gave Adam a pair, and threw the jeans in the washer. "I'll get salsa."

For supper.

Together.

CHAPTER ELEVEN

WIN SAT on the couch a few feet from Sage, wondering if it would be okay to move closer and put an arm around the man. He'd moved a little fast there before dinner, and he knew it, but damn. He hadn't been lying. He'd wanted Sage so bad it hurt. Seeing the man with his shirt off had been a revelation. Tiny, but stocky, without so much as an ounce of fat—Sage was like a little wet dream. His tanned skin stretched over compact muscles, his nipples a much darker brown than Win would have expected from a blond-haired, blue-eyed cowboy. Sage's cock was a dream, too, not too long, but nice and thick....

Was he drooling?

"Adam?" Sage's voice was like a touch. "Can I ask you something?"

He turned, meeting those pretty blue eyes with his. "Sure, man. Shoot."

"What happens next?" Sage winced, but held his gaze. "I've never done this before, and I want to do the right thing."

Oh, man. He paused, wanting the words to come out right. "Well, I don't want to push you, but I want to see you again. I want to touch you some more." That was the simple answer.

"You're not worried you'll get in trouble?"

"Nope." Shrugging, he spread his hands. "I mean, no more than I am already. My mom is the only one I give a damn about in my family."

"Okay. I think...." Sage swallowed hard. "I think I ought to get to touch you too."

Win thought that maybe that took a shitload of courage from Sage.

"You can touch me all you want, honey." He said it like he meant it, serious as anything.

"I'm gonna lock the door so my folks don't come in."

So practical. Win watched Sage move around, locking up and turning off some of the lights. He felt like he was some kind of hawk or something, perched on a branch and waiting for his prey to come back in range.

All the trash was gathered, carefully disposed of, leaving the house in its perfect state. Sage was neater than anyone Win had ever met. The place was spotless, save for the muddy boots sitting inside the front door.

It was a little unnatural, but whatever. It was better than the barracks, better than his rental with its chaos of dropped clothes and giant dust bunnies. He sat back, giving his cock a little more room in the soft shorts Sage had given him.

Sage groaned, eyes on his belly. "You're something."

"Am I?" He sucked it in a little, needing that admiration some. It had been a long time since he'd been with someone behind a locked door. Not just a quick suck in a Dallas bar.

"Uh-huh." Sage sat. "I ain't much on pretty words or nothin', but you got it going on."

"Thanks." A chuckle escaped him, and he patted the couch next to him. "Come on and touch."

Sage sat, damn near vibrating.

"You're too far away, man." Win held out a hand, hoping Sage would reach for him too.

"I am." Sage scooted closer, and then one hand brushed over his thigh.

Win actually jumped, the touch weirdly electric. He almost felt guilty at how inexperienced Sage clearly was, like he was taking advantage. However, Sage was damned near thirty and knew how to say no.

Hell, the man'd been to prison. Who knew how experienced he was? Okay, whoa. That was a sick thought. Win stamped it out, not wanting anything to wilt. This was nothing like a prison experience. This was pure want.

"You want me to stop, just say so." Sage's fingers danced their way up his thigh.

"Oh, I can't imagine wanting that." Win knew this was exactly what he needed. Stopping wasn't much of an option.

"No. No, I ain't wanting to stop. Not now." The tips of Sage's callused fingers brushed his inner thigh, barely nudged his sac.

"Good." He lifted up, letting Sage have more access. He wanted to strip the shorts off, but he didn't want to be too… what? Was it okay to say forward when a man was touching your balls?

The deep, low groan sounded so good, made his cock fill even faster. God, it was fucking heady, to be wanted like this. His belly tightened, his chest rising and falling. He wanted to hold his breath, but he forced his lungs to work. The pressure of Sage's palm against his cock drew his knees up a little, enough to lift his feet off the floor. He panted, feeling like a teenager. Hell, he'd come in his pants a while ago.

He grinned when Sage checked in with him, eyes meeting his curiously. "That feels good."

"It does." Sage measured him, base to tip. "Nice and heavy."

"Th-thanks." He started rocking his hips up, wanting more.

"Uh-huh. Can I?" Sage plucked the drawstring.

"Please. Yes." Win was—yeah. He was ready to feel Sage's touch on his bare skin.

Sage untied the drawstring, and Win lifted his hips, helping to get the damned things off. His cock was so hard a cat couldn't scratch it and red at the tip, needing attention. He stared at Sage's hand when it descended, each finger fascinating him when they wrapped around him.

Jesus.

Jesus, that was….

Whatever it was, it wasn't anything—anything—compared to when Sage bent down and wrapped those soft, hot lips around his prick.

Win jerked, his hips punching up. He wanted to grab Sage by the head, but that seemed crazy forceful for the first time he had that mouth on his cock. Besides that, Sage was doing fine—humming and licking, sucking and bobbing. Oh fuck. That was pure heaven. Win leaned his head back against the couch and tried to breathe, his balls pulling up tight. He watched every fucking stroke, refusing to miss a second of that blond head moving for his pleasure.

He stroked Sage's cheek, his mouth starting to move, words pouring out. "That's it, huh? God, that's good. Wet. Hot."

The suction got stronger, proving to him that Sage was into it, was hearing him but good. Those sweet lips shaped to fit him and pulled, Sage working his cock with the flat of that rough tongue, and Win thought he might be in heaven.

Then the man's fingers started rolling his nuts, massaging them, just hard enough.

"Oh fuck, honey. I'm gonna bust it." He was going to lose it, and he wasn't sure he wanted to yet. "I might only be good for one more."

Sage's lips popped off his cock, wet and red and swollen.

Win grinned at him, stroking that pretty mouth with one finger. "Come on up here."

He drew Sage up, tugging when those lips wrapped around his fingers and sucked. His cock jerked again, then again, reminding him how close he was to the edge.

"Kiss me, please." He groaned the words out, and Sage pushed into his arms, that tiny ass right where he could grab a double handful of it. Those strong thighs slid down on either side of his, Sage pushing even closer.

He got his kiss, hot and wet and deep. Sage was learning, and fast. Where the first kisses had been tentative, this was heated, hungry. They were rocking together fast, the friction sweet as hell. Sage's cock was like a brand, nudging his belly.

It needed to be bare, like his. He pulled at Sage's shorts.

"Yeah." Sage wiggled, letting him strip that pocket cowboy body down. It didn't take long before they were skin to skin, and Win got to look and touch and feel. Sage was perfectly formed with tiny brown nipples and a six-pack. He had scars—some big, some not—but they made Win want to touch more.

He didn't go there, though, the scars. Not yet. What if that freaked Sage out, if they held bad memories? So he went for the nipples, thumbs sliding over them.

Sage cried out into his mouth, then settled back astride his legs, rubbing on him good. Win hummed, working their cocks together, loving how it felt, the hard prick against his. He hadn't spent time with a man in years, and it felt luxurious, like he was the luckiest bastard ever.

He grabbed Sage's ass and pulled them together faster, the rhythm getting a little crazy. He loved the sound their skin made when it slapped. Sage leaked against him, pretty cock making the friction easy. Win bent for another kiss, afraid he'd start babbling if he didn't. Keep your stupid mouth busy—that was his motto.

Sage opened right up to him, tongue sliding alongside his. Shit, if this was how good Sage was at kissing in three hours, Win was going to fucking die in a week. There would be little pieces of him all over the county. No laughing, either. That would probably upset Sage. And God knew, that was the very last thing on earth he wanted. He wanted this to be the best thing that ever happened to Sage.

Kissing harder, he reached between them and got a hand on their cocks. Yeah. Oh, that was the ticket.

Sage made this amazing noise, almost swallowed, and Win nodded. That was it. *Come on, honey.* Win realized he needed to see Sage come more than he wanted to let go himself.

"Don't stop." Sage grabbed him, deepened their kiss, the man near wild against him.

No. No, there would be no stopping. Not until they hit the finish line.

The tip of their cocks rubbed together, bumped hard, and Win's toes curled. He teetered on the edge, worrying Sage's lower lip with his teeth. He pushed his thumb against Sage's slit, wanting to push the man over the edge.

"Adam." Sage curled up, shot, heat covering his fingers, his belly, his cock.

"Oh fuck, Sage...." Win came too, his balls so tight he thought they might bust.

"Uh-huh. Uh-huh." Sage blinked at him, all baby-headed, neck as loose as a shot rubber band.

Win slid his free hand up behind Sage's head and tilted the man up for one more kiss. Maybe two. These were lazy, happy touches.

Sage actually chuckled, the sound sweet, soft. "I think that was better than Blue Bell ice cream."

Win laughed, surprising himself. "I think so too."

"Good thing we can have both, huh?"

Oh. Oh, someone had a sense of humor. That made him so happy. Win nodded. "Ice cream good."

"Uh-huh. Strawberry and Cookies 'n Cream."

"With cream?" He loved whipped cream in a can.

"Are you a Reddi-wip whore?"

Win was loving these flashes of wit, of charm. "I am. I can just eat that. Oh man, did you know at the holidays it comes in caramel and peppermint?"

"Ice cream?"

"No, honey, the whipped cream."

"Dude. Really?" Sage's expression went distant, a little lost, and Win couldn't help but touch, wanting to ease whatever thought was in there. Sage jumped, cheek heated under his hand. "I just... I guess the holidays will be different this year. Better. They have to be, don't they?"

Fuck, he had a ton of questions. When had Sage gone in, exactly? What was it like, to have Christmas inside? Had there been Christmas? How in the hell did you ask that sort of thing when you were naked and sticky and leaning together on the oldest nattiest couch in history?

Win guessed you didn't ask. He would bet Sage wouldn't offer. All he could think to say was "Well, I sure hope I can help with that."

"I reckon you can." Sage grinned, eyes crinkling up. "First, though, let's make it through Halloween without someone trying to burn Daddy's barns down."

His mouth flattened into a hard line. "I swear to God, if anyone messes with your folks...."

"They won't." Sage's face was calm, quiet. "They'll mess with me. I can take it. They won't get through me to Momma or Daddy, either one."

Win wanted to jump in front of Sage and protect him from everything, but that was silly. The man could cope. Sage was stronger than anyone gave him credit for.

Sage stood up, headed for the tiny bathroom, and brought out two washrags.

"Thanks, man," Win said as he took one, then rubbed it over his skin, which was sensitive as hell.

Sage cleaned himself quickly, pulled on his shorts, and got two battered containers of ice cream out of the freezer. They settled in and grinned at each other, both of them sucking cream off their spoons.

"Ice cream's good, huh?"

"It's great." Somehow it tasted better when he sat and ate it with Sage. He really wanted to stay the night, but it seemed crass to ask.

"You have to be in early tomorrow? I got the *Batman* movie."

"Oh. No, I'm on second tomorrow. Grace is taking pity on me and scheduling me opposite the sheriff." He leaned over and put his bowl down, then moved to snuggle with Sage. "Is this okay?"

"It is." Sage grabbed the remote and turned on the TV, and the movie previews started.

"Thanks for letting me stick around." The movie would start any second, and Win thought it was important for Sage to know he appreciated the companionship as much as the sex.

Sage leaned into his side and hummed. "I'm glad you can."

He dared to kiss Sage's temple before settling in and watching the movie. All in all, the night had gone way better than he'd feared it would when he showed up to a shirtless Sage and lost part of his mind.

After all, there'd been sex and ice cream.

CHAPTER TWELVE

SAGE PULLED into the parking lot of the diner, then went inside, his book in hand. The dinner crowd was mostly gone, and he nodded to Wilma.

"Sage! Hey, stranger. How goes it?"

"Just fine, ma'am. You doin' all right?"

She beamed at him, gold tooth glinting. "Right as rain. I got chocolate, cherry, and pumpkin today."

"Cherry, please." He ignored the stares from the other tables and sat in the back with the new Lee Child book that Adam had brought him last night. They'd found out they shared not only taste in movies, but in books too.

He liked having Adam as a friend.

Momma and Daddy had been quiet on it, only inviting Adam over to the house for a cookout on Sunday afternoon with Rosemary and them. Adam had been noncommittal, saying he had to check the schedule and such. Sage got it. Rosemary's Greg was a bastard of mammoth proportions. It would be damned hard to come and listen to him growl and spit. Adam wasn't the kind to let people say awful things without stepping in.

Still, the man hadn't said no, so maybe. Who knew?

Sage pulled the bookmark out of his book, nodding when his coffee appeared in front of him.

"I'll get your pie, Sage."

He offered Wilma a smile and relaxed, then sugared his coffee and settled into Jack Reacher's world. The evening flew by, like it always did. The small crowd thinned out until it was only him, which was when Bulldog came in.

He nodded to the biker and grinned. "Evening."

"Hey, there, Sage. How goes?"

"It goes. Been working on plumbing down at the place. Y'all doing okay?"

"Not bad. Been thinking of taking Wilma on a cruise."

"Really? Y'all going to Mexico or Jamaica?"

"The Bahamas, actually. My mechanic, Hank? He says his wife loved it. We'll have to fly to Florida instead of going out of Galveston, but it'll be worth it."

"Very cool. That sounds amazing." Sage had never been on an airplane, didn't reckon he ever would, now. "When are y'all going?"

"Not sure, exactly. Next month, maybe. Might need you to do a few things for me out at the house."

"I can do that." He knew about being neighborly, and they didn't have a huge piece of land.

"Cool." Bulldog clapped him lightly on the shoulder and headed to the kitchen.

He heard Wilma's squeal, her happy sounds perfect and young, like she was a teenager again. He ducked his head and smiled, surprised to find himself with friends, real friends he cared about.

"You hear her going on? Silly woman." Bulldog was hilarious—the tattooed, fierce-looking biker teasing and playful.

Sage chuckled. "Well, that's a good surprise, man."

"It is. You ought to come out to the place over the next couple days. I'll show you around."

"I'm happy to, man." He wrote down his cell number and passed it over.

"Cool." Bulldog took it but was soon called away by one of the bikers.

The ebb and flow of the diner sounded good around Sage, tickling his ears while he read his book. He'd missed coming out, missed the pie and the coffee.

This was worth the trouble it would cause, damn it.

"You need anything else, honey?" Wilma stood there, coffeepot at the ready.

"No, ma'am. I'm right as rain."

"Well, let me top you off so I can clean the pot." She winked, and he realized maybe an hour had passed.

"Good book." The place had emptied out except for him and Bulldog, and he finished his cup and left a twenty on the table. "I'm going to head out, y'all. You're good?"

He didn't worry about leaving Wilma with her man, but he would stay and walk them out, if they wanted.

"We're on our way in two shakes." Bulldog waved him out, grinning hugely.

He nodded, stuffed his book in his back pocket, and headed to his truck. He just made it outside the ring of light from the streetlights when he heard footsteps behind him and he spun, catching the blow on his shoulder and cheekbone instead of the back of his head.

There were no taunts, no curses or name-calling. In fact, the attack was like prison, quiet and vicious and coming at him from all sides in seconds.

He fought to keep his feet, to make it closer to the truck so he could keep his back to it. Sage knew better than to strike out. That only got your arms broken. No, he kept them tight to his body, his fists up in front of his face. He wanted to keep his teeth.

"Hey! What the fuck!" Bulldog's roar was welcome, and Sage weathered another flurry of blows, a boot catching his blown knee.

A shot rang out, Sage flinching and waiting for the pain to tear through him. Instead, one of his attackers cried out and fell away, Bulldog wading in and whacking another with the barrel of a shotgun.

Two more started running even as Wilma hollered, "Win's on the way, baby!"

Sage leaned against his truck, blinking through the blood stinging his eyes, fists still up. He couldn't unclench them, couldn't stop shaking.

"They're gone. They're gone, man." Bulldog didn't touch him, which he was grateful for. He might break.

"I didn't hit anyone. I'm okay to drive." He had to go before the cops showed.

"No. No way. You need a doctor."

A siren wailed in the distance, and his gut clenched in instinctive denial. "I can't. I can't. I'll go home." He slipped into his truck, his knee screaming.

"Sage, no." Bulldog tried to stop him, but Sage pulled the truck door closed.

"I'll go home. Please. Please, I can't. You know, huh?" Bulldog had to get it.

"I'll send Win once all the mopping up is done." Bulldog slapped the hood of the truck. "Go on."

"Thanks, man." He wiped his face off and started the engine.

Home.

He had to go home.

Had to.

Just in case they came after his folks.

CHAPTER THIRTEEN

WIN DROVE to Sage's folks' ranch, hands clenched on the wheel of his truck. He'd gone home, trading the cruiser for his own ride. He hated wasting the time, but Bulldog had insisted. No cop cars.

The Reddings' house was dark, but the lights were on at Sage's trailer, so he went on up and knocked on the door. Penny hit the door like a freight train, barking violently.

"Hey. Hey, back off, sweetie. Who is it?"

"It's Win. Adam. Can I come in?"

"Are you coming to arrest me? Because I didn't do anything." Sage sounded like he'd done swallowed a frog.

"No. No, Sage. I need to know you're all right." He shifted from foot to foot. "You're not in trouble, and I won't even ask if you want to press charges if you tell me not to."

"I didn't see anything. I didn't see anyone's faces." The door was unlocked and opened. "Come on in. Do you want a cup of coffee?"

"If you've got one, sure." Win tried hard to keep his rage at bay when he stepped inside and got a good look at Sage. The bruises were vast and many, one eye swollen shut, and cheekbone ripped. The man held himself carefully, like he was afraid he'd shatter.

"God, babe." His hands clenched and Win had to stop and clear his throat. "Do you need me to look at anything?"

"I'm okay. I didn't do anything." Sage met his eyes. "I didn't start anything."

"I know that. Bulldog gave me an official report." He stared right back. "I'm not here as a cop."

"Oh, good." Sage relaxed, shuffled to the kitchen, and started pouring two mugs of steaming joe. "He scared them off."

"He did. Rubber bullets." That had been smart on Bulldog's part, not using live ammo. Fewer penalties that way.

"They didn't say nothin'."

"Nothing at all that you could make out?" Win's arms ached with tension. He wanted to reach out so bad, but Sage was stiffly separate from him.

"Nothing at all. They just wanted to whup on me."

"Sage." Win reached out, needing to feel for himself that Sage wasn't broken.

Sage stepped up and pushed into his hands with a soft groan. "Hell of a night."

"I'm sorry, babe." He didn't even know what for, really, except that he hadn't been there to stop it.

"Me too." Sage leaned against him for a second, still and heavy.

Win knew it shouldn't feel so good to have Sage's trust, but it did. He held Sage loosely, feeling the heat of bruises.

"The pie was good tonight."

"Was it?" Jesus. Sage was taking this whole thing like he deserved it, like it went with coffee and dessert.

"Yeah." Sage took a deep breath. "Yeah, it was. I think I'm gonna hurl, honey. You just hang out here a minute."

Win let Sage go, knowing how damned embarrassing it was to puke in front of someone. His first DB, or dead body, had done that to him, and he'd tossed his cookies in front of two other cops.

He put their coffee on the end table and turned on the TV. God, Sage was going to be fucking sore tomorrow. Maybe he could—hell, he didn't know what he could do. Win sat on the couch, his hands dangling between his knees.

Sage came back in a pair of loose shorts and a T-shirt, and came to sit beside him. "Sorry, man. I haven't... I don't know what to do next."

"I don't either." He shrugged, feeling oddly helpless. They were all about charting new territory, him and Sage.

"That makes it easier, somehow." Sage leaned against his side.

"Does it?" He put his arm around Sage, careful not to jostle.

"Yeah. Sometimes I'm like the only son of a bitch that's lost on earth."

"Nah. We're all wandering around in the dark." That was true enough.

"Can you stay a little while? Watch a movie?"

"I can. What did you want to watch? I can put it on." He could get more coffee, maybe a soft snack. Ice cream again.

"*Matrix*? I have it. Momma bought it for me at the Walmart in Greenville."

"I like that one. Lots of leather and ducking bullets." He could see how Sage might need a new world hero movie at the moment.

"Yeah. Yeah, I like special effects." Sage handed him the DVD case, and those square hands were shaking, just a little bit.

"I'll get some pillows and blankets, too, huh?"

"Yeah. You want me to warm up your coffee?"

"If you want to, babe. I don't want you to have to get up." No, he wanted to wrap himself around Sage and protect him.

He got the couch set up, the movie going, and then he toed off his boots. He needed to touch, hold on.

They got settled again, and he pulled Sage mostly onto his lap. "Is this okay? The heat will help with the soreness."

"It's better than okay. Thank you for coming over." Sage pulled the blankets around them.

"I'm glad you're mostly in one piece." He kissed an unbruised bit of skin. His thoughts raced around like bumper cars in his head.

"I think one day they're gonna kill me. I hope they wait 'til after Daddy's gone and Momma's sold the ranch."

How the fuck could anyone talk about losing their life so fucking calmly?

"Not if I can help it." No, if Sage's folks moved on, Win would think about taking Sage where no one knew them. He blinked, the thought unexpected but sure and solid as all get-out. He would too. If he had the opportunity, he'd take the man and run.

Win sighed. What a mess. If he ever found out who the guys were who'd done this....

"It's okay, Adam." Sage snuggled right in, 90 percent asleep. "I won't let no one hurt you."

"I know." The words came out, he hoped, with less surprise than he felt. Sage, offering to protect him. God, he was in love.

"'Kay." Sage sighed, then started snoring, like the man was worn, bone deep.

Win figured Sage had earned the rest. He'd sit there as long as it took for Sage to get some too. He was on watch, now, and he wasn't going to let anyone break his man.

HE WOKE in the dark, curled into Adam's warmth as best he could, cramped together on the old sofa, his muscles throbbing. Oh, damn.

Damn.

They could stretch out on the bed some.

When he tried to move, though, an explosive grunt escaped him. Ow! That was—Ow!

"Adam." He wasn't in the joint. He could ask for help, right?

"Hmm?" Adam jolted a little under him. "Wha'?"

"Bed. Cramps, huh?"

"Oh. Oh, crap." Adam eased him down on the couch, then stood and stretched. "Here. I can help."

"Uh-huh." He reached up, his muscles like frozen rope. "Damn."

"No worries, babe." Carefully, gently, Adam picked him right up, one arm around his shoulders, the other under his legs. Sage didn't know what to say, if anything, so he didn't speak. Everything hurt.

Adam moved them into the bedroom and eased him down as carefully as he could. It still jostled Sage's bones, and he felt oddly like a kid, but the kindness of it warmed him.

"Stay with me?" He was so sore, so sore.

"Hell, yes. You need anything? I'm gonna take a leak and be right back." Adam bent and kissed his mouth, so gentle on his lips.

"I'm good." He rested there, eyes on the ceiling as he focused on breathing. The soft noises as Adam moved around sounded a lot like the hamster he'd had when he was eight. Then Adam was there with him, warm and bare, sliding them under the covers.

"Hey." He looked over, trying to see in the dark, trying to see Adam's face.

A flash of teeth was all he could see. "You okay?"

"Sore some. Like seeing you, right there."

"I like being here." Another soft kiss made him sigh. Adam made him happy, deep inside.

This was damn stupid. Bad enough that the whole town wanted to kick his ass, now he was corrupting the local police?

He couldn't help his grin. Corrupting Adam. Right. Sweet, innocent Adam. Shee-it. The man probably knew more about gay porn than Sage could ever learn, as long a head start as Adam had.

"You look better already."

"This feels better. You look good in my bed." Could he say that?

Apparently he could, because Adam slid across the sheets, closer than his own skin, hand on Sage's belly. "Thank you."

He could feel the gentle pressure of Adam's hand, just a bit heavier on each slow breath in. If he concentrated on that, on sharing their breath, the pain faded to something bearable. Something understandable, familiar.

Real, if not right.

Adam shifted, sighed a little, and Sage thought he was asleep until Adam murmured, "What's it going to take to keep you safe, babe?"

"They don't let people like me be safe. You know that. I gave that up the day I ran off with Angel." He hadn't known then, what he was sacrificing, and he wished he could say he would have done it different, but he had been young and stupid. Nothing on earth said stupid wasn't what he'd be again. Shit, he'd spent years looking for the moment where he could have stopped, said no, and he couldn't find it, still.

He wouldn't wish being queer on anybody, not ever, but he was, so he reckoned he had to pay for it.

"Yeah." Adam snorted. "If Angel had come home, still gay and tossing it in their faces, they would have beat him down too."

"Maybe. Maybe not. Your people have money. Things are different when you do, at least a little." He would have shrugged, but it hurt too much. "Angel wasn't ever coming back, though. He wasn't meant to be here. He loved California, the city. Being high."

"Well, I'm sorry it's been such a rough time, but I'm glad I'm here with you."

"I'm glad you came." Sage's lips quirked. Smiling would hurt too much. "This is worth it."

"Oh, I'm not sure we need to go that far. People are assholes, and this should never happen." Adam laughed for him, though. "I like you, Sage. A lot."

"Good. It would be fucking weird if you didn't."

"I guess it would." Adam paused, both of them breathing. "Do you miss him? Angel?"

"No." He blushed dark at how fast he could answer. "I.... We'd broken up, that day. He wanted...." He stopped, sighed. "He'd been sleeping with Luis. Said he needed something more."

"Oh. Oh! Wow, ouch." That hand on his belly moved, Adam stroking his skin lightly.

"We were eighteen. Luis was thirty and experienced. Me? Not so much with that."

"Lord." The brush of a bristly chin on his cheek told him Adam had nodded. "When I went to basic, I thought I knew it all. Sneaking around with the guys, getting a few blow jobs, you know? The first guy who took me on there almost ruined my ass forever."

"Oh Christ, I bet. I thought I was so fucking studly, all cock and crow, not a lick of sense." He hadn't fought with Angel about fucking around, though, weirdly enough. He'd been the one who started the downfall, telling Angel he wanted to go home to Texas. He'd been the one to say the high wasn't working like it had, the buzz wasn't what it'd been. That they'd tied it up over.

California was a big, big place and was set to eat little cowboys alive.

"It's weird, when you go somewhere the first time."

"Yeah. LA was huge. I'd thought Dallas was big." He'd bet Adam got that. Adam had been all over the world.

"Dallas seemed so huge when we were kids, huh?" Adam agreed. Everyone in their high school had thought so. It had seemed so far then too.

"I know. You'd run to Mesquite to the mall, and it was like an all-day thing." Sage chuckled, and it sounded rough as a cob, even in his ears.

"Did you ever go down to Arlington? We ditched one day, and my cousin's twenty-something boyfriend took us to Six Flags. I was fifteen, and I thought I was a big deal."

"Oh hell, yes. We went for Spanish club when I was a junior. We loved it… went in the spring. It was empty, raining." He'd had so much fun. He'd ridden the coasters over and over until he was sick as a dog.

"Oh man. That had to be a blast."

They shared a grin there, brighter now that Sage's eyes had adjusted to the dark. "It was. I remember thinking that place was magical when the lights went down."

"We should go there sometime," Adam said. "I mean, it might be lame now that we're adults, but it might be fun."

"It's Six Flags. How lame could it be?" Besides, it would be dressed up for Halloween.

"That's it." Adam yawned, and Sage could hear the man's jaw cracking.

He chuckled and nodded. "You need an alarm or something?"

"Huh? Oh. Yeah. Seven?"

"I can do that." Sage would be up at five thirty anyway.

"Thanks. That will give me time to get back into uniform." Adam yawned again, making this great snorting noise.

Sage took a deep breath, ribs creaking, sore. Tomorrow would be better.

It was hard to believe it could get worse.

THE ALARM clock jolted Win right up out of the bed. He reached for it and slapped his hand down against something that was not his night table.

"Ow! Fuck a duck."

He looked around wildly. What the… fuck. Fuck. Sage's room. The little room was stark, clean, one picture on the wall—a horse. He breathed deep. Right. Sage. Huh. Where was Sage?

He heard water running, and he slipped out of bed and headed for the bathroom. Sage was a giant bruise, sleeping in the bathtub, water pounding on him. Oh man, the hot water was gone, so Sage had been in there a bit. The cold wasn't gonna help.

"Babe. Come on."

"Huh?" One eye didn't even open.

"Sage. The water has run cold." Win turned off the tap before grabbing a towel.

"Oh." Sage's teeth started chattering.

"Shh." Easing down, he pulled Sage out of the tub, gently, and wrapped the towel around that poor body.

"Sorry. Sorry. I fed the horses."

Jesus. The man was tough as nails. Feeding the animals in the wee hours of the morning when he could barely move? That was insane.

"S'okay. I think you should take it easy today." He led Sage back to bed. Win would stop by the main house and tell Sage's momma about this on the way out.

"I hurt, man, deep. The shower helped."

"Did you take some anti-inflammatories?"

"I don't take things. I won't let them catch me during a piss test with anything."

"Advil isn't going to ruin a drug test, babe." He eased Sage down. "I'll make us some breakfast, huh?"

"I can cook for you." Sage's eyes closed.

"Will you let me take care of you, babe?" Win growled a little, knowing Sage was used to going it alone, but it wasn't necessary now.

"Little bit. Maybe." That was almost a grin.

"Good. Nap." He tucked Sage into the covers. "I'll be back." He hoped Sage had oatmeal or something soft.

Sage's kitchen had eggs, oatmeal, butter, bread. Someone's momma took care of him. Adam made some scrambled eggs and some soft toast as well as some instant oatmeal. That way Sage could pick what he wanted.

He headed back into the bedroom, hands filled with plates. Sage was sleeping, sitting up against the headboard.

"Babe? I brought you food." Sage needed to eat. Then he could snooze the day away.

"I smell oatmeal."

"Maple and brown sugar."

"Yum." Sage's one eye opened. "You been busy."

"It's not much, but you can nibble." He crawled into the bed and sat cross-legged with his own plate, then handed Sage his breakfast.

Sage took a spoonful, humming softly. "You're being awful good to me."

"You look like a giant sore spot, babe." He reached out to touch Sage's cheek. "And I like pampering you a little."

"I feel like I got my ass kicked by a herd of rampaging elephants."

"Ow." Elephants might be kinder than the folks who did this to Sage. By far.

"No shit on that." Sage frowned a second. "You told me Bulldog and Wilma are okay, right?"

"They're fine. Just fine." Bulldog was utterly furious, and Win had talked hard to keep the man from going after the guys who'd done this.

"Good. They're good folks."

"They are. You have some good friends there." Sage needed friends, so Win was grateful.

"I do." Sage licked his cracked lips. "I have a good friend here."

"You do." He kissed Sage's mouth before sitting back. "Eat up. I got to go here in an hour or so."

"Eggs look good." They ate together, Sage seriously drooping toward the end. Poor guy. His body needed to heal, to rest and recover.

"You gonna be okay if I go, babe?" Win took the plates and gave Sage one last kiss.

"I'll be fine. I'll just sleep for another hour or so."

Uh-huh. Another twelve, maybe. He grinned. As long as Sage slept, Win was cool. "I'll check on you tonight, okay?"

"Okay. Okay, I'll think 'bout supper."

"You do that." He would bet Sage's momma would provide supper. He pulled on last night's clothes and stopped to drop a last kiss on Sage's mouth. Sage was sound asleep by then, so Win headed up to the main house to talk to said momma, real quick.

ELLEN WAS sitting on the front porch with the dogs, coffee mug in hand. "Deputy."

"Hey, Mrs. Redding." He took the coffee and sniffed appreciatively. "Thanks."

"You're welcome. What's up?" No nonsense. That was Ellen Redding.

"Sage had a tough time last night at the cafe. He was attacked in the parking lot." He watched her face with a cop's eye, needing to see her reaction.

She stood. "Does he need to see a doctor? Is anything broken? He didn't start it. I know it."

"No, he didn't." Win sighed. "I stayed with him last night, and he looks to be all right—beat to hell but nothing broken. He got up to feed this morning, but he's sleeping now."

"Stubborn boy." Her lips tightened. "I'll let him sleep, and we'll do the night feeding, take spaghetti over tonight. You know who did it?"

"It was too dark to see, apparently. He says he didn't see faces, and Bulldog couldn't tell me." Win spread his hands. "I got there as soon as I could."

"You're not his bodyguard, son." She sat hard, rubbing her forehead. "I shouldn't have asked him to come back here."

"Well, now he's here and staying, I think." Impulsively, he reached out and touched her shoulder and squeezed. "I'll help any way I can."

"You're a good boy, Adam." She stood up and hugged him tight. It was the first time she'd called him Adam and not Win. "You know that he… that he likes boys, don't you?"

"I do. I like him too. That way. I hope that's okay." He hugged her back.

"I think it's probably stupid of you, 'cause your family will hate it, but you're welcome here, so long as you're good for him."

"I never said I was all that bright." He winked, happy that she chuckled for him. "I have to go in. I'll check on him tonight."

"I'll bring over enough for two. Have a safe day and don't worry. I'll keep an eye on him."

"I know you will." He gave her one more squeeze and left her. He needed to call his own mom, needed to hear her voice, and needed her to tell him that he was going to be okay too. He hit speed dial, knowing she'd be sitting at the breakfast bar, sipping her coffee.

She answered as he slipped into the truck. "Hey, baby. What's up?"

"Hi, Mom. Just needed to hear you today." She said that to him a lot, but today he wanted her to know it went both ways.

"Oh man. Hard night?" He heard her coffee cup clank down.

"It was tough, yeah. Sage Redding was assaulted."

"Is he okay? Are you? Were you there?" The questions came bullet-fast.

"He's beat up. Wilma called me, and I got there when everyone was running for it." He sighed. He knew he was pushing things with his family, and he felt more than a little responsible for the attack.

"Oh man. That sucks. How can I help?"

"Just tell me it's okay? I'll believe you if you tell me." He smiled a little, the joke an old one for them.

"He's a good man and you like him. It's going to be hard, but I have your back."

"Thanks, Mom. I love you." He was almost to his place, and he needed to get dressed.

"I love you. Call me when you're having your lunchtime, and I'll drive into town."

"Yes, ma'am." That would be nice, to know he had something to do on his downtime.

"Good boy. Go get the bad guys."

"I will." He hoped to hell that didn't end up being part of his family. Today or any day.

CHAPTER FOURTEEN

SAGE LOOKED at his Daddy, his head pounding. "I got this."

"Son, I swear to God, I will put you over my knee. I can feed the fucking horses one time." Daddy looked at him, lips tight. "How many were there, for fuck's sake?"

"Four or five. It was dark."

"Tell me you cleaned at least one of their clocks."

Right, because he wouldn't be the one headed back to jail if he did. The chances of one of those men working with Adam was better than good.

"I stayed on my feet and didn't lose no teeth" was finally what he settled for. That seemed like a fair assessment.

"This ain't right."

"What do you want me to say, Daddy?" He wasn't going to fuss about this. It wasn't the first time he'd had his ass handed to him; it wouldn't be the last.

"That you didn't let them kick your ass because you were scared, I guess."

Sage looked at his dad, making himself stay easy. "I'm gonna go work in the other barn for a while. You have a good night."

Scared. Shit.

Going back to jail would kill him. He'd rather let those assholes do it quick than have the state do it slowly and even more painfully. He'd never told his folks about the beatings he took, how his first week in, his head was dunked in bleach and he couldn't see for days. About how they took his knees. About Keye.

Nobody knew, and nobody ever would. Those secrets belonged to him.

The barn, at least, was quiet, if not cool. Sweltering was more like it. Bile rose in his throat. No, he wasn't no coward. He knew what he knew. Sage put his head down and started working, the pain becoming a steady thing, something he couldn't ignore but could move through. He breathed with it, in through his nose and out through his mouth.

"Sage Marlowe Redding!"

Fuck. "Whut, Momma?"

"What are you doing? You let us do the work today. You're hurt!" She stood right inside the barn door, hands on her hips.

"I'm fine. I'm almost done here. How's your quilt going?"

"It can wait." She tapped her foot. "I told Adam Winchester I'd bring down enough spaghetti for him too."

"He's a good man." Sage put the shovel down and looked at her. "You okay with me... seeing him?"

"As long as he has your back, yes. I think he really cares for you." Her eyes flashed. "He hurts you, and I will cut off his balls."

"I'm gonna be the one gets him hurt." It would happen, like night followed day. The sheriff or Angel's daddy would make Adam pay.

Her lips curved in a smile. "He's a tough boy."

"He is. He was a soldier." Sage wanted to die, to sit and stare at the TV and pretend he was sore because he'd gotten bucked off a skittish horse, not because he had the balls to go have a piece of pie at the diner.

"Oh, Son, I'm so sorry. I know you could have stayed there in California and not had this...this mess." Her face crumpled a little, and he panicked. She couldn't start crying.

"Stop it, Momma. I'm home where I belong. Let it go."

"I know you don't want salad, but do you want bread with your spaghetti?" Her shoulders squared up, which meant she was ready to move on.

"Yes, ma'am. If there's enough."

"There is. I won't toast it hard. You go wash up." There was no arguing with her order. None.

"Yes, ma'am. Thank you for supper." Lord, his head hurt.

"I'll bring it down in a bit." She turned on her heel, left him, and marched away like she was going to take on the whole world for him.

"Christ on a crutch." He put his shovel up, made sure everything was as done as he needed it to be, then headed to his trailer. Every step sent sharp jolts of pain through his knees, and he gritted his teeth against it, hoping his hot water heater had recovered since this morning.

He stood at the bottom of the stairs and slowly crept up. Three steps, and he felt like he might sit on the second one and stay there.

No way he was going to do that.

No way.

Never.

Sage swallowed hard and made himself take another step. He collapsed right inside the front door, his legs giving out. He felt like a puddle of lava.

If there was a God, he'd die here, basically happy, pretty much home. Of course, his momma might disapprove of finding him there, so maybe he ought to drag his ass to the—

"Sage? Are you.... Whoa. Need some help?" He hadn't heard a motorcycle, but Bulldog was right there next to him, crouching down.

"Bulldog?" He blinked up and tried to stand, but he couldn't.

Bulldog obviously knew about dealing with beat-to-shit folks, because the big man lifted him without hurting him, without killing him. In fact, he was able to relax a little until his muscles started cramping. He stiffened, a cry bursting out of him.

"I know, man," Bulldog said, easing him down onto the couch. "I know. It's worst when it starts to ease off."

"Oh fuck...."

"Where's your towels?"

"B... bathroom. Fuck. Bathroom."

Bulldog headed off for an eternity, and then suddenly burning hot towels wrapped around him.

"Oh!" He couldn't figure whether he needed to fight or let the heat help him until one of the worst cramps unclenched.

"Breathe, man. Pant. It'll ease." As soon as a towel started to cool, another hot one was added.

He blew out a breath, then sucked another in, his chest working like a bellows. "Too much."

"Trust me. It works. I was in the joint for fifteen years. They hit your knees?"

"Yeah."

"Damn. Let me get another towel." This time the towel was hot and wet and wrapped around his knees. The wet heat would help the joints.

"You... thank you." He was going to puke, it felt so good.

"No worries. Wilma was fretting, so she sent me. Win is on a call over at the county line—collision with three cars."

"Oh man. That sucks."

"Totally, man. Hate to hear about it. Came through on the scanner." Bulldog kept the towels coming, then handed him a cup of some kind of tea. Time had become so fluid.

At some point, Momma came and talked to Bulldog, and Sage thought she wanted to take him to Greenville Presbyterian, but Bulldog told her to give it another day. The low murmur of voices made him blink, and he tried to get up once, only to have Wilma push him down.

Lord. Was the whole town there?

Something cold and tart wet his lips, and then Adam was there. "I'm here, Sage. I'm going to take you into the tub, okay? If you don't get this fever down, I'm taking you to the hospital."

Then he was flying. Really flying, like hovering above the floor. The world spun, but he knew it when he lay in the tub, the lukewarm water making him shiver. He reached for Adam, needing that anchor.

"Right here. Relax for me. Breathe."

"Folks keep telling me that."

"Well, it helps." Adam's face swam into focus. "You need to get that fever down, babe."

"Bulldog came. So did Wilma."

"Yeah. I appreciate them coming too. You needed the help." Adam stroked Sage's hair, smiling.

Sage closed his eyes and floated. "You have a good day?"

"Busy. There was a domestic that took two hours, then a traffic fatality. Sucked." Adam sat on the floor next to the tub.

"I'm sorry." He tried to focus, but it was too hard, so he relaxed. "Momma made supper for us, I think."

"She did." Leaning in, Adam wet a soft cloth and rubbed it over Sage's forehead and cheeks. "This first."

"I'm sorry. I'm trying to not be a pussy."

"Stop apologizing, babe. You just need to recover some."

"My daddy thinks I'm a coward, but they'd put me back in."

"You're no coward, man." Adam wiped Sage's face again, then felt his skin. "Better."

"I'm not. He don't understand." Maximum security was hell on earth.

"No, I bet he doesn't. I can't know what happened in there, babe, but I know I get it more than most people."

"I want you to know. I didn't fight back because I'm scared of going back, not because I'm scared of fighting."

"I believe you." Adam stroked the cloth over his chest.

"Good." He should be self-conscious, he guessed, but he wasn't. He felt better, his muscles unclenching, his hands no longer clawed.

"You're looking so much better, baby."

"Feel better."

"Good." Adam grinned. "You want some juice? I had Wilma go to the Walmart and get that and more pillows for the bed."

"Please." Juice sounded like heaven.

"Let me get a towel." Adam left, came back, and hauled his sorry ass to the bed. He got apple juice, which he loved.

He drank deeply, the pillows supporting him on all sides. He figured this was what real folks had. Support. People. Family.

"I'm going to make sure your folks don't need anything. Then I'll warm up supper."

"Sure." He felt his lips curl in a smile. "I'll be right here."

"You'd best be, cowboy. You rest. I got my eye on you." Adam chuckled, heading out, boots ringing on the floor.

The day had ranked at the top of the weirdest fucking days ever.

Sage let his eyes close.

Christ.

SUPPER HADN'T gone well. At least not for Sage. They'd ended up opening a can of tomato soup.

Win had eaten in the kitchen, standing up, talking to Sage's momma. Bulldog and Wilma had headed off, Wilma promising to bring doughnuts by in the morning.

"You think I ought to take him to the hospital, Adam?" Her eyes were the same color as Sage's—bright blue, sharp. "Do you like to be called Adam, son? I've always heard everyone call you Win."

"Adam is fine. Most folks call me Win, but it's okay either way." He smiled, spreading his hands. "The fever is down, so unless it comes back up or he doesn't start to ease off tomorrow, I think we're okay."

"Good. I hate seeing him like this, and then he was working in the damn barn. Stubborn boy, just like his daddy."

Win chuckled. "Yeah. He's stubborn, for sure. He's resting now, though."

"Good." She shook her head. "I shouldn't have asked him to come home. He hated LA, but he was safer there."

"Oh, now." That was the truth, but there wasn't a reason for her to feel guilty. "He's happy to help."

"I know. He loves those horses. He's a cowboy." Ellen's lips quivered, but then she pressed them together. "Is that spaghetti okay?"

"Okay? Oh, this is so much better than my mom's." Win paused. "Just don't tell her that."

"I promise." Ellen winked. "I would never upset another mother."

"Thanks." His mom was the best at everything… except cooking.

"Okay. I'm going to go clean my kitchen. Are you…." She grinned. "Do you think I should come check on him tonight?"

"I'll stay." His cheeks heated like he was talking about having sex with her son, which was so not the idea tonight.

"Okay. I've hired Bobby Christian to feed tomorrow. He can rest."

"Thanks. I'll tell him." Win had hugged her earlier today, so he felt daring doing it again, but she looked like she needed it.

"You're a good boy, Adam." She leaned against him a second.

"I try." He had his demons. Maybe that was why he understood Sage better than most folks. He woke up in a cold sweat a lot of nights, the whole combat arena close and fresh.

She kissed his cheek and headed out, leaving him standing in Sage's front room like a newborn fool. Win turned in a circle, not sure what to do next. Maybe he'd take a shower.

He heard footsteps, and then Sage showed up, naked and blinking at him. "Adam? I thought I heard you."

"Hey, babe." The damned bruises looked so lurid, so devastating in the hall light. "I was pondering whether to do dishes or wash me."

"I can do the dishes, man."

Uh-huh. Right. Sage couldn't hardly walk and was teetering back and forth. "Nah. You need to sit. We can watch a movie if you want."

"I'd like that." Sage headed into the front room, stepping so careful, so gentle.

Win took a moment to go get the extra pillows and blankets Wilma and Bulldog had brought. He'd prop Sage up good. Sage settled, staring as Win covered him. "Lord, I was naked."

"Mmmhmm. Your mom was gone."

"She done seen it all. She'd tell you she made it."

"Well, she's right." That didn't mean Win would want to walk around naked in front of his mom.

Sage chuckled, the sound sore. "Lord, I have made trouble for everyone."

"Hey, you're worth every bit." Win curled up close but didn't lean.

Sage moved, pushed into his side. Win felt tall as a mountain, just from that tiny gesture. Sage trusted him. How fucking amazing was that?

He shifted slightly until Sage's head was on his shoulder. "You good, babe?"

"I am. I really appreciate you coming."

He grabbed the remote and started the movie. *Die Hard.* Huh. So not how being a cop worked, but it was fun to watch.

It was fascinating, though, how Sage's movies were all from when they were younger. He wondered if Sage listened to music, and if that would be the same. It was like Sage had sort of stopped aging when he went in.

That made sense, huh? The thoughts spun around and around in Win's head, making it hurt a little.

"Why did you get such a hard-core sentence, honey?" Wait. Wait, had he asked that out loud? That was nosy as all hell, and rude, too, with prison being such a hard subject.

Sage sighed. "They told me that they'd go for murder one if I didn't. There's no parole for that."

"Shit. I know you didn't kill anyone." Deep in his bones, Win was sure Sage was no killer. Win knew he could have requested Sage's records and read them, but that seemed like a huge intrusion.

"I didn't. I was fucked-up, bad. I…. Me and Angel had been in a bad fight that night. Bad. He'd been cheating on me and was with this dealer. I wanted to go home and was going, one way or the other, with the truck. We got into it about that. That truck, man, it was all we had, and it was worth something. At any rate, I was screaming and crying and high, threatening to kill him if he didn't give me my keys when the blue lights showed. We all scrambled like cockroaches, but I was too fucked-up to drive off, keys or no."

"Oh God. No wonder they pegged you. But what happened at the house? It blew up?"

"Uh-huh. Few hours later, I was passed out in the back of my truck, waiting to take my keys back one way or the other, and I heard it go. Soon as I figured out what the whoosh was, I ran in, but... it was too late. Too hot. There was fire eating the place up already, like a fucking monster. It was over." Sage shrugged, moving carefully. "I should have run, but I didn't. I just stood there staring. At the end, I was in jail, five people were dead, one of them your cousin, one of them a three-year-old girl."

"Christ." A three-year-old. "One of the people who owned the house? Their kid?"

"Yeah. Angel was sleeping with the guy, Luis. His wife was Brenda, and the baby was Josie. They kept her in a little room in the back. I didn't know the other dude, Jack his name was. Vietnam Vet, at least they said so at the trial. I'd never seen him before."

Win kissed the top of Sage's head. "I'm sorry, babe. That sucks, all around."

"Yeah. It did. I fucked up, bad, and I have to pay for that, I guess. I was high, stupid, and my heart was broke."

Win shook his head. He couldn't agree with that. "You paid more than you deserved, babe. We're all stupid at that age."

"Yeah. I said I was sorry a million times, but it's only words."

"No, you mean it." That was important to him, that he knew Sage was truly sorry all that shit had happened. That Sage knew he knew. Whatever.

"Hmm-mmm. Do you think it matters?"

"I think it does somewhere." He chuckled. "I have to. I became a cop, right? I'm an eternal optimist."

"I like that about you. I don't think I'm an eternal anything."

"I think you're a tough nut, babe. A survivor." Win was beginning to realize what Sage had gone through, and he was amazed.

"Yeah. Yeah, I am." Sage smiled, and fuck, it was pretty.

"There you go." They leaned on each other, and Win thought he might be pulling as much strength from Sage as vice versa.

By the time Bruce Willis started blowing shit up, they were both laughing, and Win was remembering how much he'd loved this movie. It was almost like going back in time.

He couldn't help but wonder what would have happened if it had been him Sage had hooked up with, all those years ago.

That way lay madness, right?

There was no going backward, and he had right now, with a relaxed, dozy cowboy in his arms. So, that cowboy was all beat up, and Win knew things were going to go downhill fast once he started an official investigation.

So, nothing in life was perfect.

CHAPTER FIFTEEN

SAGE SAT at the dining room table, looking at the macaroni and cheese in front of him. God, that looked amazing. No one made food like his momma. She knew how much cheese to add, and she'd put ham in it this time. She'd sautéed his greens, too, instead of making him eat a hard salad.

He did love her for that.

Rosemary and Greg were sitting there, Rosie quiet as a church mouse with her swollen belly and thin cheeks, Greg grinning like a piranha. Asshole was a predator. A predator with a bruise the shape of a rifle butt on his jaw and bruised-up knuckles on his right hand.

Sage counted to ten. He hated that fucking son of a bitch.

"You want a blender, Sage? Your mouth's lookin' sore," Greg said.

"Nope." *Eleven. Twelve. Thirteen.*

His daddy frowned down the table. "That's enough."

"What? Everyone knows he got his ass handed to him."

"Greg, honey…." Rosie winced.

"You shut your mouth." Momma half stood, slapping her hands on the table.

"Oh for fuck's sake, he's a goddamn queer pussy, not hitting back, standing there with his hands up protecting his pretty face instead of fighting like a man."

"That's enough." Sage stood and put his napkin on the table. "Outside."

It was bad enough the fucker was giving him shit at Momma's table, but the asshole had obviously been there, helping those creeps beat him down.

"Sage." His sister reached for his arm. Not Greg's, he noticed. He also noticed the bruises on her arm, four of them. Fingers. It was time to remind a certain son of a bitch what being a man was about.

"Stay here, Rosie." He met Greg's cold eyes, feeling about as settled as he could be. "Outside. Right now."

Greg sneered and stood, jerking his head. "Sure, Pussy-man."

Sage met Daddy's eyes, and Momma wrapped her hand around Rosie's wrist when she tried to stand. That was right.

This was his to deal with.

They headed out the back door to the yard, Sage's ears pricked for Greg's footsteps. He wouldn't let the man get the drop on him, but he'd be damned if he gave that smarmy fucker the satisfaction of thinking he was scared. Sage kept his shoulders back, his head up, shaking with the need to teach Greg a lesson.

He turned, catching the sucker punch he knew Greg would throw. Christ, the man was a moron. It stung his palm a little, but not near as much as it hurt his knuckles when he slammed them into Greg's glass jaw.

Oh fuck. That felt good.

The blow to Greg's midsection was for the motherfuckers who had poured bleach in his eyes his first week in. The connection to the bastard's nose was for the day he was kneecapped in the yard. And when he kicked Greg square in the balls? Shit, that was for him.

Just for him.

The whole thing took maybe a minute and a half. Sage stood, looking down at Greg, who rolled on the ground, clutching his nuts. "Still think I'm a coward, you limp-dicked, woman-hitting son of a bitch?"

When Greg didn't answer, Sage kicked again, the impact jostling him.

"I'll kill you for this," Greg finally wheezed. "I'll kill your sister."

"Oh, I don't think so, boy." Daddy's voice cracked like a whip, and the sound of the rifle cocking was even bigger. "Son, step away."

"Yes, sir." He backed off, not at all willing to get shot.

"You get off my property," Daddy snarled at Greg. "You ever touch either of my kids again, and I'll shoot you."

"What?" Greg stared at him, eyes huge. "What the fuck?"

"You heard me, you sack of shit. I been waiting for this day." Daddy sounded damn near gleeful. "Now, git. My food's getting cold."

Greg climbed to his feet, slow as hell, that puffy face twisted up in rage. "Set your fucking house on fire."

"You come within five miles of Redding land, you fucker," Sage growled, taking a step closer, "and I'll show you what happens to men in prison."

Greg broke under the weight of his stare, under the threat of Daddy's gun. The man ran faster than he looked like he could.

Sage looked at Daddy. "You ready to finish supper?"

"I am. I never turn down your momma's mac and cheese."

"Me neither. It's my favorite." He met Daddy's eyes. "You think he'll go to the police?"

"Shit, no." Daddy held the trigger and gently released the bolt, uncocking the rifle. "I think he's a fucking coward, and he knows you and Adam Winchester are… you know."

"I hope so. I—I won't go back, Daddy." Not for anything.

"I'll shoot him first." Daddy grinned. "I'm old and sick. They won't put me in jail. Come on, now."

"Yes, sir."

Rosie was sitting at the table, tears running down her cheeks. "What am I going to do?"

He sat. "Eat macaroni."

She glanced up at him, her lower lip quivering. "That's not funny."

"I'm not joking. You eat macaroni, you get your head on, you make a plan. You're not on your own, girl. That man of yours is a fucker and a prick, and I may have ruined his babymakers for life." It had felt good too. Sage felt better than he had in years.

Rosie looked at him, and then her mouth twisted and she chuckled. "Really?"

"You know it, Sister."

She laughed a little more, the sound watery as hell. Lord, she looked younger already.

Sage sat, and Momma dished him out another spoonful of mac and cheese. He breathed deep, letting the tension roll off his shoulders. Greg wouldn't go to the police. He couldn't. That man would never want anyone to know the gay prison boy had beat him down. Daddy was right. And he'd proven, he thought, that he wasn't afraid to fight. That Momma and Daddy and even Rosie could depend on him.

He wasn't a pussy. He wasn't a bad man.

He was a fucking cowboy.

Rosie was staring at him. Momma had her head down, a smile curving her lips. Daddy just looked puffed up and proud.

Him? He wanted to call Adam.

Sage ate his supper instead. There would be time to talk to Adam later, when he was alone.

CHAPTER SIXTEEN

"I SWEAR to God, Win, I don't understand you." His Aunt Linda had cornered him at the bar, the monthly family dinner at Culpepper's one he couldn't avoid this time around. He'd been hiding out, waiting for his mom and his cousin Cheri to get there, when Linda had spotted him.

He raised a brow. "You've said that since I was five."

"Your uncles have both told me about how you're taking up with that Redding boy." She glared at him, sloe eyes sharp as a tack. "He's trouble. A bad seed."

He sighed, trying not to roll his eyes. Aunt Linda was eighty-two, and that alone deserved respect. "It's my life, Auntie."

"And I want you to have a good one. If you lie in trash, son, you start to stink in your bones."

"You think?" He didn't bite his tongue, but he pressed his lips together.

"I do, and you're a good boy. Just watch yourself."

"I'll watch my back, Auntie." It would be his uncles stabbing him there, but he wouldn't say it.

"Adam! Baby!" And there came Momma, barreling in like a force of nature. "Linda, let me have my boy."

Auntie Linda harrumphed but stepped aside. Win grabbed his mom and hugged her hard, so happy to see her no one would believe he'd had lunch with her two days ago.

"Hey, baby." She smooched him. "How's it going? Come walk with me."

"You bet." He twined his fingers with hers, his relief almost ridiculous.

"So, how many of these asshole relatives of yours have given you grief today?"

"Oh, I been hiding." He was always amazed at how he sounded so much more East Texas after being with his family for five minutes.

"I don't blame you. How's your friend doing? Better?"

His friend. Like Momma didn't know Sage's name. He supposed she had to make some concessions to the family.

"He's better. He had a few rough days there."

"I sent his folks a fruit basket. Hear the sister moved back home."

"Yeah." Lord. Sage had called him late last Sunday night to tell him about the family dinner. Win had been keeping an eye out for Greg ever since.

Hell, he'd gone with Rosie to get her things from Greg's house. Their momma had encouraged Rosie to file a restraining order. That was going to be a mess, especially once the baby showed up, but shit would come out in the wash.

The best part was Sage looking more settled in his skin. Win was all for that, no matter what else happened. The man had needed some confidence. Sage was at Bulldog and Wilma's this week at night, feeding the animals, watching the house and the garage.

Win grinned. Bulldog had an amazing TV.

"What are you grinning about, Son?" Momma looked like pure evil. "Also, do you want to go shopping after supper?"

"Shopping for what?" Had he missed something she'd said?

"There's a Target. The mall's only fifteen minutes away...." She grinned at him. "We're two whole counties away from home."

"Oh." Yikes. "Uh. Well, if you need someone to carry bags...."

"Sound a little less like you're volunteering to get neutered."

Win chuckled. "You know I love you."

"I am aware, yes sir." His momma arched a perfectly manicured brow.

"How about I agree to shop if I need an escape here?"

"Works for me." Momma winked. "We could run now. Go eat at El Chico."

He opened his mouth to agree when his Uncle Teddy walked up. "Our table is ready."

Damn it.

Win bit back a sigh. Teddy was Angel's daddy, and he rarely sought Win out. That he was doing it today meant he had an agenda. Oh hell, maybe the man just wanted to have supper with Mom. She was his sister.

"Goodie." Mom grabbed his arm. "How're you, Teddy? Having a good week?"

"Well, I suppose that depends on who you talk to." Uncle Teddy stared at Win. Hard.

Win grinned. He wasn't doing anything wrong, damn it. Not a thing. He walked his mom to her chair and held it for her.

"Thank you, Son. So, Ted, have you taken over anyone's family farm this week?" Oh, Mom was on the offensive, getting out there with the fork and knife before they even got salads.

"Not yet, no." Teddy raised a dark eyebrow. "Been thinking of calling in a few markers."

"Because, damn, you need more land to let go to seed." Mom grabbed her water glass. "Have you considered buying land down south? Somewhere on the beach?"

"You trying to get rid of me, Lana?" Teddy scoffed a little.

"God, yes. You're a mean, grouchy old fuck with a hard-on for money."

Everyone at the table cackled, including Win. He wondered what Teddy had been like before becoming a bitter old man. Win couldn't remember, because Ted had been that way long before Angel had died.

They ordered dinner—a shitload of steaks with a couple of chicken breasts for those watching their weight. Mom ordered a filet. Win got a sirloin with a potato and a salad. He worked out pretty hard.

He wondered if Sage ever liked to come out this way. It was funny, they were only seventy miles outside Dallas and all the fun two guys could need, and yet....

The distance must seem insurmountable to Sage. God knew it did to Win sometimes. Maybe he should see if Sage's parole could handle a weekend in a hotel.

Fuck, that would be fun. Swimming, relaxing, movies on the pay-per-view. Just eating out without anyone who knew them watching would be a blast. He'd ask the next time he and Sage got together.

"Are you paying attention to my story about the hairdresser, Son?"

"Yes, ma'am." Mom knew better, but Win wasn't above flat-out lying.

"Oh good. You like my low-lights?"

What the fuck were low-lights? He peered at her, trying to figure it out. Hell, he even glanced at Ted for help.

His uncle shrugged. "Just say yes, Win."

"Yes. Absolutely. You look amazing."

Mom patted her hair. "Thanks, baby. How's your steak?"

"Good." He hadn't tried it yet. Okay, he needed to pay attention.

She looked at him, then cracked up. "Liar. Where are you in that head of yours?"

"Just thinking, Mom." He didn't dare say what about.

Everyone was looking at him. Christ. Win brazened it out, grinning and then digging into his salad. No way was he going to duck his head.

TIME TICKED away, and he almost wished an emergency would happen so he could zoom out, avoid the one-on-two that was going to happen with Teddy and Jim. They both sat across the way, staring at him, not quite glaring, because that would have gotten them in trouble with the women.

It was Jim who broke first, which didn't surprise Win in the least. "I heard that the Redding boy got into a fight with some bikers."

"Did you? Strangely, the only biker there was Bulldog, who helped Sage out."

"Bill Marsh is a gang leader and a felon. It doesn't surprise me he helped. Ex-cons stick together."

Win counted to five. "Looks like cowardly assholes do too."

"That's always been true, baby." Mom was the eternal voice of reason. "Asshole calls to asshole."

He smiled at her, giving her thanks silently.

She winked. God, it was good for someone to have his back. Sometimes it felt like he was the only sane one in the family. Auntie glared over at Jim. "Why are we talking about your work, boy?"

Mom snorted into her tea, and Win bit his bottom lip, hard.

"What would you like me to talk on?" Jim asked, belligerence showing on his face.

Auntie tilted her head. "We could discuss the price of tea in China. Or the death penalty. Or why girls don't wear nylons anymore."

"We could," his mom agreed. "Or, we could talk about the supersale at Kohl's."

"Are you heading to Kohl's, dear? I need a new hat."

"I'll take you ladies down," Win offered. He'd get ice cream out of it.

"You did raise a good boy, Lana." Auntie nodded. "I'll buy us all something sweet."

"Do they have whiskey at Starbucks these days?" Mom muttered.

"No, but I have some in my purse!" Auntie cackled, tossing her napkin on the table. "Ted, you get the bill."

"That's a luscious idea. Come on, Son. I have a card to burn." Mom stood up and waved blithely. "You two old men will have to ambush Win later."

Win stood, too, looking at the rest of the aunts and cousins. "Any other takers?"

They all stared at him, a group banded together in the belief that his lover killed one of their own.

"Right. Later!" He left a ten for the tip and grabbed Auntie's arm. No sense tempting fate.

As he headed to the parking lot, he texted Sage. "Boo."

The "Eek" that came back made him smile.

"You've got it bad, boy," Auntie said, hobbling along at an amazing speed.

Win shrugged. No sense denying it. "For all the good it does me."

"I'm sorry." The words surprised him, honestly.

"Thanks." He took her to his mom's car and held the door. He'd pick up his truck later. "Who did you ride in with?"

"Your cousin Alba."

"We'll drop you off, Auntie." Mom smiled. "I'll even come in and help you feed the cats."

"Thank you. I need a hat first."

"You got it. Kohl's-ho!" He took Mom's keys, sliding into the car, his knees up under his chin. He put the seat back, ignoring her protest.

When he was fifteen, he would rather have died than gone shopping with his mom. Now? So much better than hanging out with the men in the family.

He pulled out of the parking lot and headed toward I-30 and the shops. Christ. What a fucking day. He wondered if Sage wanted take and bake pizza tonight.

He'd bet Sage would like that. The man was insistent about not messing up Wilma's kitchen.

Yeah. He'd take pizza, and they'd find something pornalicious on the satellite.

Then he'd ask if Sage wanted to spend a couple of days in the Metroplex.

CHAPTER SEVENTEEN

"SAGE? REDDING? You around?"

Bulldog's voice rang out through the barn, and Sage looked up from where he was mucking, wiping the sweat from his eyes. Damn, he was ready for fall to show up down here. "Hey, man. What's up?"

"I was wondering if I could ask you a favor." Bulldog leaned against one of the posts. "Halloween is tomorrow, and I promised my grandkids I'd take them trick or treating. You willing to close up the diner with Wilma and make sure she gets in her car safe?"

"You know it." Sage didn't even have to think on it. Halloween was mostly fun, but there was that hint of evil to it, especially in a small town.

"Thanks, man. I really appreciate it. The boys are having themselves a bonfire." Bulldog grinned a little and rolled his eyes, and Sage snorted.

Bonfire. Redneck for let's get drunk, blow shit up, and shoot shit before fighting with our girlfriends and tearing siding off a barn. Hoo-fucking-ray.

"No need to explain. I got your back."

"Thanks, man." Bulldog winked at him, bearded face all jolly. "How you holding up?"

"Good. Good. Trying to make sure all this place is ready for winter." November was coming, and there'd be blue northers with the change in the calendar.

"Yeah. Yeah, I guess it's coming on to that time." Bulldog just shrugged. "You know all we got is the dogs."

"Yeah. I have to make sure the barns are wind-ready."

"Well, I'm okay with a hammer. I'd be happy to help."

"There's one right there." Sage pointed over to the other side of Windy's stall, where Daddy's hammer was sitting. "What are the grandbabies going as?"

"One is going as a bumblebee, the other one is a superhero." Bulldog's eyes crossed. "I ain't sure which one. Not one from when I was a kid." The man grabbed the hammer and got to patching holes and shoring up boards.

"Ain't nothing the same, man." And Bulldog had twenty years on him, easy.

"Bubba? Bubba, you out here?" Rosie came in, eyes going wide at the sight of the long-haired biker. "Mr. Bulldog. Good afternoon. Momma wants to know if you want oatmeal cookies. I was craving."

"Sure. Bulldog? You want some? They're like heaven."

"I'd be happy to sample some." Bulldog gave Rosie a smile that looked much like his namesake. "Miss Rosie."

"Coffee or tea?" she asked.

"Tea for me, please. It's still warm."

"Same for me." Bulldog nodded, and they went back to work until Rosie came back with a plate and two big glasses of tea.

"You get fed like this every day, Sage?"

"God, yes." He patted his belly, which was as flat as it had ever been. He was a pocket cowboy, and he knew it. A big guy wasn't hiding inside his genes. Or in his jeans. He grinned at his little joke, thinking on how Adam would like that.

"I don't see how your gut isn't twice the size of mine, and I get pie whenever I want."

"I burn it off, I guess. Daddy's little too." Small but mighty.

"Runs in the family," Rosie agreed, nodding. "Anything else, boys?"

"I'm good, Rosie. Thank you." He watched her leave. She'd been quiet for a few days, avoided him, but then she'd started to relax around him and act like the girl he knew.

"She's got some color in her cheeks. It's been good for her."

"That bastard was mean to her. I think the morning sickness is easing up too, which helps."

"Yeah. That always makes a woman peaked." Bulldog polished off the last cookie and gulped some tea. "Anything else you need me to do, man?"

"Not a thing. I appreciate the help, though." He reached out and shook Bulldog's hand.

"Thanks. She'll close up about an hour early on Halloween. Just to keep the drunks out."

"I'll be there. I might bring Momma and Daddy to have a piece of pie. They don't get folks this far out."

"No, I bet not. My girl would love that." Bulldog slapped him on the back. "Thanks again, man."

"Anytime."

He meant it too. Bulldog was one of the good guys, no matter what the Baptists whispered about him. Bulldog had been inside too, and understood a lot of the things Sage didn't even like to think, let alone say.

Bulldog finished his tea. "Wilma wants to know what kind of pie you'd like tomorrow."

"Chocolate, please."

"Good deal. Okay, man, I'll get out of your hair. Win coming over tonight?"

Sage felt his cheeks heat. "His shift is off at six. He's bringing steaks for the grill."

"Well, good on ya." Bulldog headed off, waving as he hopped in his truck.

Yeah. It was actually pretty good, all in all.

CHAPTER EIGHTEEN

WIN SAT next to Sage on the couch, his arm around Sage's shoulders. They'd had steaks, a hand job, and half a dose of that shark movie Sage loved so.

He figured it was time to ask.

"So, I got a weekend off next week. Wanna go to Fort Worth?"

"Sure. If I can. What's in Fort Worth?"

Well, that was easy. "Well, there's a little rodeo, and there's the Stockyards. I'll take you to the Cattleman's."

"I haven't been to the Stockyards in years. I bet it's different now."

"Not that much, really. It's a fun place." Win chuckled, hugging Sage close. "Cool, then. I'll get us a room, talk to your PO."

"Sounds perfect. You'll have your hands full tomorrow, I bet."

"Halloween?" Win grimaced. "It gets hairy. High school kids especially."

"Yeah. I remember that." Sage got a naughty little look on his face, and suddenly Win could remember what little he knew of Sage back in the day—a laughing little bastard who was ready and eager for fun.

"You doing anything?" Win asked, hoping Sage would stay home, honestly.

"I promised Bulldog I would make sure Wilma got out and home safe."

God damn it. Just what they needed. "Well, stick with her. Don't separate."

"I won't. I'm going to take the folks, get them pie. She's closing early."

The cop in him didn't like this idea, not at all. In fact, he had a terrible frisson of foresight. Bad things happened to Sage in parking lots.

"You okay, Adam? You need another cup of coffee?"

"Sure." He tried to summon up a smile. It was tough to do. Halloween was a bad night as it was, and he didn't like this, not one bit.

He let Sage get up and get them coffee and all, wondering if he could slide by the diner tomorrow night.

He'd be patrolling. Hell, how could Wilma be safer?

"You're all frowns." Sage sat, handing him a coffee.

"Sorry." He didn't need to borrow trouble, so he shrugged it off.

"For what? Frowning?" Sage winked and settled. "You're allowed, so long as I didn't bring it on."

"Well, I have to admit, I don't like the idea of you being at the diner on Halloween, but you're a big boy." He wrapped an arm around Sage's shoulders again.

"Me either, but I told Bulldog I would, and I like the idea of Miss Wilma there alone even less."

"I know." He knew. Sage was a good man. He genuinely was.

"I'll be fine. I'll take Momma and Daddy. Who would mess with me, then? This is about showing me my place, not scaring them."

"That's a good idea, babe. I want you healthy for Fort Worth."

Sage grinned at him. "I'll have to shine my good boots. Momma kept them all these years."

"Will they still fit?" Very little of Win's stuff from high school would.

"Yeah. I'm the same size. Hell, my waist is a bit smaller."

Damn. That was something. Not that Win would want to use prison as a weight-loss method.

Still he didn't mind the way those lean muscles jerked and rolled under his fingers. No, he thought Sage was beautiful, so perfectly formed.

"You got needing in your eyes, darlin'." Sage's words were husky, soft, and so fucking true.

"Do I?" Win grinned a little before leaning down to kiss that mouth, loving how Sage opened right up for him. No one had ever wanted him this way. Hell, he'd never met a guy who could sit and kiss for hours, until neither of them could draw a full breath, until Win couldn't taste the difference between them. It made him feel ten feet tall and hard as a rock.

Sage's fingers slid up and down his ribs, petting him nice and easy.

His toes curled some, his belly drawing up tight.

A happy little sound vibrated his lips. Sage reached up and stroked his cheek, rough fingertips tracing the planes of his face.

Damn, but that man did it for him. Revved his engine. Floated his boat. Whatever the phrase, Sage had it going on.

"You ever had sushi before?"

Now there was a question out of left field. Win blinked. "Uh. Yeah. I mean, a couple times."

"I had it once, before the favorites dance in Greenville when I was a junior, on a dare. I loved the stuff, at least I think I did. I remember liking it. I took my cousin, Cindy, you remember her? The one with Downs?"

He nodded. Yeah, he remembered her, vaguely.

"She died from a heart attack a few years ago. It was quick." Sage shrugged. "Anyways, did you like it enough to get more? Maybe in Dallas on our way to our weekend?"

"Sure thing." Hell, he could always get hibachi shrimp. "Let's try."

"I would like that."

Christ, how did that happen, where a man was in his thirties and his experiences were damn near fifteen years old? Prison sucked. Win knew that sometimes it was a necessary evil, but God, it hurt him to see Sage be so out of sync with the world. At least the real world. No wonder so many guys went back in.

Sage wouldn't. He was a good man, and Win would do everything in his power to keep Sage from getting hurt again.

Sage kissed him. "You think I'll ever get to see your place, Adam?"

"Heck, yes. I feel like a slob compared to you, babe." He didn't want Sage to think he didn't want him coming over.

"Still, I...." Sage shrugged. "I want to know about you. Know what your life is like."

"Well, how about you come over next time and we grill burgers at my place?" He could so show Sage around.

"That works for me."

Look at that smile.

If he'd known it would make Sage so happy, he would have asked ages ago. Win kissed Sage's mouth.

"You taste like good coffee." Sage winked and dove right back in.

Win chuckled, pulling Sage up and around so those lean legs straddled his thighs. "Hey, baby."

"Hey, you."

Fuck, he did love that soft laugh. It made him....

The crack of a shot made them both stiffen, then another sounded, and one of Sage's windows shattered as the squeal of tires on dirt hit his ears.

"Shit." He pushed Sage down on the floor. He was pretty sure the shooting was over, but he wanted to be certain. He crouch-walked to the window and checked outside while he pulled out his phone to call dispatch. "I have shots fired at a residence."

Sage was on his feet, heading straight for the door. "I got to check on the folks, my pups."

"Wait." Win reached out and snagged a belt loop as Sage passed him. "Let me clear the scene, first. Just five seconds."

"Son? Sage? Are you okay? Penny? Sam, oh my God in Heaven! Sam! Someone's done shot Penny!" Ellen's voice was like a Klaxon, and the loop came right off on Win's finger.

Goddamn it.

He sprinted outside, trying to keep Sage and Ellen from getting hurt. Sure enough, Sage's pup lay on the ground not five feet from the trailer, her tail thumping weakly when Sage knelt next to her. Christ. Who the fuck shot a goddamned dog?

"Come on, baby. I got to get you looked at." Sage scooped her up and looked at Ellen, standing there in a pink pair of sweats and a T-shirt that said, "Screw you, I'm from Texas." "You and Daddy good?" At her nod, he started walking. "Where can I take her?"

Win headed for his truck. "Ellen, I've got Deputy Allworthy coming out to look around. I trust him. I know a vet in Mount Pleasant. I'll call her on the way, and she can meet us at her clinic. There are towels in the back. Wrap her up so she doesn't go into shock."

"You tell your fucking uncle that there's gonna be a war in this town, Adam Winchester." Sam Redding had his rifle in hand, a look of pure fury in the man's eyes. "Bastard has money, but he cain't scare us old-timers off their land, no more. I ain't having it!"

"Sam, honey...."

"We'll scream and threaten to burn his fucking house down later, after my dog stops bleeding on me!" Shit, Sage could holler.

"Jamison Allworthy will be here in five, y'all." Win got in the truck and hit Tiffany's number on speed dial. She was his vet, but she was also an old friend, a sister of an old Army buddy. She'd help them.

"Hey, Win. S'up?"

"Hey, Tiff. I got a dog here that's been shot. Looks like front right shoulder. She's bleeding, shocky. Can you meet me at the clinic?" He tore out of the drive, knowing Sage would protect Penny.

"Oh damn. You know it. When will you be there, buddy?"

"Not long, if I have my way. Maybe twenty?"

"I'll meet you." The phone went dead, and he stomped on the gas. Sage was murmuring to the pup, a soft, constant sound that was basically "I'm sorry" over and over.

Win wanted to reassure Sage that none of this was his fault, but he knew platitudes didn't help for shit. All he could do was get them there before Penny bled to death. This was utter fucking bullshit. What if it had been Sage? Sam? Hell, Ellen. His fucking truck was right there. Not that it had stopped anyone.

He glanced over, and even in the dim light he could see Sage's lips moving. Damn it, the man had lost too much. He couldn't lose the damned dog too.

"She's holding on. No blood in her nose."

"Good. Nothing in her mouth but incidental?" If she licked she'd have some, but that was different than coughing up blood. He'd had a shepherd who'd eaten tinfoil once. Internal bleeding was really obvious.

"She's going to make it. You got guys watching my folks and sister, yeah?"

"I do. They'll collect any evidence too. The bullet we get out of her might be our best lead." Win didn't want to handle this the legal way. He wanted to go find the guys who'd done this and beat them down.

"You'll have to look on your family tree. That's going to be a problem."

"I know." He bit off the words that wanted to come out. They were angry and not directed at Sage. "I'm sorry."

"No. This isn't your fault. I came back."

"Well, we'll figure out who all is to blame later, huh?" He grinned a little, happy when he got a ghost of a smile in answer.

"Yeah. After Penny's better and I get some coffee." Sage was trying so hard.

"That's it." They were ten minutes out from Tiff's clinic. "Tell Penny to hold on."

"I am. She's calming down, some. Hope that don't mean she's slipping."

"No." He hit the gas, pushing the truck to higher speeds. "No, she's just a little shocky, I bet. Warmer, though, with you holding her."

"Fuckers, shooting my dog. I'm gonna rain some fucking hell down on someone."

Win almost grinned. It was about time Sage started to get mad. The fatalism wouldn't help anyone. It felt good to hear him standing firm.

"There it is." Win pointed over the steering wheel. "Tiff beat us here." The lights were blazing at the clinic, Tiff's neon green pickup in the parking lot.

"What kind of vet drives a truck that color?"

He blinked. "It went with her nail polish the day she went to CarMax."

"Oh." Sage opened the door and eased out, still holding Penny in his arms. "I'm not sure what's weirder—that reason or the fact that you knew it."

"Hey, she's one of the guys." Win snorted. "Mostly. Come on." He led the way inside, where Tiff and two vet techs waited for them.

"Hi. I'm Tiffany Archer. Is she in good health other than her injuries?" Wild red hair framed her face, the woman dressed in a tank top, jeans, and a tossed-on lab coat. She hadn't changed a bit since high school.

"She's good. Young. Healthy. I gave her rabies and her other shots September first."

"Okay. Here, bring her in here. We've got a table set up."

Win stood back and let Tiff do her thing. All he could do now was hope like hell that Penny pulled through.

"So what were you two doing that you got a dog shot?" Tiffany was working, snapping orders to techs to get X-rays ready and sedatives.

"Sitting on my fucking sofa and drinking coffee. Dangerous goddamn business, that." Sage was fixin' to lose his shit. Win could read it like a book.

"Someone came on your land and shot her?" Tiff's dark eyes flashed at him, eyebrows arched up above them.

Win sighed. "Sage has some unfriendly folks after him."

"Ah. You're that one, the evil murderer." Sage got a look, up and down. "Your horns are smaller than I was led to believe."

Sage blinked, then laughed, the sound rusty as an old gate. "Yeah, well, I take them off at night."

"Good to know." She winked at Win. "And you, I bet you are growing horns, little ones."

"Oh, I have to shave them off every day." He craned his neck to peer at Penny. "She's a good dog."

"I can tell. I'm going to take some films, see how the bones are faring."

"Okay." He took Sage's arm. "Let's clean you up."

"Huh? I don't want to leave her."

Tiffany shook her head. "Let me do my job. She's not in any immediate danger. I swear, Sage, I will get you if she starts failing."

Sage chewed his lower lip. "Promise me? I wouldn't want her to be alone."

"Oh, honey, you got my word. Let me work, get her comfortable, and get that damn bullet out of her." Tiff looked over at Win. "You want it, right? The bullet?"

"I do, as long as it doesn't do her more harm to get it out than good." He would keep that fucker until he matched it to a weapon.

"You got it. There's a coffeepot up front, a bathroom." She waved them off. "Shoo."

"Yes, ma'am." He took Sage's arm and tugged him to the lobby. "I'll make coffee, if you want to wash up." Win automatically checked the danger zones, the windows and corners.

"Okay. Yeah. I'll call up to the house too."

"Good idea. Check in on your mom and dad." Win would call Jamison Allworthy and see if he'd come up with anything, but he would bet there was very little story to tell. Maybe they could get tire tracks. If anyone would care if he did.

He didn't even have time to dial, the sheriff's name coming up on his screen. "Jim."

"A fucking drive-by? What? Is he into drugs again? Are these gangbangers from Dallas? What's he running, kid? And you? You were there? Are you high? I want a piss test from you. Tomorrow morning. No question."

Win took a deep, deep breath. Counted to ten. "You can have any tests you want. You know damned well what this was. They shot his fucking dog, Jim. I swear to God, you tell them to back the fuck off, or

I'll start running people in for attempted murder. I'll call the state troopers in on it."

"You wouldn't fucking dare."

"Really?" He stared out the front door of the clinic, half expecting someone to shoot him. "I think I will. I'm sick of this vendetta y'all got going."

"You're going to turn your back on your family? Your blood? For a fucking murdering fag?"

"What has my blood done for me lately, Jim? Shot at me? You swore to uphold the law. People voted for you. You think they will again if they know you let this happen?" His hands shook with anger, his rage growing.

"He *killed your cousin*!"

"He was at a fucking meth house when it blew, man. He lived. That's what he did wrong. He fucking lived."

"I don't understand you, Adam. I swear, I don't." Jim almost sounded sad.

"Well, go you. I had to take a dog to the vet to get a bullet removed. You better hope it doesn't match anyone's in the family."

"Shit, like I'm gonna go ride out with a posse and shoot a fucking dog."

"Someone did, Jim. This is serious. You can't turn a blind eye forever. Someone is going to get killed, and you may not care if it's one of the Reddings, but I sure do."

"I'm not sure you're keeping a clear head about this, son."

"No? Well, I guess I'm glad I'm a blithering idiot. I have to make another call. Bye."

He hung up, so disgusted he wanted to scream. He needed to call Allworthy, though. Get to him before Jim did.

Sage walked through, heading out to sit on the windowsill of the big bay window, not saying so much as a word to him.

"Jesus fucking Christ." He punched numbers on his goddamned phone, getting Jamison on the line. "Tell me there's something we can use."

"A bullet from a .38, a broken gate, a scared pregnant lady that saw a dark blue or black Hemi."

"Damn." The .38 they might match, but only if they sent it to the state lab. "Did you make sure everyone else was unharmed? Take statements?"

"Yes, sir. I told them I'd stay here, to keep watch, but you know they ain't coming back. I'm more worried that they'd follow y'all."

"Well, if they did, they'll be in a world of hurt." Tiffany would kill anyone who came after her clinic. "I'll be careful. Thanks, man."

"Anytime, Win." Jamison sighed softly. "This whole thing, it ain't right, man."

"I know it. I hate getting you mixed up in it, but I knew I could trust you. Holler at me if anything comes up. We're here until we know what's up with the pup."

"Those cowards won't be back, but I'll be waiting if they do."

"Thanks." He clicked his phone off and went to Sage, wanting to—something. Hug the man. Whatever.

Sage sat there, staring at the parking lot, hands opening and closing, over and over.

"Hey." Win wasn't sure what to do. They were still feeling their way out in this whole "them" thing.

"Hey. I talked to Momma. They're okay. Pissed but okay."

"I bet they are. No one else was hurt?" He meant animal or human, he supposed.

"Not that they've seen. I only heard the two shots, but... I wasn't listening for them." Sage looked at his hands. "I'm gonna get my daddy killed, no matter what I do, man. I stay here, they're gonna keep coming. I go, he loses everything."

Win honestly didn't know what to say. Sage was damned if he stayed, and damned if he didn't. The whole situation sucked. "You know I'll do what I can to keep everyone safe."

"I know. Thank you for bringing us over." Sage snorted, the sound humorless as all get-out. "God, this sucks, man. I mean, shit, I should probably be all 'we should break up,' but one, I don't want to, and two, are we in a place where we could break up?"

"You mean are we having enough of a thing to have something to break? Yeah. Yeah, we are, and you're not breaking up with me, Sage." He kept his tone level, not wanting to sound crazed or threatening or anything, but the thought of not having Sage in his life left him in a panic.

"Nah. Nah, I'm not. You and the horses, you're the good stuff, the reason. A man needs a reason."

He found himself smiling, reaching for Sage. Yeah. A man did need something to go on.

Sage's hand met his, and he got a squeeze. "You ever wish you were straight?"

"Only for the whole I can't kiss you in public thing."

"Yeah." He thought Sage might have smiled. Maybe.

"I can here." He bent and kissed Sage lightly, knowing this was more for comfort than anything else.

"You want to know something?" Sage spoke, voice so quiet. "I never got to go into a bar and have a beer. Never. These assholes hate me, and I... shit, man. I was a kid. I was a stupid kid."

"I know." God knew, Angel had been the king of stupid. They all had been, back then. "I don't know why they have to be this way, babe."

"Because someone has to pay. That's human nature. Shit, Jesus had to pay, and I ain't even sure the gates of Heaven would open to me."

Christ.

Christ, how did a man live like that?

"Win?" Tiff called to them, and he took Sage's arm and led him to the back. She smiled at them when they got there. "Hey, we got the bullet out. She's got some muscle damage, and we have her on fluids and antibiotics. We'll have to keep her crated here for a few days to keep her as still and quiet as we can."

"But she's going to be okay?" Sage knelt by the crate, touching Penny's nose. "Hey, girlfriend. Why'd you go get shot, huh?"

"She's going to be fine. I don't think she'll even have a limp."

Poor Penny was pretty out, her tongue hanging long, her eyes a little crusty. She wagged a tiny bit when Sage talked to her, though.

"Good girl. You sleep. I bet Momma comes in with chicken for you tomorrow, huh?"

Tiffany rolled her eyes but smiled. Win grinned. Ellen would do that. Stewed chicken and rice. Win could remember his mom doing that for a pup they'd had when he was a kid.

"Let me get your information, and I hate to do it, but we'll have to talk money too."

Sage didn't so much as wince. He nodded. "How much?"

"It'll be four hundred tonight, then another two when you pick her up."

"Okay." Sage patted his back pockets, then blinked. "I didn't even get my wallet. I'm good for it. I'll come in the morning with a check."

"Of course." Tiff nodded firmly. "A friend of Win's is a friend of mine."

Sage nodded. "You want me to sign something saying I'll be back?"

She gave Sage a long look. "I see how you care about this dog. You'll be back."

"I will. In the morning." Sage wrote down his name, address, and phone number in his tiny square perfectly neat handwriting. "I told you her name is Penny, right?"

"You did." She scribbled out a bill, and while Sage was tucking it away, Win gave her a couple of twenties.

"Have supper on us, okay?"

"You got it. Take him home. Get him a stiff drink and a shower."

Right, like his Sage touched alcohol. A shower they could do, though.

"I'll see you in the morning, ma'am. Thank you for everything."

Tiffany smiled at Sage, obviously charmed. "We'll take good care of her." Tiff waved, locking up behind them.

"You want to head back or stop at the car wash and clean up the truck?"

"Better get your truck clean before everything sets in the upholstery."

"You okay?" He put a hand on Sage's shoulder, needing to feel that warm, live body.

"No, but I will be. You?"

"I'm glad everyone is going to make it." And his hands were shaking. God, he could do a murder-suicide scene without blinking, but hurt someone he cared about, and reaction set in fast.

Sage nodded, stood, and took his keys. "Come on. Let's get the truck cleaned and stop at the Village Inn."

"Sounds good." They needed some food, some fat and carbs. Then he needed to take Sage home.

It was a little odd to have Sage put him in the passenger's side, start his truck, and drive off. Win felt like he should be the one in charge, instead of the one with the goose bumps and chattering teeth. What the fuck was wrong with him?

"Breathe, Win. I'll get you a Coke at the car wash. It'll stop it."

"Stop what?" He stared out the windshield, trying to keep his shit together.

"You got the shock. The sugar and caffeine'll help."

"I don't fall apart in emergencies." He didn't. He was a cop. Of course, he'd never been in love before.

"Course you don't. Bodies are silly things."

"They are." If Sage was going to keep it light, so was he.

"When I was inside and things...." Sage's lips twisted. "...got intense, my body would just freak out. If I had the cash, I'd get a Coke from the commissary."

Oh. Oh God, he didn't want to think about that. "My mom always wants chocolate."

"I bet chocolate works, but there aren't any bubbles."

"No. Just sugar and fat." Win felt better already, his hands getting steadier. He'd take that Coke, though.

"And peanut butter. The best ones have peanut butter."

"You like a Reese's?" He would remember that. Hell, Win's mom made an astounding peanut butter pie. She couldn't cook for shit, but she could make dessert.

Sage made a yummy noise, and damn, that eased the tension, made the stress pop.

Win found himself grinning. "Well, I know what to get you for Halloween."

"I got you a bag of them lemonhead deals."

"Yum. Sour."

"I saw that you had a wrapper in your truck."

He chuckled. "Caught, huh? They keep me awake when I'm on a long shift, between the sugar and the tang."

"I bought a whole bag."

"You're good to me." And wasn't it amazing to see Sage doing something like that for him when all this crazy shit was going on?

They pulled into the car wash, and Sage killed the engine. "Well, sure. I love you."

And Sage got out of the truck, put a dollar in the machine, and started cleaning his truck. Win sat there with his teeth in his mouth for a long time. Well, it felt like a long time, but it must have been maybe a minute. Sage loved him.

Christ. They were a pair.

What the hell was he supposed to say to that?

Of course, Sage got him out of the passenger seat, handed him a Coke, and started cleaning the inside, so he didn't have to say a word.

Win stood there sipping his drink and feeling like an utter perv for watching Sage's butt while he bent over to scrub the truck seat. He felt totally off his game, like the world had tilted on its axis.

"You feeling better?" Sage grabbed some paper towels and started drying.

"I am. Thanks." He looked at his hand, which held the empty Coke bottle. "The Coke was perfect."

"Come back to the ranch with me?"

"Hell, yes." He would take Sage to his place, which was closer, but they needed to check on Ellen and Sam and Rosie.

"Good." Sage looked at him. "Let's go. It's late."

"It is." He held out his hand, intending to take the keys.

"You sure? I don't mind driving."

"I'll let you, then." He trusted Sage. He touched Sage's arm before climbing into the truck on the passenger side.

Sage got them both another Coke, then found some country music on the radio as they headed down the road. Win just sat, staring out the windshield, wondering what the hell was wrong with him. Maybe he'd finally cracked a little.

Maybe he needed a good night's sleep and to have something not happen for a few days. Too bad tomorrow was Halloween.

Win had a bad feeling that there would be no rest for the wicked tomorrow night.

CHAPTER NINETEEN

"ANOTHER CUP of coffee, honey?" Wilma was pale as milk, and Sage hated that.

"Nope. We're good." He had been too. Sitting here since five, watching everything and eating a piece of pumpkin pie. He'd worn his ass out today—hitting the pawn shop to pay off Penny's vet bill and fix his window, deal with his hysterical momma, and make sure the gate was shored up.

He was dragging ass.

Wilma summoned a smile for him. She was a good woman, but her worry about him being her protection for the evening showed in her eyes. Bulldog had been the only one who was confident. "You kick some ass if you need to, son," he'd said.

He would. No way he'd let anyone down today. He turned his coffee cup around and around, listening to everything going on.

Rick and Lena were the last customers and they left at seven thirty, and Sage got to work helping with the cleaning up. He knew tonight Wilma would want him to mop, so he started stacking chairs.

"You're a good man, Sage Redding." Wilma's voice was soft and fond, and he didn't know what to say.

"Thank you, ma'am. I try." Sage's cheeks heated and he ducked his head, working to get everything done.

By eight o'clock, Marisol, the cook, was ready, and Sage headed out with her and Wilma, telling himself that he had this. Nothing was going to happen.

Wilma looked left and right when they stepped outside, relaxing a little when no one appeared. The lot looked quiet.

"Come on, ladies, let's go. Miss Wilma, I'll follow you home."

Headlights headed for them, loud music blaring out. His shoulders tensed up around his ears, and he herded Wilma and Marisol toward their cars, wanting a barrier between them and the road.

"Get in your truck, Sage."

"I will, ma'am. Once y'all are in. They'll drive by." He had a baseball bat in the bed of his truck, and this time he would use it. He wasn't going to let anyone hurt these ladies.

Wilma bit her lip but nodded, sliding into her sedan.

The Jeep pulled into the parking lot, and the ladies both started their cars as Sage headed for his truck, one hand dipping into the bed and finding wood. "We're closed, boys."

"We're not looking for food, asshole." One of the rednecks hopped out of the Jeep.

"I don't even know you, son, and I ain't looking for trouble. I'm here to help the ladies get home."

"You may not be looking, buddy, but you got it." He knew the knuckle dragger who came at him around the other side. A friend of his soon-to-be ex-brother-in-law.

"Goodie. Well, if you insist, bring it on. I got plans."

"Sage...." Wilma came up to him, Marisol right behind her. "You boys get out of here. I've called 911."

The big guy bared his teeth and made to grab Wilma, laughing as she backed off. "Pretty girls you're protecting. Shame that Bulldog left them with just you. Kill a fag, get the deposit, and fuck the broads. Great night, huh, Charlie?"

"You know it, Jake. I'll take the beaner. You get the biker's bitch."

Sage shook his head, watching this particular two-headed snake, trying to figure which head was smarter, if one had more venom than the other. Jake was bigger, less drunk, if the swaying told a true story, but Charlie had that snake-mean look to him.

"Not going to happen, but Miss Wilma's done called the police. You ass hats best hurry, if you're fixin' to." He knew Wilma'd call Adam, but that worked for him.

He'd thought about this all day, and he'd been worried, real worried, that he'd be scared or frozen or something, but he wasn't. A man couldn't take it forever, and it was his place to protect the ladies. He'd promised. Besides, two rednecks against a real cowboy?

Shit, that wasn't fair to those stupid fucks.

The big guy, Jake, took a swing, a sucker punch, and Sage ducked it, catching the stupid fucker in the nuts with the bat, hard enough that Big Boy gave a breathy scream and went down, fingers scrabbling at Sage's boots. It took one hard stomp, and all those little bones in one hand snapped. It felt good, better than it should have, to take back some of his own.

Charlie stared at him with bloodshot eyes, the scent of whiskey on the air making Sage gag. "That was a low blow."

Sage shrugged and hefted the bat, the weight solid, comforting. "All's fair, asshole. You're up to the plate."

Jake grabbed at him again, and he kicked, hard, his toe connecting. *Come on. Come on, you fucks. I been needing this.*

A little Saturday night special came out of Charlie's jacket pocket, pointed at Sage's head, and Sage snorted. "Oh, honey. You think those worry me? What's your damage, carrying a girl's piece?"

The bastard opened his mouth to answer. Sage swung, and the bat connected with Charlie's hand. The man's arm swung wide, the bullet ricocheted off the asphalt, and the pistol skittered under his truck.

"You missed." He swung from the other side, coming in low and catching the fucker in the belly, the sound a *thud*. The blow he delivered across Charlie's kidneys when the kid bent over sounded a hell of a lot more like a *thwack*.

He could see the blue lights and hear the sirens, and Wilma came up to him and touched his arm. "Give me the bat."

"What?"

"Give me the fucking bat, Sage. Now."

He handed it over, confused as all get-out.

She gripped it, her mouth pressed tight together. "Assholes. This is my bat, right, Marisol? It came out of my car."

Marisol nodded. "*Si, señora.* Is yours."

"And I hit them because they came to steal the money."

"*Si, si, señora.* And *Señor* Sage come to help us."

"That's right."

Sage looked at them both, hating this, but hating the idea of a fucking jail cell even worse. "I'm lucky you carry that thing."

"You bet." Wilma spat on the ground next to Jake even as Adam pulled up in a cruiser.

Charlie tried to move, and Adam growled, but it was Marisol who kicked the man right in the face. "Call me a beaner, *cabrón*? You stay in the dirt."

"Adam." He nodded, just once. "Good timing."

"I been staying as close as I can." Adam grinned, then frowned down at Jake and Charlie. "Well, cousin, no end of surprise seeing you here."

"He broke my hand, dude."

"Who? Wilma, did you do this?"

Wilma nodded. "They were going to rob us, rape us. Thank God I had my bat in the car."

If he wasn't queer as a three-dollar bill and Wilma was twenty years younger or not married to the biggest baddest biker in eight counties who was working at being the best friend he'd ever had, Sage might have fallen in love with her, right then. Boom.

Win glanced at him, mouth kicking up on one side. "Marisol? That how it went?"

"*Si. Si, señor.* These is bad mans. *Señor* Sage, he sees and comes to *ayudeme.*"

"Well, boys, you heard the ladies. Backup is on the way, so be good. Roll over, Jake, hands behind your back."

"You...." Jake stared at him. "You can't believe these whores and a fucking fag over me! He attacked us! We came in for a burger, and he jumped us!"

Wilma snorted. "Little Sage Redding? Shit, I outweigh him by fifty pounds."

Sage tried not to be offended.

Adam chuckled. "Turn over, Jake. I won't say it again. I got a gun, not a baseball bat."

Sage did his dead-level best not to smile. Adam did it for him, and he was revved up as all get-out. Shit.

"You going to arrest the rest of them too?" That was Charlie, who was coming around a bit.

"Nope." Win stepped on Charlie to keep him in place. "They were defending themselves."

"That's right. Fucking cowards." Wilma rolled her shoulders. "Do I need to come in and give a statement, Win?"

"I'll need you to, yeah. Marisol, can you come in with Wilma?" Win nodded at the cook. "I can call Jameson to come get the car."

"No problem." Wilma winked at Sage. "I'll call Bulldog from the car. Sage, thanks for stopping by. I'll see you tomorrow."

Adam nodded to him. "I'll call if I have any questions."

"You got it." He'd hang until the other... there they were. Time for him to get the hell out of Dodge. No sense borrowing trouble, and Adam's backup was that nice feller who'd stayed with Sage's folks the night of the shooting.

"You sure you don't want me to follow you, Miss Wilma?" He hated feeling like a deserter.

"Nope. I'll have Bulldog call if you need to finish the grandkids' trick or treating."

"I can sure do that if you need me." No one was going to trust him to keep their kids safe. Not with people jumping out of the woodwork to beat him down.

He headed to his truck, the buzz from the fight fading quickly, leaving him empty, shaky. He sat in the cab, hands on the steering wheel. He needed a Coke. Maybe he could stop at the Woody's and get one on the way back to the ranch.

He started the engine and slowly headed out away from the parking lot. Christ. He jumped as his phone rang, and he flipped it open. "Yeah?"

"Sage? Bulldog. Talked to Wilma. Thank you, man."

"Thank me? Shit. They came for me."

"How'd they know you were there, son? You don't come in every day."

"Oh." Oh, that was true enough. Unless.... One of them was Adam's cousin. God, had one of Adam's relatives set them up? Maybe. He. It. This whole thing. God damn it!

"You need me to do anything else, man?" he asked.

Bulldog snorted. "You did great already. I owe you a piece of pie. You be safe going home."

"I will. Happy Halloween, man."

"Happy Halloween. Later." Bulldog hung up, and Sage headed down the highway, figuring he ought to get on home, check on Momma, see if she'd heard from that nice lady vet. He tensed up every time he saw oncoming lights, but he made it home without anyone running him off the road.

He parked and sat there in the truck, forehead on the steering wheel a second, trying to decide whether he was going to start laughing and go until he couldn't stop or not.

The knock on the window decided him, making him jump a mile. His momma stood there, peering in at him.

"Hey, Momma." He offered her a grin.

Her frown smoothed out. "Did you get good candy out there?"

"I did. I totally did." He slipped out of the car. "You hear about Penny this evening? There any potato salad left?"

"She's on the mend, and they're having to put her in a little kennel to keep her from bouncing." She started back up toward the main house. "There is. Hot dogs too."

"Yeah? You got enough for me?"

She snorted. "Don't make me beat you, boy. Come on."

Sage nodded, following her, a smile breaking across his face. He felt... better. Happier. He'd stood his ground.

No matter what Wilma would say, the truth would out, and that meant someone would hear that there was a cost to fucking with a Redding. Which was good. He was sick of being a damned victim.

His phone buzzed, and he answered, Adam's name popping up. "Yeah?"

"Can I see you tonight?"

"Sure."

"Cool. It may be late. If that's not cool, I can come over tomorrow, but I need to see you." Adam sounded downright intense.

"I'll be up." His body responded to the tone, jeans going tight. Something could be said for an Adam Winchester who was worried about him and wanting to show him how happy the man was Sage was okay.

"Everything okay, Son?"

"Yes, ma'am. Evenin', Daddy."

"Hey, Sage. Momma gonna feed you?" His dad looked pale. Not worried, just ill, and it made him sad.

"Yes, sir. Happy Halloween. Where's Rosie?"

"She's in her room watching scary movies with Katy Brooks. You remember Katy Brooks?"

"Vaguely. Pretty girl, lots of makeup? Scared of dogs?"

Daddy snorted. "Raises bloodhounds now."

"No shit." Huh. He guessed all sorts of leopards could change their spots. Maybe there was hope for him yet.

He sat at the kitchen table and ate his hot dogs, listening to the sounds of NCIS on the television, waiting for the evening to pass. He was waiting for Adam. That would be the best part of any day.

He headed to the trailer after the news and started the coffeepot, then cleaned himself up and stretched out on the sofa with a book, so he didn't stare at the place where the TV and DVD player had been.

Sage had dozed off by the time Adam came in, but the door woke him, making him start up.

"Relax, babe. I'm not after your blood."

"Well, damn." He stretched. "Everything okay?"

"As okay as it's gonna get." Adam chuckled. "Wilma is a hero. Of course, so are you."

"Don't know what you're talking about, Officer."

"Uh-huh. Marisol is ready to have your babies." Adam sat down next to Sage and pulled him close.

"Ew." He pushed into Adam's arms, wanting this connection, this thing they were building.

"I know, right?" Adam kissed him, hard, no gentle coaxing going on.

His entire body lit up, responding to that need, that hunger. Sage grabbed Adam's shoulders and held on, grunting when Adam pushed him down, his back hitting the couch cushions. He grabbed Adam's shoulders, hips punching up. *Oh, hell yes.*

Adam groaned, pressing down harder. The thick ridge of Adam's cock was obvious, even through the double layer of denim.

"Please." He pushed right back up, letting Adam feel him.

"I got this, babe." Adam smiled, the expression damned hot, and pulled back instead of moving closer. Sage was about to bitch when Adam opened their jeans, tugging at buttons and zippers.

His prick felt so hard it could cut glass, his balls were aching, and it felt so good, having Adam's hand on him. Adam was a little desperate for him, moving fast, but he didn't care a bit.

"More." He bit Adam's bottom lip, feeling a little wild, like he was out of his own skin, which would totally suck, given how good his skin was feeling right now.

Adam nodded, panting, and their shirts went next, then their shorts, Adam getting them naked.

"Need you, baby." Those words sounded so good, raw, like Adam didn't feel things were broke.

"Right here. Come on," Sage said.

Rearing up on his knees, Adam reached for his discarded jeans and pulled out a condom. "You got anything wet, Sage?"

He grabbed Adam's hand and sucked his fingers hard, slicking them up. That would do the trick in a pinch.

"Jesus." Adam was watching him, staring at him like he'd blown the man's mind. Maybe he had. Adam didn't waste any time, though, just pushed at him with those slick fingers, sliding two inside him.

"Oh fuck." He curled up, lips parted. "Adam."

Oh hell, yes.

All sorts of thoughts fluttered through his brain—90 percent of them unwelcome—and he batted them away. Only Adam. Only now.

"You good, babe? Can I move?" Adam had paused, staring down at him.

"Yeah. Need to feel you."

Like he needed to breathe.

"Good." Adam moved, fingers pushing in and out, spreading him right well. His body opened, letting Adam in, all the way deep. He could barely breathe, and he panted, his head swimming.

"Damn, baby. Look at you." Adam sounded wrecked, like the man could eat him alive.

It made him stretch out, made him show off a little. He'd never wanted to flaunt himself, ever. Not like he did with Adam. This was his, though, and only his. He knew it like he knew he had to get up and feed in the mornings, like he knew the smell of the ranch.

Sounds tore out of him, harsh and needy, and they seemed like they were driving Adam's need forward like the snap of reins. The man was wild for him, desperate, pushing him higher and higher.

"Please. Adam, come on. I ache." He burned for it, the need surprising him.

"You sure you're ready, babe?" Adam stared down at him, waiting for his nod. Then he was on Sage, pushing that hard cock against his hole.

He wrapped one hand around Adam's hip, encouraging him to press in deep, fill him up. The move worked perfectly, moving them together, rocking their bodies.

His entire body rolled, sliding on Adam's heat. Every little bit of skin that touched Adam's felt supersensitized, so warm he might melt. Adam's eyes were heavy-lidded, lips open, parted. The man watched him like he was the rising sun or something, like he was special. Real. He'd take it, as long as Adam wanted to give it.

When it stopped, well, he'd deal with it then.

Adam pulled him up even closer for another kiss, lips mashing down on his.

He tensed, squeezing Adam's prick as their tongues fought, pushing and sliding against each other. Adam moaned for him, body bucking, muscles working under that tanned skin.

"So hot." He stroked Adam's belly, his fingers tracing the ripped abs.

"I'm gonna explode, Sage."

He thought Adam might too.

His cock was full, begging for a touch, so he gave it, stroking from base to tip, knowing Adam would feel how good it was.

Adam gasped, eyes going wide, that whole body rippling under him. God, Adam felt fine, wide and hard, pushing in so hard he couldn't breathe.

That was all she wrote, his hand working his prick hard to push him over the edge. He cried out, spunk splattering his belly and chest. Adam was buried in him so deep he wasn't sure how they'd ever be two people again.

Please, God. Let me not fuck this up.

Adam kissed him like there was nothing else on earth to do.

He hummed, melted deep down, his entire body singing happily. Adam still rocked hard into him, moving faster and faster. It only took a few more moments for Adam to fill him up deep.

Sage held on tight, memorizing every second of this, letting it erase the other ones in his brain. This was nothing like the rest of his life. This was a lot like hope.

CHAPTER TWENTY

WIN HATED paperwork.

Oh, it was a necessary evil, and thank God all the forms were on a computer now, but he still sucked at it. He felt like he was all thumbs. Or maybe all two-fingered hunt and peck.

"Winchester! In my office." Jim loomed over him, glaring like a big old ogre.

Looked like it was time to pay the piper for daring to arrest his cousin.

"Sure." Win stood, leaving his weapon in his desk drawer. That way they couldn't shoot him and call it self-defense.

Grace winked at him as he went, and it felt good having someone at his back. She was a staunch supporter of reason, which Jim seemed to be lacking.

Win stopped right inside the door when he saw his Uncle Teddy sitting there too. "What's this, an intervention?"

"I want to know what the fuck is wrong with you." Uncle Teddy stood up, tanned face all florid and flushed. "Arresting your cousin? Letting the murderer walk away?"

Adam breathed deeply and counted to ten in his head. "No one murdered anyone, and you know it. As for Charlie, he should be lucky no one pressed charges."

"He's been beaten half to death."

Adam had to fight his grin. Sage had torn the stupid son of a bitch up. It had been a beautiful thing. "Wilma has one hell of an arm."

"Wilma my ass!" Jim burst in. "I know it was that Redding boy."

"Well, now, that wasn't how it was reported to me."

"What is your fucking deal with him?" Teddy stood, staring at him. "I swear, son—"

"Back off, Ted. I ain't your son." Win shook his head. "Hell, the more I have to deal with you, the more I can see why Angel ran off and left home."

"He left because of that evil Redding bastard! You wait until I get their land and that fucker will be living with his folks in a truck!"

Evil? His Sage. Bullshit.

He waved a hand at Teddy's face, then looked at his other uncle. "You're foaming a little. Jim, if you try this on work time again, I will file a formal complaint."

"You put an innocent man in jail."

"Innocent? Charlie went to the cafe with the intention of starting shit. We have that on taped confession." No one had ever said his kin had two brain cells to rub together to spark off a thought. Hell, if Teddy hadn't had money, Jim Dale wouldn't have been elected to office and the county knew it.

"You—"

"No." Win held up a hand. "I'm done. You want to write me up, fine. Otherwise, let me go do my job." He felt utterly calm and thoroughly disgusted.

It was his Friday, and he was taking Sage to Fort Worth. They were going to have steaks and goof off and, if he was lucky, have wild monkey sex. He wasn't going to think about work or beatings or drive-by shootings.

Win stared at Jim, then Ted, who looked like explosion was imminent.

Jim waved him off, and he managed to get the door shut before Ted started screaming.

"Thank God." He shook his head. Maybe he should take his paperwork out to his truck.

"I got you all loaded on the laptop, Win." Oh, Grace was a winner.

He bent to kiss her cheek. "You're a queen among women. Thank you."

"Enjoy your days off."

"You know it." He hit the door at warp speed, hopped in his truck, and dialed Sage.

"'lo?" Sage was laughing, and the sound made him smile.

"Hey, babe. I got out a little early. You about ready?"

"I am. I'm watching Rosie try to teach that little dog of hers tricks. Funniest thing you'll ever see." Oh, now, how fucking fine was that? Hearing Sage simply enjoy something? He loved the side of Sage that was slowly emerging these days, the laughter and the teasing.

"I'll swing by my place, then, and change, and then I'm on my way." He couldn't wait to get out of town. Win was ready.

"Sounds good to me. I got a bag packed."

They hung up, and Win headed home, hating that he felt like he had to look everywhere for some of his family who were hunting him. He grabbed his little suitcase, all packed, and his good hat. He might not be a cowboy like Sage, but he was Texan, after all.

He looked around at the mess and shook his head. At some point, he needed to bring Sage over, show him. He hated the idea of his favorite neatnik reacting to his place. Whatever. Sage would either cope or clean and either way, it'd work. He headed out the door, whistling along with the happy tune in his head.

Win tossed his little case in the toolbox, then headed down the road to the Redding ranch. He made it there and groaned as he saw his Uncle Teddy's truck.

Goddamn it.

Why the hell was Teddy harassing these people? It wasn't right.

He hopped out of his truck and stormed around the house to where Ellen Redding was reading Ted the riot act. "...get off my land before I shoot you. I'd let this land go to Satan himself first!"

"Ted, what are you doing?" Win knew Ellen could handle herself, but damn it, he wanted his uncle gone.

"Just talking to your new best friends and making them an offer on their land."

"They're not interested." Win slowly, carefully put himself between Ted and Ellen.

"He knows we're not interested." Ellen stared Ted down. "I will shoot you if you don't get off my land."

"I see where your murdering son gets it from," Teddy snarled.

"Sage, get me my shotgun."

Sage sighed. "Mr. Dale, I think it's time for you to leave."

"Don't make me call the state in on this, Ted." Win wasn't above using that threat over and over. His uncles didn't want state troopers messing in their business, not in this tiny corner of East Texas.

"You fucking traitor. I hope the piece of ass is worth it."

The sound of a shotgun cocking had Win spinning around. Rosie stood there, little baby bump just showing, staring Ted down as Sam leaned against the doorframe. "Get. This is Redding land. It'll always be Redding land until me and my kids and my grandkids are in the ground."

"I'd go if I was you, Teddy." Ellen looked viciously pleased. "My Rosie can turn you from a bull to a steer in one shot."

Win bit back a grin, trying not to chortle at the color Ted's skin turned with his rage. *Lord.*

The Reddings stood there, staring as Ted backed off, cussing and threatening the whole way. Finally Teddy just got in his truck and left, spitting dirt and gravel out from under his back tires.

God, he loved this family.

Win rubbed the back of his neck. "Would it help if I say I think I'm adopted?" He grinned, hoping it would lighten the mood.

"Oh, honey. I know your momma. Your apple dropped from her tree." Ellen grinned. "Y'all heading to town? I made y'all some cookies for the drive."

His smile widened into something real. "Yes, ma'am. And thank you. I'll call Allworthy to keep an eye out while Sage and I are gone."

"That'd be a blessing, son." Ellen kissed Sage's cheek. "Run get your bag, now, and get on before your daddy finds you more work."

Sage laughed but nodded and headed off to get his bag.

Win glanced back at Ellen. "Seriously, you call if anything happens. Okay?"

"You know it. We're not stupid. Or scared."

"I know. I just worry." He nodded at Rosie. "You're a stud."

"Totally. I'm tired of every asshole in town fucking with us."

"Rosie!" Sam's voice was shocked, but the look was approving. "Good on you."

Sage came back with his duffel, and Win felt something tighten in his chest at how amazing the man looked. He couldn't wait to go have some time alone.

"We'll have our phones. Y'all be good. I'll bring him back in three days."

"Have a good time, Son." Ellen waved at Sage before herding Sam and Rosie back in the house.

"You ready to play, man?"

"Hell, yes." They slid into his truck, and he squeezed Sage's hand down beneath the dash. "Sorry about Ted. I pissed him off this morning at the office. He and Jim ambushed me."

"He comes back once a week to ten days. He's a prick."

"Shit, you never told me that." He frowned, so damned pissed. Win didn't want to start the weekend that way. "I guess I can see why, but it makes me crazy."

"I didn't want to put a thing 'tween you and yours."

"Shit. Ted and I haven't been family in a long time." His uncle hated the whole world. "What are you looking forward to most?"

"Taking a shower with you."

Well, then. He grinned. "I thought you'd say the Stockyards or Six Flags. I like how you think."

"I'm looking forward to that too, but that's the big one." Sage gave him a little grin, and Win's body surged a little.

"We can start and end with that."

"I like that." Sage chuckled, hand sliding over his thigh. "A lot."

Oh, ho. Look at his man, being all forward. He hoped to God he didn't run off the road.

The hand stayed put, mostly, teasing at the seam. Sage wasn't trying to make him crazy. No, the man was just touching, letting him know that anticipation was a fine thing.

"Thanks for inviting me out."

"Thanks for coming." Win meant it. They needed to get out of Sage's trailer, be real people together.

It seemed like every mile away from things eased the worry from Sage's face. It was stunning how every time he glanced over, Sage looked younger. Happier.

Lighter.

Christ, how hard was living there on a day-to-day basis? It had to be a little like prison. Sage would say jail was far worse, he knew, but damn.

"Penny for your thoughts."

"I'm thinking how glad I am we're getting out of town." He'd take Sage to the Cattleman's Steakhouse for supper. They had a room in the old hotel right in the Stockyards.

"God, me too. How much money do I owe you for the hotel?"

He was hoping Sage wouldn't ask. Hell, the man had hocked his movies and TV for the vet bills. Win knew he was broke-dick. Time to tap dance.

"I'll let you get the tickets to Six Flags, babe."

"Is that fair? I want to be fair to you."

"It's more than fair." Sage had that damned cowboy pride, so Win would have to work hard to make Sage understand. "I asked you to come with me. It's like me paying for a date."

"One day I'll have my shit together."

"I think you're doing great as it is."

"Yeah." Now that didn't sound convinced.

"Hey." He curled his fingers around Sage's where they lay on his leg. "You are. I know it's hard."

"Parts of it, yeah. The horses, though? That's all I ever wanted to do with my life."

"Yeah? Always wanted to be a cowboy?" Win had wanted to be an astronaut. Maybe a firefighter. Then Indiana Jones.

"Every day of my life. It's even why I got my degree."

"You got a degree?" Win had heard of those kinds of programs, but he was woefully undereducated about Sage's life.

"I have a master's in accounting."

Okay, that was unexpected. Sure beat his bachelors in criminal justice. "So, accounting so you could do the books?"

"Yeah. I mean, I can't work as an accountant or anything, but at least my checkbook is balanced."

"I should get you to look at mine." Win did all his banking online. He never overdrew, but he never really knew what he had either.

"Sure. I'm pretty good at it. I ain't scared of math."

"Good deal. I have some savings. I might have you look at how much, though, see what I might have to invest." He knew accountant and investment banker wasn't the same, but he had to know what he had before he could do anything with it.

"Sure. If nothing else, I can tell you about the tax part."

"I'll take you up on it." He squeezed Sage's hand. "Though this weekend, I'm feeling spendy."

"Lord, it's sure grown up 'round here. I haven't been this far from the farm in eons."

"I guess it has, huh?" Win was used to this stretch of road; he never thought about it.

"You must think I'm like a hillbilly or something, to never even drive out to Royse City." Win hated that hint of shame, of embarrassment.

"No, sir. I think you've had a hard row to hoe." He didn't want Sage to think he pitied him. He didn't. He thought Sage was a stud, but Sage's life made him sad.

"Just been caged a lot. Once you're in prison, it follows you, they say."

"I'm sorry, babe." He didn't know what else to say.

"It's okay. It's not like I didn't earn the problems."

"All teenagers do stupid shit."

"No shit on that, darlin'." Sage laughed for him, though, and that made him smile.

"You hungry?" They weren't but a little ways down the road, but he could totally stop in Rockwall and eat at El Chico's.

"Not yet, no, but I could use a cup of coffee."

"We'll grab some Starbucks, then." Win would get some lemon cake. Or a scone.

"My mom loves Starbucks and their fancy coffees."

"Does she? So does mine." He chuckled. "I like the cake."

"I like the lemon one. Momma brings it to me when she goes."

"That's my favorite too." Win liked cinnamon scones, though, so if there was only one lemon, he'd let Sage have it.

"The chocolate cinnamon one is not as good."

"Neither is their banana bread." Of course, what Texas boy didn't love his momma's banana bread best?

"Mmm. Banana bread. You like walnuts in yours?" The conversation was easy, lazy, and they pulled into the Starbucks parking lot in Mesquite, near the mall. It was huge, crowded, and they were just two dudes getting coffee.

"I do, but pecans will do in a pinch."

Sage headed in, humming along with the music playing. Win hung back, admiring the movement of Sage's ass in those Wranglers.

Tight, lean—*Jesus, Win. Get it together.*

He headed inside so Sage wouldn't wonder what the hell he was doing.

There was an older man standing at the end of the line, scowling at a smartphone. "You boys know anything about this fancy coffee shit? My daughter sent me for her. She's in labor and wants a flippy-chinaman."

Sage's head tilted. "No, sir, but I reckon we can figure it. Adam?"

Win chuckled. "Maybe a Frappuccino? Auto correct can be a bitch."

Sage read the board. "Does she like vanilla? Can girls in labor have coffee?"

"Shit, son. Girls in labor can have whatever the hell they ask for."

Sage snorted. "Got it."

Win cackled. "We'll have to remember that with your sister."

"I bet I will. Hell, I remember it now."

They got the old guy set up with a vanilla bean Frappuccino, and there was just enough lemon cake for all of them.

Sage and Win sat down together and ate, watching each other across the table, the tension of anticipation delicious. Win felt brave as all fuck when he pushed his foot against Sage's under the table.

Sage looked up at him, eyebrow lifted. "Daring."

"I know, right? Starbucks is supposed to be equal opportunity."

Sage snorted into his "just drip coffee, please," but grinned. The expression was fucking adorable, especially when Sage's ears went red. It was so easy to be stupid over this cowboy, all the little quirks, the expressions.

Hell, Win was hard in love.

"Holler when you're ready to go. We want to be through Arlington before rush hour."

"I'm good. I need to pee."

"Good deal. I'll throw the trash away."

They split up for those few moments, and Win had to admit, he expected someone to attack while Sage was in the head. Starbuck's only had one-holers, though, and he stood in line for his turn. Never knew what the traffic downtown would be like.

When he got out from doing his business too, Sage was standing outside the coffee shop, talking to an older lady about her bright green-and-pink scarf, the sweet thing blushing and fluttering with pride.

"You ready?" He left off the babe in deference to the old lady.

"I am. You have a good day, ma'am, and best of luck with your surgery tomorrow. I'll pray for you."

"Thank you, son." She tottered off.

"You charmed her."

"I was just being polite."

"Nah, you were being you." He copped a quick feel of that sweet ass.

Okay, the little deep sound rocked his socks. Win was beginning to like this "get out of town" thing. A lot. Just the freedom to admire.

And he could see the pressure lifting from Sage's shoulders with every mile. That was worth every penny, every hour spent on the road. He wanted to take Sage away permanently.

The thought startled him.

Did he? Really? Was that even an option? Ever?

He'd gone home to be a cop a long while back, and he thought that was what he wanted to do. Now he knew better. He wanted to be with Sage.

"Come on, Officer! We got the whole Stockyards to explore."

"Hell, yes. We can even go to hear some music."

Sage grinned at him, eyes twinkling. "I've been known to listen to music."

"You have? I didn't know." The teasing made him so damned happy.

"No?" Sage snorted, belting out a few lines of "Back in Black."

He laughed and sang along, driving with one eye toward the cops that might be lurking out there on the road. God knew, he didn't need a ticket. No. This was their fucking vacation, and Win wasn't going to do a damn thing to fuck it up.

"You okay?" Sage asked, and Win glanced over, realizing he was frowning.

"Sure. I was being all fierce about not messing up our trip."

"No messing. We'll have a ball." Sage sounded so sure.

"We will." There was a hotel bed and shower, just waiting. And while he was gone, he was paying his mom's friend Stella to clean his house.

After this, he was bringing Sage home to visit, like he'd promised. "We need to find something else on the radio to sing to."

"I'm on it."

They pulled up on I-30 and headed into the depths of Dallas. By the time Sage found KSCS, they were singing with George about Amarillo and having a ball. Win felt like he was seeing a whole new side of his lover.

One that he found himself being protective as hell about.

He'd just have to make sure no one ever hurt Sage again. Including him.

CHAPTER TWENTY-ONE

SAGE SAT on the edge of the bed, staring at the room, which looked like an old Western movie had come in and thrown up all over. Damn, he'd never seen anything so cool.

He'd unpacked his clothes and Adam's, put everything away in the little dresser, and stowed the suitcases away so they weren't messy while Adam did his business in the restroom.

Fort Worth was bigger than he remembered. A lot bigger. Good thing the Stockyards took a man back in time. There'd even been a little cattle drive down the street. He'd seen it through the window right after they'd checked in.

He moved to the window and looked down at all the folks wandering. It was warm today, but the man on Channel 8 had said there was a blue norther coming down the pike around dinnertime.

He sure hoped that meant snuggling.

Adam came out of the bathroom, smiling easily. "Hey, you."

"Hey, darlin'." He stood and headed right over to Adam's open arms. "You did good with the hotel."

"Did I? It looked all cowboy."

"It's the neatest thing I ever did see."

Adam smiled for him like the sunrise coming up, and well now, that was a fine thing. One hand came up, massaging right at the base of his neck, fingers digging in, and his eyes crossed. Damn. Damn, that was fine.

Sage leaned into Adam's touch, and they ended up sitting on the bed, him on Adam's lap. He grinned, got him a long, slow kiss that liked to burn him to the ground. His arms were looped around Adam's neck, his legs straddling those strong thighs. Oh, yeah. He could ride.

"Damn, baby. Look at you." Adam's voice was all rough and raw, his eyes on Sage like he was something else.

He knew better. Sage was what he was, but if Adam thought he was all that, well, that worked for him.

It was how it was supposed to be.

"So you want that shower now or later?"

"Can I have both?"

"Hell, yes." Adam grinned, lifting him to his feet and standing.

Adam's shirt was already off, and they'd both tugged their boots off when they got to the room, so it was easy to start working open belts and flies. Adam's fingers tangled with his every few seconds, and they got to laughing, both of them tickled.

"Look at us, getting naked during work hours." He tugged the dark hairs at the base of Adam's tight belly.

"Uh-huh. No one to worry on, just you and me and that shower." Adam's muscles worked, rippling under his skin.

Sage nodded. He wanted to touch, to soap Adam up and let his fingers trail over the man's slippery body.

They finally got naked and into the big shower, which was all marble tile and showerheads. Way more modern than the room itself.

"Wow." They got the hot water going and the soap unwrapped.

Then it was a free-for-all. Adam got rubbing on him, the soap easing the way. Those hands felt so good on his skin. The soap bubbled up, catching on the mat of hair on Adam's chest, his tiny nipples hard as pebbles.

Sage rubbed at them with his thumbs, watching how the deep flush climbed Adam's chest. He did that. Him.

"Fuck, you're fine." He kissed Adam's jaw.

Adam laughed, turning to take his mouth, kissing him good and hard.

He hadn't had so much fun in eons.

They slipped and rubbed, goofing around more than getting off. The suds built up until they were so slick they could barely stand on the tile. Sage laughed, stealing sloppy kisses. "Adam."

"What, baby?" More and more he said "baby" instead of "babe," like Adam was really getting serious.

"You make me happy, bone deep."

"Good." Adam reached around and grabbed Sage's ass.

The touch made him goose pimple up, made him rub a little harder. He would have thought that touch would make him nervous, but this was Adam. His Adam. He leaned up and nibbled on Adam's earlobe. "More."

"Hell, yes." Adam pulled him closer, and silly went very serious. And hot. And hard. Adam leaned back against the tile, keeping him there, and he climbed up the slick muscles.

Holding him steady, Adam let him climb until he could start rubbing, getting their cocks together.

Fuck. Fuck, this was real. Him. Adam. Wet and slick and naked. The tiles pressed against his sore knees, cold enough to make him yelp and pull back.

Adam chuckled and shifted a bit, but those sure hands didn't waver a bit. "I'll keep you warm."

"I trust you."

Eyes going dark, Adam pressed in for a kiss. A hard kiss.

He opened up, his cock rubbing against Adam's belly, Adam's prick on his hip. He loved how they felt together, how strong Adam was. How his man made him ache, made him a little stupid.

"I like your skin all wet."

"This is...." Better. It was erasing things that he didn't think of. Sometimes Sage needed that more than breathing.

"Uh-huh. It so is." Adam might not know what he was thinking, but those eyes told him that he wasn't alone.

He leaned forward and fastened his mouth on Adam's throat, tasting soap and salt and fresh water. He wanted to leave a little mark there, and he figured he could. They had days for it to fade.

"It's okay. I won't tell."

Sage chuckled. Who was there to tell? Still, that was all the encouragement he needed to fasten onto Adam and give the man a hickey.

Adam grabbed him, dragged him closer, a raw sound bouncing off the tile. God, that was stunning, the way Adam needed him, wanted him. He bit a little, and Adam groaned, spun him around, cock rubbing against his ass. "Tell me this is okay?"

"Uh-huh. This ain't... this ain't nothin' bad."

"Good. God, I'm going crazy, baby."

"Fuck me, honey. I want to feel you again." That had rocked his world.

"I can so do that." Adam let Sage's feet slide to the floor, leaving him blinking for a moment, alone while Adam got the kit bag.

Sage leaned back into the spray, throat working, one hand slowly jacking his cock.

"Fuck. Sage." Adam came back and stared at him a moment, condoms and lube in hand.

"Uh-huh. Excellent plan."

"I thought so." Adam's laughter was better than all the soap and water out there.

Sage grinned over his shoulder and winked. "You're awful far away."

"Not anymore." Adam slid up behind him, cock rubbing his ass while Adam struggled with the lube.

He didn't help. He wiggled and rubbed back, teasing, playing some.

"Make me drop this stuff, why don't you?" Adam laughed for him, rubbing two fingers against his hole.

"Hmm? Me?" He didn't do innocent so well. Maybe it was the cowboy in him.

Adam chuckled and goosed his ass but good. He whooped, hands smacking the tile so he could keep his balance.

"You're a turd." Sage loved this son of a bitch with all he was.

"Nope. No talking about stuff like that at a time like this."

Sage cracked up, laughing like he hadn't since he was a kid, the sound pouring out of him. Oh God, that was funny, keeping him chortling, even when Adam slid two fingers right into him.

He spread, his balls swinging between his thighs. Damn, that felt good. His back arched, his body bowing, and Adam played him like a fiddle, in and out, back and forth. He let himself feel it, let himself go with it, like never before.

Adam had him. Safe. Sound. Driving him higher and higher.

He pushed back, riding the touch, missing it when those fingers disappeared. Then he squeezed his eyes shut and tried to relax everywhere else, because Adam was pushing inside him, cock heavy and wide.

"Adam." He bore back, throat working, hands sliding on the tile.

"Baby. God, you're tight. Sage. Need you."

"Got me. Swear. Come on, honey. Let's make this happen."

"Yeah. Yeah." Adam gripped his hips and moved, thrusting hard enough that their skin slapped together.

His eyes rolled, his ass holding that thick cock tight. He tried to rock back and forth, but it was too wet, too slick.

"Gonna have to let me make it good, baby."

"I know." He did. Sage trusted Adam. Didn't keep him from wanting to move.

Adam chuckled for him and bit the curve of his shoulder. The touch of the hard ridge of Adam's teeth made him rise up on his toes. That made Adam gasp and jerk into him deeper.

Fuck, this was what he wanted to be doing when he died.

One hand wrapped around his hip, and they moved faster, Adam guiding him. They were going to set this whole place on fire.

"Need. Fuck, Adam, I'm aching here."

"I got you, baby." Adam reached around, grabbed his cock, and stroked it in time with his thrusts.

Oh hell, yes. Just that. Just like that. His eyes rolled, electricity slamming up his spine. He panted, working back and forth as much as he could. Adam kept moving, hips spanking his ass.

Sage shot hard, spunk spraying up over the tile.

"Oh God. Yeah, baby. I feel that." Adam rocked into him twice, maybe three more times and boom. It was all over.

He leaned back into Adam's arms, grinning like a newborn fool. The water was about to get real cold, he'd bet, so maybe they ought to turn it off. When he could move.

"We should nap before supper." Adam's lips brushed his ear.

"That sounds good. I got a candy bar or two in my bag."

"Perfect." They stumbled out of the shower, dried off, and tumbled onto the bed. The mattress was firm but pillowy on top, which was nice.

Adam stayed right next to him, their legs all tangled up in each other and the sheets. The whole idea of a midday nap seemed... decadent. Like a real vacation.

He pulled the covers up over them and kissed the top of Adam's head, offering the good Lord a quick prayer of thanks.

"HEY, SAGE, you like the blue shirt or the green?" How silly was it for Win to be nervous about supper?

Sage looked over, head tilted. "The blue."

Well okay, then.

Win tugged on the light blue button-down, hoping he didn't look like an idiot playing dress the cowboy. He was a Texan. His boots were worn in.

Sage's eyes fell on him, watching as he tucked himself in, refastened his belt, everything. He tried hard not to puff up like a peacock, but it was tough. That gaze was nothing but admiration.

"You're the finest man I ever seen." Sage's lips quirked in a little smile. "Swear to God."

"Thanks. You clean up good too." Sage looked like the real deal. Cowboy to the bone.

Sage was wearing white, the shirt and jeans both pressed 'til they squeaked. Win stared a little himself, tickled as hell that this was his. Sage sprayed on the tiniest bit of smell good and smoothed the shirt over his belly. "You ready?"

"I am. I could eat a steak as big as your head."

"Yum." Sage put his wallet in his pocket and grabbed his hat.

Win grinned, snagged a room key, and stuck it in his jeans, then headed out. "You like a baked potato or are you a fries guy?"

"A baked potato with bacon and green onions."

"And cheese." Win loved cheese and sour cream.

"Uh-huh. Butter. We can't forget the butter."

"Oh man." His mouth was actually watering a little. His belly rumbled.

"Rolls. Butter. Steak."

"Yeah. Oh heck, yeah." They got downstairs and headed outside, the broad street that ran through the stockyards filled with people.

No one looked twice at them as they ambled. They didn't have far to go, just down the street and around the corner, the scent of yeast rolls like heaven on the air. The place was all old school, wooden rails and pictures of prize cattle on the walls.

"Look at that. Daddy was talking about getting some cattle, but I'm not for it. I'm thinking llamas."

"Seriously?" Adam raised a brow. "Why's that?"

"They go for good money. They make solid watchdogs. The babies sell, and they aren't hard to keep fenced."

Listen to his cowboy. He knew his shit. "Well, llamas it is, then." He could so see Sage expanding the ranch.

"Maybe. I'll try a couple three first, see what I think. I'll always be in this for the horses."

"I know. You're good with them." They got seated and got menus. Win knew you had to love a steakhouse with like, five options. All meat.

"I want the rib eye, I think. The T-bone is a bit dear."

"I like a big sirloin." He wasn't much on the fattier steaks. "But you have what you want, baby."

"I think I'll take the littler rib eye, so I can enjoy my potato."

"There you go." Win ordered an iced tea. The soft yeast rolls came, and they both smeared butter on.

"Oh God." Sage fell on the rolls like a starving man, snarfing the bread up.

"You are a bread fiend." Win loved it. Loved knowing these weird things about Sage.

"I am. Love it. Also, I missed breakfast."

"Well, shit, you should have said. Did you say?" Had he missed that?

"We were busy threatening your uncle." Was that a joke?

Win blinked, then grinned. "We so were. Your sister is a stud."

"She's knocked up and has a concealed carry license. It doesn't get much studlier than that."

"I guess not." In fact, Win's background in law enforcement sort of reinforced that fact. Hell hath no fury like a woman protecting her baby.

"You ever miss being in the service?"

Where the hell had that come from? Win tilted his head. "Not really, no. I'm pretty good at what I do, but as a cop, I do it way more on my terms. In the military, there were always orders."

"Cool. I never thought about being a soldier, but I might have been good at it."

"I think you're good at being a cowboy, huh?" The salads came, and Win munched away, the bread having whetted his appetite.

"It's what I know. Cowboying and... well, there ain't much call for professional convict."

He frowned. "Which you aren't. You're doing fine, Sage."

Sage nodded. "I know. I know, it's just.... Everyone pretends like it didn't happen, and... I did hard time for eight years. I'm fixin' to be twenty-nine and.... You know?"

"I know." Win paused, trying to decide what to say. "I think about it sometimes. About how you seem to have been abducted by aliens when it comes to some stuff."

"Weird, huh? It's like I was in a foreign country, sort of. I mean, I could have had any drugs I wanted, smokes, but I couldn't get a Domino's pizza. Then they let you out into a halfway house and... that shit's filthy, man. The joint is less scary."

"Lord." Win grinned a little. "I like Pizza Hut."

"I like pizza. Period." Sage chuckled. "I love real Mexican food and good steaks and…. One day I'll be able to have a beer, even."

"You will." He would bet Sage would be supercautious when he could drink. Jesus, when he could drink. The man was twenty-nine fucking years old, and he'd never had a legal fucking beer, never got to vote. Hell, Sage couldn't tell a goddamn police officer no on a drug test. It was never going to go away, that fucking cloud, the stain of being young, stupid, and in the wrong place at the wrong time.

The roll in his hand made a wet sound, and when he looked down, he'd kneaded it back into dough.

"Maybe. Maybe I won't. They say that addictions are addictions, so maybe I won't." Sage nodded to the squished roll. "They better that way?"

"Shut up." Adam rolled his eyes and dropped the mangled bread on his little plate. "And for the record, I don't touch cigarettes." He was an ex-smoker, had been for six years, but he always knew he could fall back.

"Cigarettes are nasty. I hate the smell."

"I used to love them." They'd calmed him down. "Now the smell makes me sick."

"I bet." Sage leaned back as their steaks came. "Look at that."

"That's amazing." The potatoes came on separate little plates, all covered with sea salt. They got more rolls too.

They ate hearty, telling silly jokes and reminiscing about high school football games that Sage had been too tiny to participate in and Win had been too shitty to start in.

"You know, they might take our Texan cards away, man? Neither one of us started in varsity." Sage's eyes were twinkling.

"Well, you're a cowboy, and I'm a deputy. We have the stereotype exemption," Win said, deadpan until Sage cracked up.

The waitress came back and refilled their teas. "Y'all look like you're going good. Y'all want something sweet?"

He looked at Sage, who shook his head. "No, ma'am. I'm fixin' to take a long walk and then find some ice cream."

His man did love ice cream.

"Thanks, though." Win loved the idea of ice cream too. "Tomorrow they said we ought to try that barbecue place. Is it any good?"

"Totally. Go early or late, or you'll have to wait in line. There's good ice cream in the coffee shop in the square."

"Cool. Thank you." Adam grabbed the bill neatly when she slid it over, not even letting Sage see it.

Sage pinked, sighed the slightest bit. "One day, Adam. I swear."

He knew. Sage worked his ass off. "It's no big, baby. I told you this vacation was on me."

"Still. One day." Sage's boot nudged his under the table.

"One day you can take me to the Caribbean." His heartbeat kicked up, his cheeks heating.

"My hard-core probation should be over in a year, give or take. Then, yeah, I can request permission to leave the country. Then I just got five years of calling in, for the most part."

"Where would you like to go most?" Win thought maybe they should go where they could hold hands.

"I don't know. I've never thought about it. I like the idea of the ocean, though. I used to walk the beach in California."

"Hell, we can go down to Galveston without leaving the state." Win liked the beach. And the seawall.

"I went once when I was a teenager. We got so sunburned I liked to died on the way home."

"I went a few years ago to some law enforcement conference. There was this little place that did pancakes...."

"Yeah?" They headed out into the crowd, the music floating on the air. The place had a real old boomtown feel to it now that evening was on them.

They headed into Billy Bob's, paid their cover, and went to sightsee. They had the tiniest bull riding ever, the arena so small the clown was the one bullfighter.

"You ever been on a bull, Adam?" Sage watched the cowboys closely, eyes sharp.

"Oh hell, no. You?" He could see Sage do it.

"Yeah. Yeah, when I was a teenager. Junior rodeo, you know." His lips twisted. "I bet I could do it again, though."

"Bullshit." One of the big old boys sitting below them snorted. "You're an old man. You could not."

"I ain't that old."

"Old enough to be scared."

Win saw Sage's eyes harden. "I'm not scared, boy."

"Oh, now, you're just tiny. You should be."

Win didn't know whether to flash his badge even though he was off duty, or let Sage handle this. The man could look out for himself.

"You gonna get your ass up there, kid? Put your money where your mouth is?"

"He's not signed up." Adam had taken enough. He half rose, slipping his badge out of his jeans pocket. "Back off."

The kid's eyes went wide. "Dude, I don't want trouble."

"Neither do we. You were the one acting like you did." He sat back down, hand brushing Sage's leg.

Sage stared the kid down, never looking away until he backed off.

Then they settled in to watch the rest of the bull riding. Sage didn't say another word, just watched the cowboys quietly.

Win hoped to hell their night wasn't ruined. Maybe he shouldn't have flashed his badge. Shit, he wasn't sure if Sage was pissed or was glad. Whatever. All he knew was Sage was quiet.

When the bull riding was over, they headed out, watching the dancers a moment. "Do you line dance?" Win dared to tease.

"I'm a Texan. Of course I do." Sage shook his head. "It's a little more complicated now."

"It is. I always get my feet all tangled up."

"I don't think I'll probably be dancing anytime soon." Sage chuckled. "I need a Coke, I'm thinkin'."

"Cool. I could use a drink." Nothing alcoholic, but he could wet his whistle.

They headed up to the bar and Sage slid in between two groups of frat boys to order two Cokes from the harried little bartender. She smiled at Sage, though, obviously liking what she saw.

Sage nodded, tipped her, then headed toward him, drinks in hand. "Ta-da!"

"Thanks, babe." He took his Coke and sipped. Lord, bar sodas were always too cloying.

"Surely." Sage drank deeply, nose wrinkling. "Whoa. Sweet."

"Yeah." He grinned a little, feeling brave. "Wanna go wander back toward the hotel? See what's at the arena?"

"Absolutely. It's smoky in here."

"Cool." Win drank a few more sips before setting the glass aside, not willing to waste Sage's money.

"This is nasty." Sage placed it aside and nodded toward the door.

Win laughed. "It was pretty bad. We'll find somewhere to have that ice cream too."

"God, yes." They headed out into the midsized crowd, the night surprisingly chilly.

He moved a little closer to Sage, enough to not be obvious, but to share warmth.

"That blue norther is coming sooner than they thought."

"It is." He took a chance, nudging Sage with his elbow. "We could get the ice cream room service and watch a movie."

"Oooh. I've never had room service. Can we get coffee?"

"We can get anything you want." He'd do about anything to keep that smile on Sage's face.

"Sounds perfect."

Weirdly enough it was.

SAGE HADN'T had such a good time in all his life. They'd walked and eaten, wandered around museums, and then, yesterday, they'd hopped in the truck and driven around, looking at all the little towns around Fort Worth.

They'd thought about Six Flags, but Sage figured they ought to pace themselves. They would do that when he could pay.

He packed his little bag, putting everything back in its spot. They still had today to wander home. Adam had some sort of thing they were going to, but hadn't told him what it was.

It was kind of exciting and a little unnerving. A surprise.

He hadn't had a good one of those in too long. Well, he'd had a few in the last few days. Like how stunning it was to watch Adam eat ribs. A lot of licking was involved. Licking lips. Licking fingers. Moaning.

He rubbed his cock through his jeans, jonesing on it a bit.

"You okay, baby?" Adam came out of the bathroom and leaned against his back.

"Uh-huh." He was. He pressed back, biting his bottom lip some.

"Whatcha thinkin'?" The slight hint of laughter told him Adam knew exactly what he was thinking about.

"About you and your mouth."

"Yeah? You like it when I kiss you, Sage?" Adam was rocking against him.

"Uh-huh." His eyelids got heavy. "I like when you do lots of things."

"Me too." Adam reached around and put one hand over his, pressing his cock. "I like your things, as well."

"Uhn." He went up on tiptoe, eyes rolling back in his head.

"Uh-huh. Checkout's not for two hours."

"Cool." He lifted his chin and kissed Adam's jaw.

Adam twirled him around as neatly as if they were dancing, kissing him on the mouth nice and easy.

His hips pressed against Adam's thigh, his belly against that sweet prick. The brush of cloth couldn't hide how happy Adam was to be there with him.

"Can't believe how bad I need you."

"I'm glad."

He got him another kiss, then another, and Adam finally pushed him down on the bed.

Sage laughed, the sound bubbling out of him. Fuck, he wished life could be like this all the time. 'Course then he guessed he wouldn't appreciate it when things went so good.

"Good vacation, baby?"

"Best. The best." He cupped Adam's cheek and took a deep kiss. "Let's see if we can end it with a bang."

"Oh, we can so do that. The question is who's doing the banging?"

THE IMAX theater was remarkably empty for a Sunday matinee. Win was tickled to death, because that meant he and Sage could sit close without too much worry. They had a row to themselves, and everyone was hiding behind 3D glasses.

His cowboy was like a kid, with popcorn and soda, staring at the screen in awe. "Dinosaurs. How fucking cool."

"I know, right? I love this movie." The dinosaurs were stunning in 3D.

Sage reached over, squeezed his arm, then ate another bite of popcorn. Win grinned, feeling like the most amazing boyfriend on earth. Dude. Did he call himself a boyfriend?

Win worked that one over in his mind, like he was chewing gum. Boyfriend? Lover? Fuckbuddy? Partner? He wasn't sure. Partner sounded like a Western. Of course, Sage was pretty damned Western. The man wore tighty-whities and starched his jeans. The hat was a dead giveaway too.

He snorted. Howdy, partner.

Sage looked over at him, eyes huge behind the 3D glasses. That blinky expression made Win smile.

"Having fun, man?"

Was he having fun? Shit. He was having a ball. He loved to see Sage relax and have fun. "I am."

"Cool." Sage offered him more popcorn, fingers barely brushing his.

He grabbed a handful, his arm tingling. He kept thinking about earlier in the day, back at the hotel. Standing there and bending Sage over the bed. He hadn't imagined Sage would be so eager, so horny and in his face with it.

The whole thought threatened to give him a happy, and that might be awkward. Even in a dark theater.

The tyrannosaurus roared, and Sage laughed, clapping.

Yeah. This was so totally worth the trip and the time off and the money. It was worth the shit he was gonna take when he got back to work.

This was hope, and it was something he'd been hunting. He needed to believe that he and Sage could have a life outside their little town. Had to believe.

He just had to figure out how to make it happen.

The popcorn made him thirsty, and he grabbed his Coke and sipped, pondering things.

At least until the velociraptors started eating people.

Then he was all about the dinosaurs.

CHAPTER TWENTY-TWO

WIN WHISTLED, feeling damned good. Damned good.

His little vacation with Sage a couple weeks back had gone so well that he couldn't stop grinning, and he hummed to himself as he flipped through e-mails.

"Win, you got a sec?" The sheriff breezed by, heading toward the private office.

Goddamn it. So much for the good mood. Jim was smiling, which boded ill for Win.

"Sure. What's up?"

"Sit." Jim moved behind his desk and settled. "I have some information you need to know. I know you and the Redding guy are hooking up, and I just want you to have all the news."

Win raised a brow. "Do you, now? For my own good, no doubt."

"I called in a favor and got Redding's records. I thought you ought to know that he had a steady in the pen, one that still writes him. Some big black dude. Apparently they tried to separate them twice and this 'Bear' guy got him returned to the cell, both times." Jim's lips twisted. "Sounds like true love."

A sick feeling settled in the pit of Win's belly. Not about Sage, but about his uncle. "What possible good do you think telling me this will do?"

"I reckoned you should know if you have competition."

"Competition." His hands felt icy cold. "Tell me something, Jim. Just tell me what I've ever done to you personally that you hate me."

"What? Shit, son. I'm trying to protect you. You've lost your fucking mind over that asshole. Think of the diseases he could have, man."

"He's not an asshole." He clenched his teeth, spitting out every word. "He's a man who made a mistake. I wish to hell you would admit everyone is being crazy about this." He used to like his Uncle Jim just fine. They'd clashed over politics and religion occasionally, but that was normal. God, he was tired.

"No one is being crazy. He was there when your cousin died, Win."

"So? Angel was a drug addict flopping in a meth house!" Win stood, done with this whole thing. "Is there something work related, Jim?"

"Nope. Go on. I thought you ought to know your cowboy was somebody else's bitch."

"Jesus." He turned on his heel, so disgusted he was about to explode. "Just leave me alone."

Grace didn't even say a thing as he stormed out and stomped to his truck. *Motherfucker.* He slammed the door and sat with his hands on the steering wheel. He stared at his white knuckles, not sure where to go from here.

Somebody else's bitch.

Asshole.

Sage was no one's bitch, no matter what had happened to him. Win knew that.

He did wish he'd known, that Jim hadn't been able to ambush him. Hell, he didn't know anything about Sage's time inside. Nothing. Win could infer a lot, from the sore knees to the way Sage jumped when someone touched him from behind without warning, but he didn't know the details.

He sighed, starting his truck. Maybe if he went to see Sage, got some questions out of his system, it might help.

Win headed out to the Reddings', his mind going a million miles a minute. He didn't know what the hell to do about his uncles. They weren't going to let this go, and he wasn't going to give up. Sage was worth fighting for, though, worth holding out for.

The gate was closed, so he hopped out and let himself in, grinning about how he knew the combination to the padlock now. He was the only person not named Redding who did.

He drove up to the house, parked beside Sage's old work truck, and headed toward the barn where he could hear Sage whistling. The sound made him smile, and he pushed down his worry, hoping this whole thing was nothing. And what if it wasn't? What could he do about someone Sage used to know in prison? Hell, what business was it of his, anyway?

Except that it was his business, a little, right? They were together. They were a couple. They were supposed to tell each other things.

He blew out a breath, trying to get rid of the negative energy Jim had brought to him. Then he went to find Sage.

Sage was behind the barn, repairing a saddle, whistling tunelessly. Win stopped and admired a moment, trying to collect his thoughts. He couldn't just blurt out something stupid.

Sage looked up. "Hey, Adam. What's up?"

"Hey." He stood, shifting from foot to foot. God, he felt like an idiot.

"What's wrong?" Sage stood up and came over to him. "You look pissed."

"I am." He put an arm around Sage and kissed the man's temple. "At my uncle."

"Oh Lord. What has the sheriff done now?"

Win wanted to smile back, to match Sage's tone, but he wasn't sure he could. "He was telling me shit about your time in prison."

Sage's head tilted. "Okay. What shit did he tell you?"

He drew a deep breath and let it out slowly. "He was going on about someone you knew in there. Someone who still writes to you. I didn't know you were... close to anyone."

"They don't call it 'close.' They call it being someone's bitch."

Win drew back, kinda feeling like he'd been slapped. "What?"

"In the joint, it's called being someone's bitch or a meat-wrangler. Sometimes they tell you you're a pole sitter." Sage's voice was even, quiet, steady.

That almost made what he was saying worse, like it was something people said in normal conversation. Win had no idea how to reply, so he shrugged. "I didn't know."

"No. I don't think about it." Sage's pale eyes looked right at him. "Come with me for a second."

"Okay." He followed Sage, feeling numb all the way to his toes.

Sage led him to the trailer and up the stairs. The TV was still gone, but there was a stack of old paperbacks there. Westerns. Some Clive Cussler books. Sage went back to the bedroom, went to the dresser, and pulled out a little stack of letters, then handed them over. "His name is Darryl Keye. He's a lifer. Homicide. Multiple offenses. I belonged to him when I was in."

Win stared at the letters, all neatly addressed in pencil, the name and identification number of the prisoner on the return label area. None of them had been opened. "Why would he write to you?"

"He fucked me for six and a half years, off and on, so I guess he's fond of me." Sage shrugged. "I honestly don't know. You're welcome to read them and find out."

Win wasn't sure what he wanted—for Sage to deny it, to scream. Something. Anything but this calm, almost bewildered expression. He opened his mouth. Closed it. "You haven't read them."

"I haven't. I never will." Sage rubbed his forehead. "I was nineteen when they moved me into maximum security. On the first day, they poured bleach in my eyes. The next week they made me choose— teeth or knees. I chose, and they broke my knees and three of my fingers. Keye worked in the infirmary that week. He liked little white boys with teeth, so I still have mine."

Bile rose in Win's throat. He'd seen the stupid shit that went on in the county lockup, but this was something else. "Bleach."

"Yeah. Stings like a motherfucker, and you can't see for days. The knees were the worst part. Still are."

How the fuck could Sage stand there, so even, almost flat?

"You never talk about it. It's like there's this whole you that I don't know." That was the crux of it, finally. He'd been thinking about it like Sage went into cold storage all those years, that he hadn't had a life. He'd had a life, just not one Win could even fathom.

Sage shrugged. "There is. There's a whole me you aren't interested in knowing. Do you want to know about how the guards would hit you if your cell wasn't clean? I was nineteen and scared when I went in. When they let me out, I was twenty-seven going on twenty-eight, and I can make a bed, figure taxes, and tell when it's going to rain."

"What I want to know is why you're not more pissed off about it." Win clenched his hands to keep from shaking Sage.

"What do you want me to be pissed off about?"

"Losing half your life? Not having a choice about a goddamned thing?" He didn't know. All Win knew was that he didn't understand this… acceptance.

"I had a choice. I could have stayed here. I could have told Angel no. I paid my dues. I did my time. There's enough anger there."

Win searched Sage's face, looking for something. Some tightness around the eyes, some lines around the mouth. All he got was a watchful gaze, Sage waiting for him. Waiting to see what he'd do.

He had no idea what to do. Or feel. He looked at the letters he still held in his hand. "I need to go. I'll—" God. He'd what? Call? Apologize. Whatever. For now, he needed to go somewhere not there.

"Okay, Adam. You be careful on the road."

He wanted to scream. Stomp. Something. Instead, he turned on his heel and left, still holding Sage's letters.

His truck was sitting there, right next to Sage's worn-out Ford. Win got in it and drove, only stopping to open and close the gate. He didn't know where he was going, really. Just driving.

He couldn't do this.

SAGE WENT back outside and sat down to finish his chores, listening to the sounds of the horses whickering out by the fence, tails swishing as they fed.

The tack was in shit condition. He reckoned he'd be on this, fixing it all winter. Maybe he'd set up a stand in his little front room, work inside when it got colder.

"Bubba, you and Win didn't come in for lunch. Momma set out plates when she saw his truck."

"He wasn't here for lunch." No. Adam had come to see if he'd been ass-fucked in the joint and whether he liked it.

"Oh. I…. Everything okay?"

"Nope." Everything was not okay.

"Oh." Rosie picked her way over, past all the leather and metal, and dusted off a bench. "You want to tell me?"

"I was in jail. His family hates me. Mainly though, I was in jail for a long time. He's a hero and a cop, and I'm an ex-con."

She sat there for long moments, looking at her hands, which she twisted in her lap. "I think you're the best man I've ever known. If he doesn't, he's not the one for you, Bubba."

He nodded. "Whatever happens, happens, honey."

Sage loved Adam and he knew it, but he was an ex-con. He'd let a man fuck him so people didn't beat him up. He wasn't a good man; he was just a man. If Adam couldn't handle that, well, who could blame him?

Rosie snorted. "I used to say that too. Sometimes you got to stand up, Sage. Fight for things."

"There's no fighting the truth, baby sister. Right now I'm just trying to keep this outfit afloat. Adam will either come back, or he won't. I can't be more than I am."

"Well, just make sure you're not being less on purpose." She patted his leg when she stood. "You ought to come on and eat."

"Okay, honey. I'll be in in a couple. Keep Momma off my ass? I cain't do this with her."

"I'll tell her to lay off. That will buy you a day, at least." She winked, heading back to the main house.

Sage sighed, gathered up the tack, and put it away. Sometimes he wished….

Shit, what did it matter? If wishes were fishes, they'd all swim away. Time to go eat some lunch and keep his head down.

Maybe later he'd go get a pizza for supper and read a book. That part of his life was way better than prison.

He'd take what he could get. Sometimes that was the best you could do.

CHAPTER TWENTY-THREE

WIN DROVE. He drove until he was almost out of gas, burning up the back roads. Then he got some gas and headed for Wilma's diner. He had a feeling Sage wouldn't show up for pie, so he could sit and decide what the hell to do. Turn off his radio and his phone and try to clear his head.

The parking lot had a couple of bikes, no pickups, so he parked, figuring he was safe enough. Shit, how crazy was it that he was worried about assault when he went out to eat in his own town?

He stomped inside and just headed straight for the back. He'd sit at the counter, have some coffee. Be by himself.

Wilma smiled at him and nodded. "Afternoon, Win. Coffee?"

"Hi. Thanks, yeah."

He got a cup, Wilma busy enough to not stand and chat, thank God. He wasn't wanting to be ugly, but he sure didn't want to talk.

His reprieve didn't last long as someone came to sit right next to him. Damn it. Win glanced over, fairly relieved it was Bulldog.

"Hey, man. How's it going?" Bulldog grinned at Wilma and nodded when she held up the coffeepot.

"Kinda having a shitty day." He kept it short, hoping Bulldog would get the message.

"Sorry to hear that." Bulldog fixed his coffee and asked for a patty melt. "How's Sage?"

"Probably pretty unhappy." He felt damned guilty, even as he was pissed.

"Ah. Okay. You… you want to talk or just grunt at each other?"

Win grimaced. "I don't want to insult you, Bulldog, but can I ask you something?"

"Ask away. I'm not terribly sensitive."

Win grinned a little. No, Bulldog wasn't a delicate flower or anything. And way more of an open book than Sage. "Is it normal to be so… emotionless about prison?"

Bulldog's lips twisted, and he looked like a whistle had sounded. "You mean, like, quiet?"

"Do I?" Win sighed. "I mean, there was some pretty awful shit that happened to Sage, and he's not even mad about it." He couldn't help wanting to go hit that guy, the letter-writing guy, right in the face.

"Ah." Bulldog nodded, like he got it. "Are you mad at your drill sergeant for making you do pushups?"

"What does that have to do with it?" That was the military. Even if you hated it, you did it.

"It's the same thing. You do what you have to, to survive." Bulldog shrugged. "He's little. He was young. He had no chance. They were going to break him. That's how it works."

"That's fucked-up." Bulldog seemed just like Sage. Blasé. Win didn't get it. "They poured bleach in his eyes, Bull. How does someone do that?"

"How does someone look at a kid and stab them just because they're a different color than you? How does someone fist fuck a guy dry to 'loosen him up'? These people are criminals and they're locked up together, and the rules are basic. The big guys win over the little ones. Three big guys win over one big one." Bulldog leaned back and gave him a long look. "What did you find out, man? That he had a protector? That he whored himself out?"

"Don't say that!" Even if it was the damned truth, it sounded so fucking dirty when Bulldog said it. Sage was better than that. "I'm not that much of an asshole, Bulldog. Am I? I mean, I don't even know how to tell you why I'm so mad."

"Because he's a good man and he deserved better and it hurts to know that he has to live with this shit, the shame of it? That's a fucking decent reason."

Win nodded slowly. Shame. God, Sage was ashamed, wasn't he? He shouldn't have to carry that, damn it. "Yeah. I guess—that's it, huh? That's why he doesn't get all het up."

"He did what he had to, to survive 'til the end, but he's still a man. No one wants to admit that they had to bow down to someone else." Bulldog turned his coffee cup around. "I'll tell you, from my time in, the guys who hooked up with someone for protection, that's survival. Everyone looks on them like they're property. Redding was a cowboy, before and after, but inside, he was no more than someone's bitch, because he was small and young and white. If you can't deal with the scars that leaves, you should walk away."

"I'm not saying I can't deal. I'm just saying I have to figure it out." Everyone and his neighbor wanted him to walk away. Christ.

"Good." Bulldog grinned, that one gold tooth that matched Wilma's shining. "You make him a little stupid. That's got to be worth something for both of y'all."

"He's worth a lot, Bull. I mean it." Maybe he ought to take those letters back to Sage, unopened, and apologize. Hell, he didn't know. "Maybe some pie will make me feel more settled."

"Pie helps everything. Shit, have a piece, then take one back to him. I've never seen a person with such a sweet tooth."

"He missed out on a lot, I guess." Win nodded slowly. "I'll have mine here. Tell Wilma to pick something yummy for Sage, though."

"Baby, pie for the deputy and something for Redding."

"You got it. Chocolate silk for here and cherry to go."

"Thanks, man. How's everyone holding up this way?" He knew Bulldog and his biker friends were catching a little extra hell for being friendly with the Reddings.

"Good. Good, we're having a big ride for toys after Thanksgiving. We'll bring them to you to dole out."

"Good deal. I look forward to that every year."

"Me too, man. I fucking love it." Bulldog gave him a glinting grin and a wink.

"I bet. You get to ride, and no one can harass you."

"You know it. Sometimes you have to remind close-minded assholes that they don't know everything."

"I did that today." Win grimaced. "Then I freaked out."

"Now you'll get over it." Bulldog passed him a plate and a to-go box.

"I will. I hope Sage can too." Win wondered when Sage would have enough of him.

"He will. He's one strong son of a bitch."

"He is." One way or the other, Sage was strong, good, and deserved a chance at happiness.

Damn it, so did he. Win loved the fine, stubborn bastard.

Maybe it was time to go back and tell him. The past could stay where it belonged. They had a future to work on.

CHAPTER TWENTY-FOUR

THERE WAS a storm coming down on the ranch. Fucking wonderful. Sage could see it, just hovering up to the north, the blue sky damn near black on the other side of the front yard. God damn it. It was just what he fucking needed after his morning.

He whistled up the horses, hurrying to beat the rain that his knees insisted was coming. "Come on, you evil bitches. You don't want to be out here in this shit, and neither do I!" His lead mare, Sugar, lifted her head, her ears swiveling. Then she snorted, her head bobbing like she was nodding, before heading toward the barn.

"Good girl." The others started following, and he looked around, making sure there wasn't anything else to tie up or wrap up before that storm hit. Momma and Daddy were back from town—he could see their good F150 sitting up there. Sister was in town with girlfriends, and he had a pot of chili to warm up on top of the stove.

He shivered, feeling like the wind was blowing no damned good. Sage hated that feeling. It had been showing up less and less, so when it happened it hurt, down in the pit of his belly. Today had been all about hurting. "Come on, everybody."

He started flinging feed, the wind dying down, like the world was waiting to let loose. In the end, the microburst beat him to the house, drenching him to the bone, the wind lifting him right off his feet.

He crashed into the little front porch, holding on with one hand, his knees screaming. The door. He had to get the front door open to relieve the pressure, or he'd lose his windows.

Come on. Come on, Sage.

He stumbled up, the trailer beginning to shake, the walls damn near breathing. No way. He got the door open, and it slammed against the wall, his all-healed-up Penny jumping up and whining at him, tail wagging a little.

"Stay, baby."

Please, God. Please. Let Adam be safe. Momma and Daddy too.

A sound like a freight train started, filling the air like all the angels in Heaven were screaming. Oh, sweet Heaven. He knew that sound. No way it was anything but a tornado. His trailer would be no damned good against it. He and Penny needed to get Momma and Daddy somewhere safe.

"Come on." He grabbed her collar. "Now. Move!"

Penny barked once, then crouched down, whining, and he pulled hard, making her come. There'd never been a longer run from his place to the main house.

Not once.

His knees creaked with every running step, and it was Penny dragging him by the end, his hand clenched around her collar so hard he couldn't let go. Debris was flying, stinging his back and neck.

The front porch peeled away as he reached the side door, and he hit the dirt, covering Penny with his body. She shook and whined, but she didn't try to struggle away from him. They both knew.

"Shh. Shh." *Please God. Please, let my family be safe.* He squeezed his eyes shut, breathing dirt filtered by Penny's fur.

The earth shook so hard he thought it was gonna open up and swallow him. He might deserve to go to hell, but Penny didn't. He felt his feet lift up, and for a split second, Sage thought he'd be sucked right up, like Dorothy in Kansas.

Then something smacked his head, and he blacked right out, everything going quiet.

THE SOUND of crying pushed into his ears, and Sage frowned, coughing as icy water bashed down against him. "Momma?"

"Oh God, I thought you were dead. Sage. We need you to get up."

"Is it past us?"

"The rain is bad, but the rest is gone by." She tugged at him, her hair plastered down, her chin smeared with blood.

"Where's Daddy?" He tried to stand, but his left knee buckled, the pain washing the color clean out of the world.

"I need your help, Son! He's in the rubble!"

"Daddy?" Shit. Okay, his knee could just fucking wait. He set his teeth against the agony and started crawling. "Daddy! Daddy, where are you? I'm coming!"

When he got no answer, Sage scrambled, trying to get where Momma was, back at work digging. Penny barked, running back and forth, scratching at what used to be a hunk of the porch.

"Good girl. Good girl. Find him. Find Daddy." He made it over, dragging his leg with him. "*Daddy!* Goddamn it! You answer me!"

His scream sounded foreign, scared. His mother was no better, her gulping sobs a terrible counterpoint to the pouring rain.

Penny yelped sharply, starting to dig furiously at the rubble. There. That had to be it.

He dragged himself over and tore at the wood. "Here. Momma. Here."

Daddy's fingers were right there. *Fuck. Fuck!* "Daddy I got you. I'm coming."

"Oh God. Oh God, please." His momma turned into a superhero, tossing wood and shingles aside that she shouldn't be able to lift.

He got Daddy's face uncovered, then pulled, getting him out of the rubble. "Daddy? Daddy, come on now. Talk to us."

Don't you fucking die on me. Not now. Not today. Please, Daddy.

He scrabbled in his back pocket, praying that his phone wasn't broke-dick, that he could call someone. He got a screen, the emergency number right there. Momma had to hold Penny, so Sage dug with his other hand while he shouted into the phone.

"We need an ambulance. Please. My father is buried here, and he's not responding." How did he sound so coherent? "Tell 'em to hurry! Daddy? Daddy, can you hear me? I'm getting you out. Right now."

Momma was sobbing, cussing in between. That was his momma, tough even in the hard times. The lady on the phone was telling him to stay put, to tell them where he was exactly, that cell phones weren't like landlines. He just babbled, giving her anything that might help.

They got him mostly uncovered, and Daddy was gray, blood on his lips. Momma was holding Daddy's hand and talking hard, and Sage's eyes were on the clouds as he prayed. *Please, God. Jesus. Take me instead. I ain't worth shit no more. I'm just an ex-con that ain't never gonna catch a break. Take me. Daddy's a good man, and Momma needs him.*

It seemed to take years for the sirens to show up, and somehow he expected one of them to be Adam. None of them were, and it wasn't fair to be disappointed, but Sage was. He needed a rock.

Hell, at the moment, he could use a friend.

His phone started ringing, and he grabbed it. "Whut?"

"Bubba, the radio said… I'm driving that way," Rosie said.

"Don't. Meet us at Presbyterian."

"Are you…?"

"Daddy. Just hurry. Ambulance is here."

"Oh God." She gulped, her voice shaking. "I'll be right there."

"Pray. Pray hard." He hung up and tried to stand, screaming as his leg buckled, the sound from the bone making his eyes roll back in his head.

"Sage." His momma was trying to reach for him and hold on to Daddy. "You're bleeding."

"Sir, you need to sit down." The EMT was there, and a fireman Sage knew from Bulldog's bike brigade. "We'll get your father loaded and get your leg splinted."

"You just work on Daddy. His name's Sam. Sam Redding."

"We'll get him out. I promise." The boys went to work, and Sage slid in and out of consciousness until someone touched his leg.

"Fuck!" His eyes popped open. "Don't fucking touch it."

"I have to, Sage." Denny was a big, grizzled biker, but he was steady as a rock and had gentle hands. "We have to get you in the bus."

"Is Daddy gonna be okay, Den?"

Denny's mouth flattened into a hard line. "I don't know, Sage. I ain't gonna lie. He's bad off. You need to let me get your leg immobile so we can get you both in."

"Fuck. Okay. Okay, whatever you have to do, do it. Let's get him to the hospital."

He set his teeth, eyes on a piece of soffit that was dangling from where the porch roof had pulled away. He'd have to fix that, when it came time. Momma would make a list.

Denny wrenched his leg into position, and Sage screamed, flashbacks of prison breaking into his brain like glass shattering.

"Okay. Okay, you got it. You got it. We're moving you now."

He was soaked—with blood and sweat and rain—and beginning to shake. The jolt as they lifted him into the ambulance made him fight not to puke. Daddy was on the stretcher, so he had to sit in one of the wells.

He closed his eyes and prayed. It was all that was in him to do. The rest was in someone else's hands.

CHAPTER TWENTY-FIVE

THE FIRST sign of trouble was Jamison Allworthy pulling up outside the diner and braking hard enough that gravel flew up against the front window.

"Goddamn it, Win," Jamie snarled when he threw open the door. "Where the hell is your radio? Why is your phone off?"

"What? Why? What happened?" Shit. He scrambled for his phone.

"Tornado. Touched down a few times, cut a swath just north of town." Jamie grabbed his arm, tugging him out, even as Bulldog and Wilma called out to him.

"Injuries?" He had a dozen voice mails. God *damn* it.

"I haven't heard too much, man. I was working traffic at the south end of the county."

"Fuck." He put the phone up to his ear and headed toward his truck. The first voice mail was from Jim.

"Win. Me. Funnel hit the Reddings'. Everyone is heading to the hospital. I need you out at the county line. There's a teenager missing."

Fuck.

The second message was from his boss-uncle too. "Do not go to that hospital yet. They're all alive. I need you."

Win nodded. He knew his job. Didn't make it any easier.

"I'm headed south. I'm on it, Jamie."

"Good. I'm going to the school."

He nodded. "Check in."

Fuck.

Fuck.

He put his phone on speaker and started going through the rest of his voice mails, waving at Bulldog as he squealed out of the lot.

Jim. Jim. Jamie. Jamie. Jamie. Then there was Rosie. "Hey, Win. It's Rosie. I'm heading to the hospital. Everybody got hurt. Sage says Penny is still at the ranch. Is it safe for me to go out there after, check the horses?"

Shit. He hit call back and waited for it to ring.

The damn thing went straight to voice mail. She either had her phone off or the storm was screwing with the signals.

Speaking of storm, he hit a wall of rain and had to focus on keeping the truck on the road. *Shit.* Win remembered he was supposed to be talking to Rosie.

"Hey, hon. Hold off going out. Penny will be fine. You know Sage didn't let her get hurt. As soon as I can, I'll check in."

This was becoming the shittiest day in the history of days. Win's head started to pound, and he gritted his teeth against it. He had a job to do.

Then he would find Sage and hold on until he was sure the man was okay.

"AS SOON as we can, we'll get that knee in surgery." The doc shook his head. "It might be tomorrow, though, unless you want to pay to go to Dallas."

"I'm fine. How's Daddy?"

The doctor's face went all blank, like doctors did when things were bad. "He's in critical condition, Son."

"I need to see him. Now." He pushed up, the balloon-cast-deal on his leg squeaking.

"You need to rest." The doc frowned now, putting a hand on his chest. "You're showing shock symptoms."

"*Sage!*" Momma's voice rang out, and he pushed out of the bed, almost blacking out when his leg hit the floor.

"Momma. Please. Please, Rick. Help me."

The big old nurse—who was one of Bulldog's friends like the EMT had been—grabbed him up and got him into the hallway.

That evil son of a bitch was there, Angel's daddy, right in Momma's face. "…take that property. If you don't accept my offer, I'll leave you homeless."

"You leave her alone, you motherfucker."

Teddy turned on him. "You sorry son of a bitch. You had to come back here, you murdering asshole."

"You leave her alone. You'll never get Redding land. Ever. I didn't kill Angel. He was fucking another guy, getting high. The meth lab blew."

Teddy's hands clenched, and he took a step toward Sage, face mottled with ugly rage. "You don't say that. You don't talk about my boy."

"Talk about him? I fucking spent eight years in the pen because he took my fucking keys!" He stumbled forward. "I was leaving his cheating ass, coming home! He was a fucking whore!"

A loud roar filled his ears, Angel's daddy rushing him, fists swinging.

Oh, he didn't think so. He backed up a half step, stumbling, crying out as he put weight on his knee.

"Son!" Momma rushed forward, reaching for him, and that sorry son of a bitch popped her, right in the face. His momma. His *momma*, goddamn it.

Sage lost it, hitting the old man with ten years of fucking rage, of shame, of knowing that Adam was fucking gone, Daddy was dying, and the house was trashed. He didn't even know if his dog was still alive.

He kept on hitting until his knuckles were bleeding and his knee was screaming.

Security grabbed him, dragged him back, and Ted was on the floor, calling for someone to get 911.

"Sage. Sage. You leave my boy alone." Momma was fighting to get to him.

"You stay with Daddy. I got this." He looked around and met Rosie's eyes. "You don't let anything happen to that land."

"That's Redding land." Her hand was on her swelling belly. "It ain't going nowhere."

Sage smiled, even as the cops showed up. "That's my girl." She was so much braver now.

"They're going to take you in, man." Rick's voice was soft. "What do you want?"

"You call Bulldog. Tell him what happened. Tell him Momma needs him."

"I can do that. Keep yourself in one piece until I get you help." Rick was a good guy. Solid.

"I got this." No matter what. Rosie had the land. The bikers would have Momma and Daddy's back.

Him? Hell, he'd been on his own a long, long time.

CHAPTER TWENTY-SIX

WIN DIDN'T really know what time it was. He wasn't sure he knew what day it was. If this was what happened when a twister touched down and bounced a few places, he didn't want to see what happened when one took out whole towns.

Of course, the nagging worry for Sage and the rest of the Reddings was right there, poking at his brain.

Nobody'd called, but to be honest, with all the shit hitting the radio, Win wasn't surprised.

He needed a drink of water, a few minutes to call Sage, and possibly some headache pills. He got in his truck and headed back toward town and a gas station for a drink, when his phone rang, Sam Redding's name showing up.

"Hello?" His heart thudded against his ribs.

"Adam? This is Ellen." Sage's momma sounded totally blown. "I need you to listen to me and say yes, ma'am to every single word I say to you."

"Yes, ma'am." The words fell out without him even trying.

"Sam is dying, and they took my boy to jail without even letting him have surgery on his knee. I swear by all I hold holy, if he doesn't get to tell his daddy good-bye, I will never forgive you. Ever. You go get my son and bring him to this hospital, and you do it right now."

"They took Sage to jail?" He hopped in his truck and headed to the sheriff's office. They wouldn't have had time to take Sage to county lockup yet. He'd be in holding at the office.

"Your asshole uncle came to threaten us, hit me, and Sage beat his ass down. I need him, Adam. We're losing Sam." There was pure panic there, devastation.

"You tell Sam to hang on. I'm going to get Sage. He'll be there, no matter what happens."

"Good boy." The line went dead.

Jail. Jesus. What the fuck was Ted thinking, going to the fucking hospital? Knee surgery? Fuck. Win called Bulldog as he burned up the road, not sure who else to trust.

"Win? I'm at the hospital. Rick called. You need to go get Sage," Bulldog said without even a greeting.

"I'm heading there now. Y'all keep everyone but me and Sage away from Ellen and Sam."

"Rick and I have it. I sent the boys to the ranch to start cleaning."

"Can you make sure Penny is okay? Sage's dog?"

"I'm on it. Hurry, man. Shit's looking serious in there."

"Got it." Win put on his siren and stepped on it. Gravel flew as he fishtailed into the parking lot.

He stormed into the office. "Where the hell is Sage Redding?"

Grace looked up at him. "Hank's got him in the back. It's not pretty."

"His father is dying, Grace. I'm taking him back to the hospital. Log it for me." He would try to do this as much by the book as he could.

"You got it." God love that woman. She was solid as a rock.

He headed back and heard Hank say, "You want a bottle of water, man? You look rough."

"Fuck you. I want a goddamn lawyer."

He'd never—not once—heard that harshness in Sage's voice.

"I'm taking him back to the hospital, Hank." Win didn't let himself really look at Sage. Not when all he could see was bruises.

"Back to the hospital? I don't…. You sure, Win? There was a bad fight. Your uncle's still in there getting checked out."

"His daddy is in a bad way, Hank. I won't let him miss his chance to say his piece." Win held out his hand for the keys, then unlocked Sage's cell.

Sage limped out, face gray as a squirrel's butt.

Win wanted to touch him, wanted to hold on tight, but he knew he couldn't. "You need to lean?"

"I cain't make it all the way to the truck. It's broke." Sage met his eyes. "Daddy still with us?"

He ducked under Sage's arm and put his shoulder right there for Sage, holding him up. "Right now, yeah. Your momma sounds scared, baby." He wasn't gonna lie.

"Okay. This gonna get you fired?"

"Possibly." Win grinned a little, despite the situation. "I don't care."

"Oh."

Sage was covered in blood, in tears and scratches, and Win wanted to scream.

He needed to suck it up, though. This wasn't about him. He got Sage in the truck and hit the siren again, booking it to the hospital.

Sage never said a word to him, just sat there, eyes closed, still as death. Win wanted to ask what had happened, what Sage needed, but he choked it back. Time for that later.

He pulled into the emergency lane, and Sage opened the door, legs buckling as they hit the ground.

"Shit!" Win circled the truck and picked Sage right up, his pocket cowboy not weighing enough to even slow him down.

"Sam Redding?"

The tiny slip of a nurse buzzed him in and pointed, and Win ran.

Rosie was in the hallway, sitting and sobbing, face in her hands. "He's...."

"No." Sage shook his head. "No. I have to say good-bye. God can't have this too."

Ellen came out, white as a ghost. "Sage. Hurry. He's waiting for you, I know he is."

Win rushed Sage in, Ellen behind him. Sam Redding was still, as close to dead as anyone he'd ever seen who was still breathing.

"Daddy." Sage sat on the edge of the bed and grabbed his father's hand with fingers that were more meat than skin. "I'm here. I got this.

I'll take care of things. You're okay now. I got this, I swear in Jesus's name."

Sam didn't say a word, didn't open his eyes, but the man took a single, deep breath and then was gone.

Win held his breath, feeling like an intruder.

Ellen stood there, tears streaking her face. "I… I don't know what to do now."

"Adam will help. He'll know." Sage put Sam's hand on the blue blanket, stood up, and then collapsed.

"Doctor!" Win knew what to do. It was like battlefield triage. Get help for the ones still alive. Sage needed care. Then he could help Ellen do what needed done.

"Sage! Adam, oh Jesus, help." Ellen was fixin' to lose her shit, and no one on earth would blame the woman.

"Get a doctor in here, damn it." He knew when it registered that Sam had died out there at the nurse's station, they turned off the alarms and let the family have time. He needed to make a fuss. "We have a collapsed family member in here!"

"What the hell is he doing here?" A doctor came in, frowning. "Why isn't he in surgery?"

"They took him to jail, Doc." Win clenched his hands to keep from hitting something. "He needs care. I'll deal with any issues."

"He needs surgery. Get me a gurney and some orderlies! Get these people out of here!"

Win took Ellen's arm. "Did you need to sit with Sam, Ellen?" Some people needed long good-byes, and he didn't want to step on toes.

"I…." She looked at her husband for a long, long minute. "I slept with him for thirty-two years. I reckon it's all done now. Someone needs to call his brother."

"I called Uncle Seth, Momma. He'll be here with Mona and the boys in a couple hours." Rosie came in, face all red. "There's a lady here that can help us. Where's Bubba?"

"He's going into surgery." Win put an arm around both women, his heart sore for them. "Let's go sit somewhere."

"Is he going to go back to jail, Adam?" Ellen looked at him, her pretty eyes lifeless. "The man hit me first."

She turned her cheek, and he saw the black bruise on her jaw.

Hope bloomed in his chest. "Are you willing to play hardball with that, Ellen? I think we can work a deal if you are."

"I just lost my husband and my house. I am not losing my son. You haven't seen hardball yet, boy."

Atta girl. Win nodded. "Good deal. I'll talk to Jim about just who gets to press charges. You'll have to give your statement to Hank or Jamie, and they'll have to take pictures of your face."

"Okay. Just make it happen." She swallowed hard and closed her eyes. "I don't know what to do next."

"I do." Win had dealt with this mess on the job, more often than he wanted to admit. They didn't talk on it much, but he knew what to do.

"Good."

He got his phone out and started making a list of things he needed to do for Ellen and for Sage. The counselor from the hospital would come soon to let Ellen know what her choices were for funeral homes, in case they hadn't planned that in advance. Some folks did.

"Win? Win, they told me you removed someone from the office?" Jim came down the hall, all bluster.

Leaving Ellen to Rosie, he pulled Jim aside, not brooking an argument. "I did. We don't deny anyone medical treatment, and you know it."

"Medical treatment? What the hell?"

"Teddy tried to attack Sage Redding, Jim. His daddy is dead from the storm, and Sage needs surgery on his knee. They hauled him in, but he's got every right to press charges against Ted."

"You sure Sage didn't hit him first?"

"Ted hit Mrs. Redding, Jim. In the face. There are a dozen witnesses." Win hadn't had a lot of time, but he'd seen people nodding when he talked to Ellen.

"Jesus Christ." Jim winced and shook his head. "Stupid asshole. He knows better."

"He should." God, it was good to see a glimmer of Jim's reasonable side. "He's losing it. Screaming at Ellen about that land while her husband was in there dying."

"She pressing charges?"

"Not as long as we leave Sage alone."

"Done."

He felt his eyebrow arch. "You sure about that?"

"Am I still sheriff here?"

"I sure hope so." Something eased a little in his chest. Jim was still a lawman, thank God.

"You deal with that wreck out at the county line?"

"I did. I got that trailer court well on the way too. Hank is out now, since he doesn't have anyone in lockup, and I'm on call." He was going to stay and help the Redding women.

"Okay. You stay here, make sure no one comes and harasses Mrs. Redding about anything. I won't have it. The woman lost her husband." The turnaround didn't surprise him. Jim didn't hold with hitting women or messing with folks when they'd lost their breadwinner.

"Thanks, Jim." He held out his hand and shook with Jim, feeling like part of the world had righted himself.

Ellen sat there, staring down the hall, Rosie orbiting her like a pregnant satellite.

Win went to them, sat, and put his arm around Ellen. "They're going to ask a bunch of stuff. Do you need some coffee or a sandwich?"

"No. No, I don't need anything. I have to go clean up the mess at the house."

"Bulldog and Wilma have people out there now. They'll do what they can until you can come. Sage needs you."

"I shouldn't have ever asked him to come back to this place. I was selfish. God is punishing me."

"Oh, Momma, stop it." Rosie snapped the words out.

Win understood how she felt. He really did. Rosie was right, though. Ellen needed to keep it together. "Rosie, can you get some coffee and some chocolate? Helps with the shock."

"Chocolate. Right. Sure. You want coffee too?"

"I'd love some." He took her hand and squeezed it.

"It's going to be okay, right?"

"It is." He knew it would be hard, but they'd get through it.

"Okay. I believe you." Rosie was fixin' to break down, he could see it.

"Chocolate. Get some for you too."

"Yeah. I'm on it."

"When can we see Sage? Is he in surgery already?"

There was no way they had him prepped already. Win stalled. "I'll check as soon as Rosie gets back, okay?"

Ellen nodded, and then the hospital people started coming with papers and questions, and suddenly Win was up to his elbows in it. It took almost an hour, two cups of coffee for him, and three candy bars for Ellen to get through it.

When they got done, though, the doctor was there with news about Sage.

"Mrs. Redding, the previous damage to his knees was extensive. I went in and cleaned that up on the right, but we had to replace the knee on the left."

Her lower lip quivered, and Win could tell she was about to lose it. "Well, as long as you fixed him. We'll figure it."

"He'll feel considerably better than before, I imagine. He had to be in real pain. After he heals, he's going to feel like he's ten years younger."

Ellen nodded, blinking rapidly. "Good. Good."

Win patted her back awkwardly. "When can they see him?"

"He'll be in recovery for an hour or so, then they'll move him to a room."

"Thanks." That would give Ellen and Rosie time to clean up and get some food.

He needed to get them a hotel room and some clean clothes. Mom. Mom could help. Win moved off to one side to call his mother. She always knew what to do.

"Son? Son, is that you? I'm heading into town. Grace called and said the Reddings got hit. Her sister June is caught in Rockwall, but she's trying to get to Ellen. How can I help?"

"We're at the hospital, Mom. Sam…. He didn't make it, and Sage had to have surgery. Everything is fucked up."

"Okay. So I need to get clothes and toiletries for Ellen and… shit, I can't remember the girl's name."

"Rosemary. Rosie." He glanced at Ellen, who was staring at the nurse's station, face stony. "She needs help with all the people who want a piece of her too. And Uncle Ted hit her right in the face."

"Rosie?"

"No, Ellen."

"Christ. Let me stop at the Walmart, and then I'll be there."

"Thanks, Mom." His relief knew no bounds. Sometimes women needed women.

He headed back over. "Ellen, that was my mom. She says June's heading over to see you."

"Oh. Well, good." She stood up and hugged him. "I'm sorry about all this mess."

Win hugged her back, holding on. "Don't you dare apologize. I'm just happy I can help." He was pretty invested in the Redding clan these days.

"Me too. Sage is lucky to have you."

"I sure hope he still thinks so. I was going to talk to him tonight, and then all this…."

She looked at him. "I don't want to know. Lovers fight. It happens. You fight, you make up, you go on."

"That sounds good. Not the fighting." He smiled a little, feeling some hope.

"It is." Her eyes filled with tears. "And you'll not know what to do when it's taken from you, so hold on."

God, his mom needed to hurry. He wasn't good at this part.

"Momma, come on. Come sit." Rosie took her hand. "Win don't need you bawling over him."

Ellen sniffed and went to sit, holding Rosie's hand. Wilma showed up then, about five minutes ahead of his mom.

When crazy June showed, he knew they were safe, and he started worrying about Sage.

Maybe he could see what was going on, when they could see the man. When he could see Sage's eyes again. It had to be soon. He needed to know at least one thing was going to be okay.

He needed Sage to know that he was in this for the long haul. All of it.

And that he'd made that decision before any of this ever happened.

CHAPTER TWENTY-SEVEN

THE WHOLE fucking world was fuzzy, distant, and his throat hurt. Bad.

Come on. Come on, Sage. Where the fuck are you? What is going on? His eyes tried to open, but felt like they was glued shut.

He wriggled a little, his legs screaming and stiff and wrong. Wait. Wait, was this a dream?

"Mr. Redding? I'm Cari, the day nurse." The woman had a soft, super-drawly voice. Sounded oddly like Rosie. "Would you like anything for the pain?"

"Nurse?" Fuck, his throat hurt. "Where 'm I at?"

"You're in the hospital, Mr. Redding. Some water?" She pressed a straw to his lips.

He sucked hard, the cool liquid feeling like pure heaven. Hospital. Not infirmary. Okay. Okay. So….

Everything crashed in on him in a rush—the storm, the fight, the jail. Daddy. "My dad."

Her mouth flattened for a moment. He could finally focus on her. "Your mom would like to see you. Should I let her know you're awake?"

"Uh-huh."

"I'll go get her." The nurse hightailed it out, and he lay back, sighing.

He knew Daddy was gone. He knew it. He needed to get up, go check on the ranch. He pulled the covers back and stared at the wires and tubes and bandages and shit. Oh damn.

His heart started racing, blood pumping hard.

"Sage. What the hell are you doing?" It wasn't his momma. It was Adam.

"I.... My legs. There's tubes." He didn't understand. At all. "I got to get up, man. I got to get home and fix Momma's house."

"Hush, baby." Adam pushed him back down. "They had to do surgery on your knees. One had to be replaced altogether. Your mom is napping, and I told them not to wake her yet."

"Surgery? I don't... what? Adam, the house is broke, Penny's there, the horses."

"Penny is okay. The ranch house is bent, but it's watertight right now, thanks to Bulldog and his buddies." Adam touched his cheek. "And you're not in jail."

"He hit Momma. He hit her, Adam, and told her he was going to take advantage."

"She told me. Jim cleared the arrest today off your record, baby. Teddy is crazy." Adam stroked his face like the man couldn't stop touching him. "I'm so sorry."

"Daddy's gone. Is Momma hurt? Is she okay? Fuck, I'm hurting."

"He is. You got to say good-bye. Ellen is fine, as much as she can be." Adam's hands kept moving, nice and easy, making his eyelids heavy.

"There's tubes in my legs."

"They have to make sure stuff drains and all. The doc said it went really well."

"I don't... they took out one of my knees?" Could they do that? "Am I going to have to use a cane?"

"Actually, the doc says you should have way less pain now." Adam was smiling about that, so it must be true. "You will have to do some therapy."

"Yeah? That sounds pricey. I ain't got nothin' left to pawn."

"Don't worry about that right now." Adam's face tightened up, just a little, but he didn't say anything else.

"Yeah. Thank you for everything, man." God, he was sleepy, sore, and everything seemed so far away.

"You think I'm going away that easy?" Adam took his hand. "I'll be here."

"I hoped not, but...." Shit happened. Bad shit.

"I know, baby. We'll talk on that later, okay? There's a lot more to process now, and you and me? We're solid."

"Solid." He held onto Adam's hand and worked hard to stay there, stay focused, but it was like he'd worn himself to the bone, worn himself plumb down.

"Yep. Sleep a while longer, babe." Adam leaned down and kissed him, right there in the hospital.

"Gon' get in trouble. Can't kiss up on me."

"Shh. Sleep. I promise I won't molest you while you nap."

"Shut up." He laughed, though, and the sound followed him down into dreams where he was a kid again and hadn't fucked up so bad.

WIN SAT, staring at Sage's face. The lines cut deep around Sage's eyes and mouth, the pain evident. He sure hoped Ellen wouldn't be mad at him and Rosie for not waking her to see Sage, but they both needed their rest.

He couldn't believe, looking at those poor legs, that Sage would walk better now. No way. They were Frankenstein legs. Those scars would be epic.

"How's he doing?" A deep voice interrupted him, and he looked up to see a big old boy in scrubs. Oh, that was one of Bulldog's boys.... Rip? Reg? Rick. Rick. It was Rick.

"Sleeping. Wigged out when he's not." Win smiled a little, feeling odd with it on his face.

"Yeah, no kidding." Rick went over, checked some shit, and then pushed a button on the IV. "Morphine drip. Push as needed. They'll have him walking by the morning, for sure."

"Seriously?" He looked at Sage's legs again.

"They look swollen, but the doc cleaned it up in there a lot. Give him a couple days, and he'll be amazed." Rick sighed softly. "I'm sorry about his dad. We're having a fundraiser for costs for the family. Guys are coming from Houston, Dallas, even Louisiana."

"That's amazing. If I can do anything, let me know." The bikers had been so good to Sage. Win had a whole new appreciation for them.

"Surely will. You going to stay in here with him? He might have bad dreams. Don't worry about waking him up."

"I am. His mom is out like a light, and Rosie needs her rest."

"I'll get them to bring you supper. It's not good food, but it's food."

"Yeah. The menu says there's a BLT?" He could so eat some bacon.

"Totally. Coffee? Coke?"

"Oh, Coke. That would rock." Adam shook Rick's hand. "Thank you."

"No problem, man. Sage is a good guy."

"He is." No matter what else happened, Win knew that fact deep down in his bones.

He settled back in his chair, taking Sage's hand when it searched for him. "I got you, baby." Christ, what a day.

"Adam." He did love how his name sounded like a prayer in Sage's voice.

"Rick says you have a morphine drip if you need it." That was inane, but he didn't want Sage to hurt.

Sage made a soft sound, squeezed his hand, smiled a little. Win grinned. God, he loved this man. So much. If nothing else came of this rotten day, he knew that was the most important thing now. He would have to do things day by day.

He wasn't stupid. His family was going to come after him, after the Reddings, and there was no real avoiding that, but they'd deal. They had a whole lot of more important shit to deal with, like Sam's funeral.

God, he wasn't ready to think about that. Thank goodness for Mom and her practical self. She'd walked Ellen through all the funeral home paperwork and the call from organ donation. Man, they asked a lot of questions.

"Adam, I need to piss. Help me up."

"Let me get the nurse." Win hit the call button.

Rick was back in a second. "What's up?"

"I need the facilities, man. I need to get up." Sage tried to sit up, swaying dangerously.

"Whoa. Whoa, hold up. The catheter's probably kinked. Stay. Stay right there." Rick went to the side of the bed, fiddled, and Sage sighed. "Better?"

"Uh-huh."

Oh man, he was glad he hadn't tried to get Sage up. He'd thought the cath bag was there, but he wasn't sure. Hospitals were damned confusing.

"The doctor will have you up in the morning, man. For sure. For now, you hang out, watch TV. Play cards with Win."

Uh-huh. Like Sage could see cards right now. They could so watch TV, though. They had proven to be good at that.

"'Kay." Sage leaned back. "Did someone feed the horses?"

"Bulldog's people have been out there all day." He could call, he guessed, but those guys were good as gold.

Rick nodded. "Everything's taken care of. Wilma took Penny to her house for the night. She was worried."

Sage made a satisfied noise. "She's a good girl, my dog."

Win knew he was smiling like an idiot, but Sage did it for him, 100 percent. He patted Sage's belly, needing to touch.

Sage made a soft sound, easy and peaceful and happy.

Rick murmured something and slipped away, and they were alone again. Win had to admit, he was savoring this time. Soon enough they'd be crazy busy.

"This has been a really fucking long day."

"It has, huh?" He met Sage's eyes, staring intently. "I love you."

"That's probably bad for you." Sage nodded, though, and squeezed his hand. "I'm sorry about earlier. About not being... right."

"There's no right or wrong, baby. We just have to deal with all the weirdness." He ran his thumb over Sage's knuckles.

"You're always going to be a good guy, and I'm always going to be an ex-con."

"Mmm. And I'm always going to be the one with the crazy family."

"You musta had a lot of sane genes in your daddy."

"Mom too. She's a rock. She's been here with your mother."

"Good. Momma needs help, and I'm stuck 'til the morning."

"At least, yeah." It would be a few days.

"They're not lying about my legs, right? They're going to work again?"

"They'll work better, if the Doc is right." He'd repeat that as long as Sage needed him to.

"Okay. I don't want them blowing sunshine up my butt."

"This is Texas, babe. Not likely." He winked, trying to get him a smile.

Sage chuckled. "You're the only one I want dealing with my butt."

"I like your ass. It's tight and tiny."

"Everything about me is little, Adam. I'm a pocket cowboy."

"Not everything, babe." They both cracked up at that, and it felt good to laugh.

Win's food came, along with a bit of soup and Jell-O for Sage. It smelled like bacon and potatoes. Suddenly he was viciously hungry.

He dug into his BLT while Sage picked and basically ignored the food. He didn't blame Sage for not wanting the Jell-O. Finally Sage gave up, eyes closing. "I want a Reese's cup."

"I can do that." He could, if Sage would be willing to let him go.

"Okay." Sage held his hand.

"Did you want it now, babe?" He would call Rick in. He wasn't ashamed to admit he didn't want to leave Sage alone.

"In a minute, maybe."

"Sure." Man, he wished he could lie down with Sage. Maybe once the man fell asleep again, he'd stretch out in the little convertible chair.

"Love you." The words were fuzzy, Sage already sleeping.

"Get some sleep, babe." He'd hold on a while longer. Then he'd have to get shit done.

He had to. He didn't have any choices. He had people to take care of.

CHAPTER TWENTY-EIGHT

WALKING WAS possibly the scariest thing he'd ever done.

Ever.

He wasn't sure if it was because he was on legs that didn't even feel like his or because Momma was waiting there at the end of the hall. Sage felt like a two-year-old might, all wobble and stop and start.

Momma just watched, her face set in determined lines, and he made himself do it, not flinch, not panic.

The first step made his heart race. The second felt easier. The knee that wasn't his actually hurt less than the other, and that unnerved the hell out of him. Momma smiled a little, the lines around her eyes easing, and that made him work harder. One step after another, and he was sweating like a lathering horse by the time he reached her.

"See? I ain't broke."

"That's my boy." She was beaming, catching his hands.

"Yes, ma'am." He held on, shaking with it, and that little torture girl brought him a wheelchair. Easing himself down was pure fucking hell, and he fought the scream with all he was.

"There you are, Mr. Redding," the little gal chirped. "That was a great first day."

"Fucking fabulous," he muttered, biting the words out.

It spoke to Momma's state of mind that she didn't even bitch at him. She just nodded, then tried another smile. "Rosie is bringing a sausage biscuit."

"Yay, Whataburger." They were waiting for the funeral until he was sprung from the hospital. Momma had Daddy cremated, saying she couldn't bear the thought of bugs eating on him. They were going to take him to the ranch, sprinkle him along the tree line that he'd loved so much.

It made Sage want to scream.

Hell, he'd apologized a dozen times, and he opened his mouth to do it again, but Momma glared. "Don't. Don't, Son. Just stop. He's gone. God took him home."

"I just—I should never have come home."

She frowned harder. "He'd never been happier than he was working with you on the ranch. You gave him that, Son. Besides, he didn't have a long, slow fade. He went fast. He wanted that."

"Sure, Momma." He didn't know what else to say, so he was grateful for the chirpy lady who came to take him to hydrotherapy. Sage was even happier when he found out that was sitting in a hot tub.

He could fucking handle sitting and bubbling with a bunch of old guys from the VA. Even if they had to wrap him in plastic like a prize turkey.

They were cooking him up.

Bubble bubble.

God, he needed out of here.

He needed his couch and a movie and maybe Adam to love on him a little. Adam had been pulling doubles after spending the first day with Sage in the hospital.

Momma was staying at her friend June's. Rosie was staying at the house, making sure that no one messed with it. His place was gone, from all he could gather and how no one was saying shit about it.

Penny, though—Rosie had been sending pictures of that silly mutt in her big, new fuzzy bed.

Not a scratch on her furry body. Thank God for small favors.

"Are you ready to go soak, Son? I can go grab a muffin."

"Yeah. Yeah, Momma. I'm good. You should go rest, have real food."

"Oh, they don't have that here, honey. That's why Rosie is coming. She should be here when you're done."

"Has the doctor said anything about when I can go home with you?"

"Not yet. I think they were waiting to see how well you walk."

"Yeah. Well, I'm walking. There's work waiting on me."

"Now, Mr. Redding, I have to make a recommendation first," Torture Girl said, wheeling him off.

"So get with it. Daylight's burning."

"And you're fighting infection. Be nice."

"I'm not feeling nice." He wanted to apologize, but he'd be lying.

"No. I don't imagine so. If I were you, I'd hate the whole world."

"I'm trying hard not to."

She patted his shoulder. "Your family is great."

"They're better than great." He found a smile for her that was almost real.

"And your, uh, friend. He's pretty."

"Adam? Yes, ma'am." Adam was better than pretty. Adam was also his. He would fight for the man now that he knew Adam was gonna stick around.

"Rick says he stayed all night when you had your surgery." She wheeled him into the hydro room and started getting him wrapped up.

"And he'd been working his ass off." The man still was. The storm had hit the county hard.

"Here we go. You have about fifteen."

"I'll just bubble."

He sat there, his eyes closed, everything fading away. God, it felt good. The weight dragging him down seemed to fall right off.

He forced himself not to think on this mess, not to stress it. He'd do what he'd do, right?

Right.

How in hell was he supposed to not worry on things? His daddy was gone. His sister was pregnant, and he was nothin' but a broke-dick cowboy ex-con.

He didn't have a house, he couldn't pay this hospital bill, and he wasn't 100 percent sure he could walk right. Fuck a doodle doo.

"Hey, Sage. Your time is up, and someone brought you breakfast." Thank God it was Rick instead of that tiny girl trying to lift him.

"Hey, man. I think I'm fixin' to move in here."

"Yeah? Pretty comfy, huh? Come on, though," Rick eased him up and out then wrapped him with a big bath sheet.

His knees were screaming by the time he got back to his room, but he didn't bitch. He wanted to go home.

"Hey, you." It wasn't Rosie waiting for him with breakfast. It was Adam, looking tired but smiling.

"Adam. Weren't you on call last night?"

"Yeah, but I figured I'd stop by before I went home. Saw Rosie at the Whataburger and told her I'd bring breakfast." Adam touched his arm, fingers warm and callused.

"I want them to let me go home."

"They have to be sure you can heal, babe." Adam handed over a bag of breakfast.

"I can. I will. I can't afford this, man. I'll never be able to pay it off."

Adam's eyes flashed for a moment, something sad in them. "Don't worry about that right now, okay? You can talk with your mom later on that."

His head tilted, his brain catching on to that look. "What did she do?"

"She didn't do anything unusual, baby. Your dad had some insurance, is all. I feel like that's her deal to tell you about."

"So long as she didn't sell the land. That's hers. It's Redding land." He didn't want it, but he'd give his soul to keep it in the family.

"Rosie has plans for it, I think. The house, well, your dad had good home insurance too." Adam's mouth twisted. "Your trailer is a bust, babe."

"Yeah. I reckoned that. No one's said a thing about it. Figured that meant it was in Oz." Still hurt to know it, though. He imagined it would hurt again to see it. "Momma will let me stay in the guest room 'til I can move to the barn, I'm sure."

"Shit, you can stay with me. I have a better TV."

"Yeah? I wouldn't mind that at all." Hell, he might love that, a little bit.

"Hell, yes." Adam's grin, well, it went megawatt. The man meant it.

Sage's cheeks stretched with his smile and, for the first time in days, something felt right. Adam and him, living together. Lord. "It's okay if I bring Penny?"

"Yes. I mean, if my landlord doesn't want dogs, we'll go somewhere else. Down Fort Worth way. Or Stephenville."

"You think? Could we do that?" *Leave?*

Adam paused, seeming to give the idea the thought it deserved. "I think so. Hell, it might be best, babe. Just start over. I'm not all that much more popular here than you are."

God, that was like a fucking fantasy. To be able to go, be where no one knew him, no one was watching him every second. He could talk to his parole officer. Move. He could.

Couldn't he?

Surely the good Lord would let him have this. Just this.

"Talk to me, Sage?"

He met Adam's gaze. "I want this, more than anything. That means I won't get it."

"Don't." Adam moved, shifting to hold his hand. "Don't do that. We've earned a little happiness."

"I'd hook my wagon to yours, Adam. You know I would. I ain't worth shit, so far as the world thinks, but I'd work to put my pennies with yours, the rest of my life."

"That's what I need to hear. I'll start putting out feelers on the jobs, okay? I can work anywhere, and if Jim doesn't give me a good recommendation, I'll turn his ass in to the damned state police."

"I need to find someone that needs an old cowboy." Maybe a day laborer.

"I got this crazy idea." Adam ducked his chin, cheeks pink. Shit, Adam wasn't the shy one between them.

"Can't be any crazier than this last week, Adam." He knew that.

"No. No, I know." Adam's laugh held a tiny note of hysteria.

"So? Just tell me. It'll seem less weird out loud." Lord, Adam was fixin' to lose it.

"Well, you know I rent my house, yeah? I have some money put back. A good bit, actually. And I know you want to train horses. Raise them. I was thinking of a plot of land, investing in a few good mares...."

"Adam, I got nothing. I couldn't help with the money part. The work, yes, but...." He shrugged. If a guy looked up broke-dick cowboy in the dictionary, there he'd be.

"Well, I sure don't know anything about horses, so that will be your job."

"I know all there is to know about training them, sure as shit, and Rosie wants to run cattle." Something he didn't quite recognize started blooming in his chest.

"Well, then, maybe you can take a few of the stock you have now." Adam's smile kept growing.

"Maybe. I'll talk to Momma and Rosie." He reached for Adam's hand, but barely touched him before backing off.

"No one's looking." Adam took his hand back, holding on.

"I don't want to get you in trouble." He twined their fingers together.

"Well, babe, I'm already kind of there." Shrugging, Adam stroked the back of his hand, fingers drawing little random shapes.

"Kind of." He reached out, cupped Adam's cheek, thumb moving slowly. "You need some rest, Officer."

"I do. I'll have breakfast with you first, though."

Right. Whataburger. "Chicken biscuits or sausage? And tell me there's coffee."

"I got some of both, and yes, there is."

He could just have the coffee and ignore the food.

Not that Adam ever let him do that. In fact, the man gave him a knowing look. "I also got a couple of plain biscuits."

He felt his cheeks heat. "I'll take a sausage one, thanks."

"Cool." Adam pulled back to open up the food bags, and they smelled good all of a sudden.

"Mmm." His belly started growling.

"There you go, babe." Adam handed over an unwrapped biscuit before pulling out a chicken biscuit and starting in.

Sometimes a man just craved a greasy biscuit.

"This is what I needed."

Sage wasn't sure if Adam meant the biscuit or the talk about moving away. Either way, he was suddenly starving. He bit deep, still fucking smiling around the bite.

"You still want llamas?" Adam asked around a mouthful of food.

"I like llamas. They're good watchdogs."

"Then we should get them too."

"You think?" He'd like that. He loved the critters.

"Yes. You had a good plan when you were talking about that for your folks' place."

"I did." That seemed like a million years ago. He could still do it, though, this time on his own land.

He rested back, full, head spinning with ideas. His eyes drooped, but Adam stayed right there with him.

"We're going to get land together."

"We are. Just you and me." Adam laughed. "My family can go fuck themselves. My mom can visit, though. She'd love llamas."

"I met her. Your mom. She brought me socks."

"Yeah?" Blinking, Adam sort of sat there for a moment, surprised. "Did you like her?"

"I did. She's like you. Or you're like her. She made me laugh."

"Oh, good." That seemed to make Adam happy.

"Do you look like your dad?"

"I do, yeah. Mostly."

Sage nodded. That's what he'd thought. Adam's mom was sure pretty, but she and her son looked nothing alike. Kind of made him happy that Adam didn't look like Angel.

Funny, but he rarely thought about Angel these days. His brain was full of life and Adam. He guessed that was how it was supposed to be when you were happy and getting on with your life, right?

God, he sure hoped so.

"What? You're grinning, babe."

"I'm happy. Don't tell anyone."

Adam shook his head, all solemn. "Not a soul."

"Thank you. I need to hold it tight."

"God, you make me happy."

How weird was it that all the things they never said, they were saying here, in a hospital room, of all places. Sage guessed they needed to be said after all that had happened.

"I miss Daddy, huh? Momma wants me to speak at the funeral, and I don't know what to say."

"That's tough." Adam balled up the wrappers from the food. "I mean, I didn't know what the hell to say when my dad went."

"Yeah, but you're smart and you thought it was hard and you were still mostly a kid."

"Stop that." A frown crossed Adam's face. "You're plenty smart. This is your dad, though, and he's gone."

"Yeah." And Sage couldn't stop thinking about whether it was a good thing or a bad thing. Daddy didn't want to fade away with the Parkinson's, but... Sage wasn't done needing him.

"Then it's going to suck." Adam's petted his arm, fingers moving in a figure eight.

"Funerals suck. All of them."

"No shit." They sat there for a long while, because what else could a man say about that?

He could feel himself blinking, nice and slow. Maybe it was the effort he'd put into walking, or the hot tub had done its job, but he was relaxing. It was probably Adam, though.

Whatever it was, he'd take it. He needed to rest. Maybe Adam would stay.

WIN WOKE up with the imprint of hospital sheets on his cheek, his mouth all pushed to one side. Crap, he'd fallen asleep right there, leaning on Sage's bed.

Sage's fingers were in his hair, his lover sleeping hard, snoring.

Thank God the man had finally gotten some rest. The real food had helped, he'd bet.

"You ought to get some real sleep, Son." His mom's voice was so soft. "I stopped in to check on Sage."

"Hey, Mom." He gently disengaged from Sage's grip and sat up all the way. "I hate to leave without telling him, and he's sleeping good."

"He is. He's looking better. He's got color today." She handed him a Coke.

"Thanks." He opened it up and let it burn him all the way down. No one brought him Coke, no one but his mom. "How's Mrs. Redding?"

"Sad. Crying a lot, but that's normal. She's grieving."

"Sure." He felt so damned bad for the whole lot of them. Rosie was pregnant and getting divorced. Ellen had lost damned near everything, and Sage was laid up and feeling helpless.

"She's a strong woman, though. She's going to move in with June, I think, try city living for a few months."

"No shit?" Well, that was good for Ellen. He hoped it was good for Rosie and Sage too.

"Yeah. That girl of hers is on the warpath, getting things done." Mom grinned. "Christ."

"Nesting, huh?" He grinned back before lowering his voice. "Are you getting flak from our side?"

"I haven't heard a fucking word, Son. Not a thing. I have to say, I expected to hear from the girls, at least."

"Huh." That was either really good or really bad.

"Yeah. I keep expecting to have the house blown up or something."

"Oh God." Win stared at his mom. "You don't think Teddy would…."

"If he does, I'll cut his balls off."

"Good on you." His mom was something else. "We're thinking of moving, Mom."

"Good. This is a shitty place for you and a worse place for him. This entire county is resting on a Good Ole Boys network, and it will strangle you both."

"Yeah." That wasn't going to change anywhere, but at least he wouldn't be related to them.

She shrugged. "What do you want me to say, Son? You are who you are."

"I know. I'm a little sick of being sorry for it too." She got it. She'd never been anything but his biggest fan.

"I bet. Wherever you go, there'd better be a guest room."

"Oh, that I can promise." Ellen would want to come too, if she went to city living. Sage's mom was a ranch lady.

"There will always be a place for moms at our house." Sage's voice was raw.

"Well, good deal, boys. How are you feeling, Sage?"

"I want to go home, ma'am. I'm worried about the horses."

"Well, you have a whole host of folks out there helping." Mom laughed. "I've never met so many bikers."

"They're good to me." Sage took a deep breath, wincing a bit. "I'm so tired of being in the bed, y'all."

"We have to get the physical therapy folks to sign off on you, babe." Not that Sage would be up and around a lot at home to begin with.

"I know. I'm ready. I'll cope and stuff, I swear."

"I know you will."

Win's mom nodded. "Of course you will. But you got to give your sister time to clean up."

"Sage is coming to my place, Mom."

"He is? Oh. Maybe I'll get someone to go clean up your place."

"Mom!" God. His ears got hot.

"What? You're a shitty housekeeper."

Sage snorted.

"I'm not dirty. Just…."

"Lazy." His mom and Sage said it at the same time.

"Oh, you both suck."

Wait. Wait, did he say that? They grinned at him, so he must have. Whoops.

Sage started chuckling; then the chuckles turned into full-out laughter. That was a damned fine look for his lover, and Win laughed right along with him. And Mom.

"Okay, boys. I'm off. I'll have someone deal with your house, Son."

"Thanks, Mom. You know, I did hire a girl."

"Uh-huh. What? Once?"

He guessed. Lord. At least it was one less thing he had to do.

Sage was still laughing at him. Fucker.

"You're fired," he said.

"Out of a cannon." Sage winked at him.

"If I thought it would get you home sooner, I so would." He patted Sage's hand, yawning.

"I know. You should go rest. I'm going to lay here like a worthless thing until someone lets me out."

"No, I'm good." He wasn't, though. He was exhausted.

"Bullshit. Go sleep. I'm fine." For a second, Sage sounded just like Sam.

Win chuckled, then stood and dropped a quick kiss on Sage's mouth. "I do need some sleep. I wanted to be here when you woke up."

"Thank you. I want to go home, sleep in your bed."

"God, I want that too." They would hide under the covers and hold on, watch movies, and eat popcorn.

"Maybe I'll be home tonight."

"I'll cross my fingers."

"Me too. Go sleep. I'll call you if something happens."

"Okay, babe." He lowered his voice. "Love you."

"I love you." Three little words again, simple as fuck. They made everything in his body stand up and take notice. Whoosh.

Sage loved him.

Sage loved him and they were going to find a place.

Damn.

Win walked out of that damned hospital feeling ten foot tall and as high as a mountain.

CHAPTER TWENTY-NINE

"I'M WALKING out of here, man, whether or not y'all get your heads out of your asses and sign me out." He'd had enough. Momma needed to put Daddy to rest, and she swore she'd not do it without Sage there. So, he was getting out of this place.

He'd done walked, he'd bent the things the doctor swore were still his knees. He'd pooped on his own, and he'd managed to hold down the shit they considered food. He was done.

"Mr. Redding, your insurance can deny your claim if you go against doctor's advice."

"My insurance? What fucking insurance, man? I'm a goddamn cowboy! They don't just come around in happy insurance trucks going, shit, you make no money, you work with petulant thousand-pound critters with teeth and hooves and tempers, let me help your hick ass out!"

The nurse stepped back, blinking rapidly, her mouth opening and closing. Hell, he figured she had to be in from some other town too, not to know he was also an ex-con. You didn't get dental with that once you were out.

"Really, Son? This woman's going to think you were raised in a barn without doors." Momma leaned against the doorframe. "I assure you—" She peered at the nametag. "—Stella. The barn had doors. Find Dr. Franks for me. Now."

"But...."

"Was there a syllable in the word 'now' you missed?"

Oh, yeah. Momma was ready too. She'd always hated hospitals, his momma.

The nurse hightailed it off, muttering.

Okay, that was fun.

"I brought you some clothes. Can you manage jeans, or do you want sweats?"

"I'll wear my jeans." He was a cowboy, damn it. "You bring my boots?"

"Oh, honey. No. There's no way. Look at your feet. You'll have to wear sneakers for a bit longer. Least 'til I can afford you some lace ups."

He stared at his momma, then down at his swollen feet. Damn it.

"He can wear slippers." Dr. Franks came in, looking him over critically. "Sweatpants, Sage. I want as little friction as possible on your dressings."

"Okay. Okay, I'll wear them. I swear."

"And you have to finish the antibiotics and keep your feet elevated. No riding. Not for eight more weeks."

"Eight weeks!" He was about to explode all over again.

"Yes. It's the holidays. Relax. Be with your family."

Like it could ever be the holidays again. That wasn't the Doc's fault, though, so he swallowed the words.

"You'll drive him, Ellen?"

"Of course I will." She nodded. "We'll take care of him."

"Well, then I'll sign you out. I expect to see you in four weeks for X-rays."

"Fine. I'll be here. Momma, give me my jeans."

"Sweats."

"Right." The big vein along his right temple was going to go. Bang.

"You want me to help?"

He gave her a look. "Go away, Momma."

"I'll be outside, baby." She gave him a wink and a smile and left the room.

He got the sweats over one foot, but not the other. Damn it. He was gonna fall right over, and he sighed, wanting to stamp his feet, which would be straight-on stupid.

"Momma?" He hadn't needed her help dressing since he'd been three.

The door opened, and it was Adam there. "Hey, man. I came to give you a key."

Oh, thank the good Lord. "I can't get my pants on."

"I can help with that, babe." Those fingers felt good on his sore legs.

"I'm coming home. That's okay, right?"

"Hell, yes. I can even take you. I mean, your mom is here, but she can come too, make sure you're settled." Adam's smile was like sunrise.

"That sounds good." He was so ready to get the fuck out of here.

"Well, come on, then." Adam knelt and got both his feet in his pants, working his legs gently.

With Adam's help, he was dressed, slippers to ball cap, feeling like he'd run a mile. Adam slung an arm around him and helped him to the wheelchair that waited for him.

"Thank you." He was sweating like a lathered horse.

"No problem, babe. They insist on the wheelchair."

"I don't hate it."

Adam laughed. "No, I guess not. They said we could buy one at the pharmacy down the way."

"I'll manage without. I will." He didn't have a dime. Not a single fucking dime. The Red Cross had got him some jeans, and he'd had his boots on during the storm at least.

"Hey." Adam turned to stare at him, their faces inches from one another. "We're in this together. If you need it, we'll get it."

"I'm scared that I'm never going to pull my half."

"Bullshit." Squeezing his ribs, Adam led him to the wheelchair. "You're the hardest working man I know. If it makes you uncomfortable depending on me to begin with, then we can sit and work out a plan. But not today."

"Not today." He eased down, his heart racing.

"That's it. Today we get you home, get you settled. I have to go back in after lunch, but I'll be there for supper. I can stop at Wilma's and get pie."

"Oh, I'd like that. Can…. Penny?" He felt like an ass asking about his dog.

"Oh heck, yes. Do you want me to get her on the way home too? Or should I ask…." Adam chuckled. "Uh. Have you talked to Rosie lately?"

"Rosie? No. No, why? She's okay, huh?"

"She's good. Really. She's just… I mean, I was going to ask if you wanted Chance to bring Penny over, and it occurred to me you might not know."

"Chance? The redhead mechanic? Friends with Bulldog?"

"Yeah. He's been out at the house. A lot." Adam began wheeling him out into the hall.

"Huh. He's a solid guy." Rosie? With a biker? Huh.

"He is. I mean, who knows? But I figured you ought to know. He's in it to win it."

"Lord have mercy." Still, the guys were decent, and he wasn't one to pass judgment. "I'll call up to the house and see if they'll bring me my pup."

"Okay. Then all I have to do is get supper. Ellen, are you staying for supper?"

"No, Son. I'm tired, and I'm going to go to my bed at June's and rest."

At some point in this whole thing they had, Adam had gone from Officer to Adam to Son.

"Well, if you need me to get anything, I can so do that." Adam was good to his momma. Sweet.

"I think I want a day of rest. Tomorrow I'm going to have to deal with things, and then the funeral will be the day after. I need to close my eyes."

"Then go and do that, Momma. Adam's got me."

"I do. He'll want to rest once I get him home." Adam went to hug Momma and kiss her cheek. "Mom says to call her and tell her when you want her and Auntie to come help with the food and all."

"I will. I love you, boys."

"Love you, Momma." God, he was tired.

Bone tired.

"See you later." Adam wheeled him out to the truck, and it was actually quieter in the parking lot.

He felt every bone in his body try and relax, just from being outside in the sun. Sage hadn't realized how much he'd missed it.

Adam chuckled. "Gonna have to set you and Penny up a cot on the porch, huh?"

"A place to bask." He looked at the truck and forced himself to move, to get himself up and in. His new knee wanted to go the right way. His old one wanted to go backward. He managed not to keel over, but only because Adam steadied him.

"The doctor says the other knee's going to be replaced at some point too, probably." Stupid thing.

"Well, you said the new one feels better, right?" They pulled out onto the main road, and Sage was a little surprised the world didn't implode or something.

"The new one feels amazing. To be honest, except for the tired, the knees don't grind like they had."

"Well, I'm glad." Adam glanced over. "Does that make me selfish?"

What? "I don't follow, Adam."

"To be tickled that something good came out of the last week."

"Don't we deserve something?"

"We do." One big hand settled on his leg, Adam's touch warm, easing the tension his stitches were pulling.

His eyes crossed. "God, that's the most wonderful thing."

"Really? We can do some heat tonight. My mom got me some of those bags that go in the microwave when I broke my elbow a few years back." Adam didn't rub or squeeze. He gave Sage all that warmth.

"Uh-huh." *Anything. Just stay right there.*

Adam did, all the way back to the little house he'd only seen the once. Shit, once had been enough to know he hoped Adam's momma had really sent someone to clean. Oh, Adam wasn't nasty at all. Just cluttered.

"Here it is. Home sweet home." Poor Adam sounded so damn nervous.

"It's great. Thank you for letting me stay."

"Well, we're throwing in our lot together, right?" Adam helped him inside.

"We are. I am. Yes." Adam had the most comfortable recliners in history. When Adam eased him down, he sighed, his muscles relaxing.

"I'm going to put the footrest up, babe. You want a Coke?"

"Please. A Dr Pepper, if you have one."

"You got it." Adam put Sage's feet up and got him a drink. "Here's the remote, baby. And the phone."

"Thank you." He found Adam a smile.

"You're welcome, babe. I have to get back to work, and I forgot to get you food. You want those cheese crackers?"

"That's fine. I'm just going to sit a bit. Go work."

"Okay." He got crackers, an apple, and a kiss. Adam was beaming, silly man.

"See you tonight, huh?" He was exhausted, all the way to the bone.

"Absolutely. And then I will bring food. I promise. Pie. And Penny."

"Good deal."

And it was. It wasn't great, but it was good, and it was his, and he couldn't ask for more than that.

CHAPTER THIRTY

THE OFFICE was jumping, the donation barrel for folks affected by the tornado almost full, the phones ringing off the damned hook thanks to an early-morning Amber alert. Win had about an hour of paperwork to do, and he kept getting called out for this or that, and it wasn't getting done.

He'd also put in three applications that morning, so he needed to talk to Jim about the reference calls he was fixin' to get.

Man, was he dreading that. He and Jim had an uneasy peace right now, which mainly meant they were talking through Grace's desk and text messages.

Sage was settling in at the house, mostly. It felt a little like having a houseguest, more than a live-in. All Sage's clothes were new from the Walmart, the man's toiletries were from the hospital. Hell, even Penny's dog bowls still had tags on them. Poor guy. Adam hurt for him every time he watched Sage pull out a too-stiff pair of jeans or hunt a movie that wasn't there anymore.

There was a tiny ball of rage, right in his belly, that wanted to explode, rail at God about how Sage had paid enough, damn it.

They needed to get through the funeral. He needed a new job. Everything was in flux. And there was Jim. "Hey. Got a minute?"

His uncle looked exhausted, old, and for a second Win thought the man would blow him off, but Jim just nodded. "Sure. Come on in. Is there any coffee, Grace?"

"You bet, Sheriff." Grace bustled around and got them coffee and a big plate of cookies.

"Such a mom," Win said, settling across the desk from his uncle.

"I keep saying I'm going to retire when she does."

"I can see that. She's the glue in this place." He straightened the seam on his pants.

"What is it you want, Win? Everyone's too busy to cause trouble."

Win raised his brows. "I'm not here to bitch, Jim. I need to tell you that I'm looking to get a job somewhere else. I hope you can give me a good recommendation."

"Where are you looking to go?"

"Down toward Fort Worth. Maybe out Stephenville way. I applied for the state too." Sage's parole officer had a judge willing to sign off on a move to anywhere in state. What did the old song say? Anywhere but Here?

Jim sighed softly. "You're one hell of a cop, man. One hell of a cop."

"Thanks, Jim. That means a lot." It did. He hated asking what he was about to ask, as tired as Jim looked. "Ellen Redding is moving too, but Rosie is taking over the farm. She needs…. Teddy needs to leave it be, Jim."

"I know. The man's just… he ain't right."

Win stared a moment, reading Jim's face. Then he nodded, relief sharp in his belly. "No, he's not."

"Losing a kid messes with folks. I ain't going to apologize for him. He's my brother."

Win tried not to grit his teeth. "I'm not asking that. I am worried that he's gotten dangerous, though. He attacked the Reddings in the hospital, you know? I know I haven't made it easy, getting involved, but this has to stop."

"Yeah. I know. I've spoken to him—about leaving both Redding women alone."

"Have you?" Not that Angel's dad would give up if he was that bad, but who knew? Jim was the law. It might work. "Thank you."

"I'm not a fucking monster. I got no beef against Mrs. Redding."

"I know." No, that was all reserved for Sage, who represented the shame in Angel's dirty little secret.

Sucked to have a meth-addicted homosexual slut in the woodpile. He snorted out a chuckle before he could stop himself.

Jim looked at him, eyebrow arched. "You know, you've always been a shit."

"I know. At least I didn't say what I was thinking out loud." He shrugged. "I appreciate all your help, Jim. I do. I know it's hard."

"I just want this fucking drama to cease. Tornados, beatings, hell, I found a fucking hydroponic tank deal at Cooter William's place." Jim was building up a head of steam, face red. The man was at the end of his rope.

"I hear you," Win said. "I'll be here at least a few more weeks, maybe a month. I'll still be helping with cleanup."

"I'll start looking around for a replacement too." Jim sighed. "You're going to take the Redding boy with you, aren't you?"

"I am. Does this get me uninvited to the Memorial Day picnic at the lake?" He had to tease. He'd had a good relationship with Jim once.

"Probably. I don't know how to explain that to folks." Jim looked him right in the eye. "All I got is my reputation, Win. What you and Sage are.... What do you want me to say? It ain't natural, to look on another man like you look at a woman. No amount of numbers is going to make that right, but if you don't flaunt it, no one will bitch. It's hard to not know about the Redding boy."

Right. Because Sage was a rainbow-waving prancing queen. Christ. Win shook his head, knowing that was how it was. He'd known that about his family from the time he was old enough to know he was queer at age fifteen. "We'll stay out of the way."

"I'll not stand in your way. Go on now, and get your paperwork done."

"Thanks, Jim." He stood and shook his uncle's hand, feeling like he'd just slammed a big old book closed.

There was some sadness, but not as much as he'd thought. He had his momma, Ellen, Rosie. Hell, he had Sage. Penny. How long had it been since he'd had a dog?

He found himself walking past his desk, heading out to his truck, thoughts swirling like mad in his brain. He had his radio. If they needed him, Grace would put a call in.

Win headed home, where Sage was waiting, where their dog was. He wanted to see Sage's face, make sure the man was eating.

Get a hug and some silent reassurance that….

He turned the corner onto his road and immediately started growling. Sage was taking out the trash. Limping like crazy. The damned doctor had said no physical labor. None. Not some.

Not a little.

None.

Zero.

Zilch.

He pulled up and hopped out of the truck, about to tease that Sage was under arrest for not following doctor's orders. Good thing he opened his mouth after he thought that might be a shitty joke.

Sage looked over at him and smiled. "Adam! I saw your neighbors had their cans out."

"Well, thanks, babe. You shouldn't be out working. Doc said." He walked over and grabbed Sage's hand.

"I wanted to make sure they were out. Are you home for lunch or the day?" Sage looked a little hysterical at the edges.

"I told Jim I was looking for another job. I think he's happy to give me a day. I have my radio."

"Oh, good. I didn't know what to do in there by myself."

"No?" He let Sage lean on him, the warm weight of his pocket cowboy perfect.

"No. I hate being useless and I kept thinking."

"Thinking is dangerous, babe."

"No shit on that." There was a book on the little table beside the chair and a cup of coffee. Someone was bored out of his mind.

Not that Win could blame him. "You want to watch a movie, babe? Something else?" He scratched Penny's ears. "Go for a ride?"

"Can we just go, Adam? Just somewhere not this goddamn town for a cup of coffee and a burger?"

"You know we can, baby. Let me change." He'd go in civvies.

"Okay. Thank you." Sage was holding onto his shit with both hands, Win could tell. Barely. Like clinging with his nails.

"Hey, you're not used to being cooped up, huh?" Well, he guessed Sage knew all about cooped up, and that was the problem.

"I don't feel trapped. I just don't know what to do." Sage shrugged. "My schedule's blown to shit."

"Well, yeah. I don't have a lot to feed." He winked, heading for the bedroom, which was neat as a pin. "Babe? My jeans were on the floor."

"I washed them. They're in the closet."

Washed. Dried. Starched and pressed. Like George Strait. Lord.

"Well, then I ought to wear my boots." He laughed, thinking how his mom had tried to get him into this look for years.

"I like the way the boots make your butt look."

His cheeks heated, his pleasure at the way Sage looked at him making him worried his jeans wouldn't fit.

"You know, babe, washing and ironing jeans is work."

"Hmm?" Sage looked about as innocent as he could, which, really, was not very.

"Just be careful, huh? You're important."

Sage beamed for him, at him. God, Sage was like a parched desert when it came to affection. Good thing Win had a lot of it to spare.

"How do I look?" Win asked.

"Like I wish my knees were better so I could show you how good you look."

"Oh." That was.... Sage could knock him over with a feather sometimes.

He got a grin and a wink. "My jeans aren't going to look as good. They're baggy."

"I'll give in on the jeans if you forgo the boots, babe."

"I have tennis shoes. I don't think my feet fit in my boots yet."

"Cool." They got all dressed, and he took one more kiss. "Ready to go?"

"I am. Penny's got water."

"Good deal." He stayed close to Sage, not wanting those knees to give out.

Sage got to the truck, climbed up carefully, face paling some.

Win kept his mouth shut for the moment, but he was watching carefully. If it got bad, they'd eat in the truck or something.

Sage settled and sighed softly. "I think they're getting better."

"Absolutely. You're moving a lot easier." It was true, even if he worried.

"Yeah? You can tell?"

"I can. You're limping a lot less, and you're more sure your feet are under you."

"You'll be there tomorrow, right? All day?" The question came out of the blue.

The funeral. That had to be weighing on Sage's mind. "Yeah. I will. I got the day off already."

"I want to go out to the ranch in the morning before everybody heads there after the funeral. I haven't seen it, and I don't want to be shocked in front of people."

"Okay, babe." Shit. He hadn't even thought about that. Tonight wasn't the time, though.

"Thank you." Sage reached out, fingers brushing his thigh. "Drive, Adam. Let's go let the wind blow."

He nodded, rolling the windows down in the cab. Anything to make Sage smile like that. "You got it."

Like the song said, the road was made for people like them.

CHAPTER THIRTY-ONE

SAGE SAT on the edge of the bed in a pair of new jeans, the new black jacket on his aching knees. He'd forced his swollen feet in his boots, and he kept swallowing past a lump in his throat that wouldn't go away.

He wasn't sure if he was more dreading the funeral or going home. He'd never had home be where Daddy wasn't, and he wasn't sure he could face it. He wasn't sure he could see the house, broken and different, see the front porch and know that it was there—right there— where his daddy had been home for the last time.

No wonder Momma had said she was going to stay over to June's.

Adam poked his head into the bedroom, hair still wet and combed back ruthlessly. "Babe?"

"Yeah?"

"You okay?" Adam came in and sat next to him. Adam had already talked to the sheriff about not wearing his uniform.

"I will be. Probably. My boots don't fit no more." *And my daddy is gone, and I have to stand up in front of people that hate me like it don't matter.*

"They'll fit again. Mine are bigger, if you want to try them." Adam knew, right? He'd lost his dad.

"I think if you pull them off, I'll hit you. I got them on." They were never coming off.

"We'll have to put your feet in the freezer to get them off."

"There's another blue norther coming. Been a cold bitch of a fall. I'll just sit outside." *Please, God. Let it be tomorrow soon.*

"You'll do no such thing." Adam reached out and hugged him.

"I'm glad you'll be there." What else could he say?

"I'm sorry you have to do this at all." That warm body all along his side felt good. Right.

"God, me too, but I don't reckon we have a choice."

"Nope. You need to be there for your mom. Everyone else can take a flying leap."

"Okay. I guess we should go to the ranch so I can see."

"Yeah." Adam stood and helped him up. "Rosie's had the crew working night and day."

"Yeah. I should be there helping." He just… hadn't.

"Rosie would have made you sit and drink iced tea."

Sage chuckled. Rosie was getting her bossy on these days. "Rosie's so swollen everyone's being nice."

"Could be." Adam widened his eyes comically. "She is like a house."

"Uh-huh. We're going to be uncles, and Momma's betting on twins."

"Twins?" Adam blinked. "Oh, man."

"Rosie says no, but Momma's… Momma."

"Moms know." Adam reached out and hugged him. "Come on, babe."

"Yeah." He forced himself to walk to the truck without limping or mincing. It took some damned hard effort too.

It was still easier than looking at his parents' house when Adam pulled up.

Oh God.

It was standing—hell, it looked good. But it wasn't home.

The porch was gone, the paint was different, the windows in the front were different. One of the barns and his trailer were gone. Just gone.

Sage sat there, staring, his brain trying to understand what was breaking his heart.

Rosie came out to stand on the step, staring at him, her eyes looking almost bruised. She would know. Understand.

"Hey." He didn't reach for her, because he didn't have an ounce of comfort to spare, not even for her.

"Hi." She offered a ghost of a smile. "Momma's here."

"Okay." He made himself walk to the house, made himself do this because he was a grown man and his family needed him. "How are the horses?"

"Good. Only Wednesday got any real injuries, and that was splinters. She's all patched up."

"I should go see them." Anything rather than going inside.

"Take Adam. There's still a lot to clean up."

"Yeah. You and Momma need me to do anything?"

"Go see your fucking horses, Bubba. Adam, I swear to God, I will unman you if you let him so much as touch the tack." Rosie rubbed the small of her back. "Chance? Can you make coffee, baby?"

Baby? Huh.

"Sure." Bulldog's mechanic friend waved from right inside the screen door.

Go Rosie.

"Hey, Sage. I…. Hey."

"Yeah, go make coffee before you get hurt."

Chance disappeared, and Adam came to take his arm. "They have the horses temporarily in the old lean-to, babe."

"I…." He walked out, eyes taking everything in, everything that was different, broken. God, he needed to ride fence and….

The horses saw him and went wild, calling for him, kicking and stamping and tossing their heads, telling him that things were wrong and they didn't like it.

He left Adam behind, galumphing out, feet like dead things at the ends of his legs. "I know. I know, I'm sorry. Oh, guys. I've missed you."

Warm, soft noses poked at him, the big bodies and horsey smell comforting.

He stroked and petted, muttering as they surrounded him. If his cheeks were wet and his shoulders shook, they weren't going to tell on him.

Neither was Adam, who hung back and let him have this time.

When he backed off, his white shirt wasn't pristine, but his jacket would cover that. "It's going to peak at some point, right?"

"What's that, babe? The grief? Yeah. It will be like a fucking tidal wave, and then you'll rebuild."

"Okay." He had to believe that. He had to.

"I'm here when you need me, huh?" Adam came to him and slid an arm around him. "I'm so sorry, baby."

"Don't be. Not now. Not here. After, when we're home. Then."

"Anything you need, babe." Adam squeezed. "I know you don't want to go in there, but you need to sit."

He opened his mouth to argue, but what was he going to say? He was scared? Fuck that. He was Sam Redding's boy. He'd missed a lot of his Daddy's life in prison. He wouldn't miss this.

"Let's go." He just needed to get through this day. That was all.

CHAPTER THIRTY-TWO

THE LAST distant cowboy cousin left the Reddings' house, and Win let out a sigh of relief. That just left Rosie and her new man, Bulldog and Wilma, June and the two moms.

Win glanced at Sage, who doggedly washed dishes, face set and pale, the deep lines of pain etched hard in his face.

"You need to get him home and lying down, Son," his mom said, coming to hug his neck.

"I do." He hugged her tight, so ready for all this to be over.

Sage had been fine at the funeral, quiet and sure, walking up to the podium and looking out over the crowd, simply saying, "Sam Redding was my daddy and I loved him, and he loved me, no matter what." It had damn near broke his heart.

Rosie sang. Ellen cried. Jim had showed up to pay his respects. Sage's cousins from over near Will's Point had lead Sam's favorite horse at the head of the procession, empty boots tucked into the stirrups, cowboy style.

"I'll take Ellen back. June says she'll take the flowers no one wants to the hospital and get some groceries so they don't have to go out for a few days."

"Oh, good." He glanced around, lowering his voice. "Do you think I need to worry about Teddy? He didn't show up, but I want to make sure he doesn't bother Rosie."

"Ain't no one bothering my girl." Chance's voice was rough as a cob, pale eyes meeting his. "No offense, ma'am, but I promised her I'd keep her and her land safe, and she said she believed me."

Adam had gotten to like Chance today. The big mechanic seemed solid, over the moon for Rosie.

His mom laughed. "No offense taken, Chance. The family has threatened to have him committed."

"Now that would be entertaining." Win liked that idea.

"Adam? I'm sorry, but… I'm worried about Sage. He needs his pills, rest. He needs you to take him home, please." Ellen looked like she'd aged thirty years in two weeks.

He went to her and kissed her cheek. "You make sure you eat some supper, huh?" They had plenty of casseroles and salads, but he knew Ellen had just picked at stuff. "I'll get him now."

"Good boy." She hugged him tight. "Love you, Son."

Sage was heading out onto the back porch, with a bag of dog food in hand. "Come on, guys. I got kibbles."

The barn dogs came running and barking, wagging up a storm.

"Hey, babe, let me do that. You give scritches." They'd feed and then head out.

Sage looked over at him, and those poor eyes looked bruised. "Yeah?"

"Yep. Your mom is heading out with mine, and Chance has Rosie in his sights. We do this and we can go."

"Sure." Sage's hands were shaking some as the dog food was passed over.

Adam pressed his lips together. This was no time to berate the man, but they'd talk about stubborn later.

Stubborn, prideful, vain cowboys.

It didn't take him thirty seconds to feed the dogs and get Sage to the truck. His lover stood there, staring, the man still.

"Come on, babe. You need to get in." He would help Sage bend if need be.

"I don't think I can, Adam." Sage sounded… shocked. Like someone had wounded him.

"Okay. We'll put you in the backseat with your legs straight out." Thank God for king cabs.

"I'm sorry." Sage looked at him, eyes purely panicked. "I think… I could sleep on the porch."

"No. No, we need to get you home. We'll get you in the shower to steam and then get iced." He opened both truck doors in the back. "Here. I'll get your butt up and then pull you from the other side."

By the time he got Sage in, the man was the color of milk, but was laughing at them. That had to be good, right?

"You got it, babe?" He shut one door, then the other before hopping up to drive.

"I feel like an idiot, but I appreciate the help."

"Everyone overdid a little." Ellen had seemed almost transparent by the end, and Rosie hadn't been able to stop crying.

"Yeah." Sage was so quiet, so still.

"Long day. Did you eat? Did you want to order pizza or something?"

"I want french fries and a milkshake. Can we do that? I.... Shit, I don't have a fucking dime to my name, man."

"We can do that, babe." That would be so much easier than trying to cook.

A quick stop at the Dairy Mart and they'd be set. Onion rings, burgers, shakes, and fries. Something so Sage could take his pills. Adam smiled at the girl in the window. "Hey, Annette."

"Win. What can I get you?" She looked back at Sage. "Sorry about your daddy, Sage. How you holding up?"

"I'm good. Long day."

"I bet. What can I get you?" She grinned, the expression sympathetic.

"Two double cheeseburgers, two fries, two onion rings, two cherry fried pies, a strawberry milkshake and a Dr Pepper the size of my head."

"No problem, Win."

Sage met his eyes in the rearview mirror. "We having company?"

"Nope. We're hungry. You have a hollow leg. Once you get a pill in you, you'll eat." It took a shocking amount of food to keep that little body going.

Sage chuckled, the sound rusty, like an old hinge. "I could eat I guess."

"Uh-huh. You can. You're good at it."

That got him another laugh, this one a little easier. He passed the shake back when Annette handed it over.

"Thank you." Sage took it, sucked on the straw, the sound oddly comforting.

"No problem, babe." He took the rest of the food, ready to get home.

"No charge, Win. Sage. Y'all have a good night."

"Thanks, Annette. So much."

He let Sage nod his thanks, but left before the man could protest.

"Smells good."

It did—greasy and spicy and salty. His stomach rumbled, his mouth watering. Man, he was starving all of a sudden. Good thing home was close.

He pulled into his driveway and hopped out to help Sage out of the truck. Each step looked like pure hell, but his cowboy never even grunted. They got settled, got Sage a pill, got Penny out and in.

Then, finally, they could eat. He'd get food in his cowboy, then get after Sage's boots.

"You want me to get some ice for your legs? Might help get those boots off."

"I'm scared to try, to be honest."

"Well, let's ice and eat and let those pills kick in." He got two bags of frozen peas and set out the food, shooing Penny away.

Sage ate, not as good as he'd hoped, but better than he'd feared, munching on french fries and nibbling on the burger. Hell, he even got a few onion rings into the man. Win devoured the rest, feeling bloated as hell, but a little calmer.

Ready to tackle the boots.

Sage didn't say anything, just watched him like a kid watched a dentist or a clown. Wary and exhausted, poor Sage couldn't even tense up when he pulled one off in a rush.

"Oh fuck. Do the other. Hurry, love. Please."

"I got you." Like ripping a Band-Aid, he pulled the other one off, *whoosh*.

Sage leaned back, panting hard, fingers curled in tight fists. Okay. Okay, the worst part was done. He could cut the socks and jeans off if he had to. Sage would fuss, saying they were the only ones he had, but Win could get more.

"You good, babe?"

"I don't know." Sage chuckled, and it sounded forced. "I'm scared to wiggle my toes."

"You want me to?" He pulled off those heavy socks and made sure there was color in Sage's toes.

They were blistered and raw, swollen, and Win helped Sage take his jeans off before propping those poor raw legs up. The man's knees looked better than he'd feared they would, although Sage was going to have to take it easy tomorrow.

"I got an idea, babe." He had some amazing oil that his mom had gotten him for when he had to stand all day doing crowd control. It felt amazing on blisters. He grabbed it from the bathroom and washed and dried Sage's poor feet. Then he rubbed.

"Adam. Adam, oh God." Sage's head fell back, throat working. Poor baby. Those feet flexed, muscles jumping. "Tell me today is over. That I never have to have today again."

"Never, babe. This is a one-time deal." That he could promise. They would outlive other family members for sure, but there was no way there would ever be this sequence of events.

"Every single thing I have hurts."

"You look worn to death." Win chuckled. "I'm not trying to put you down, I'm just worried."

"I am too." Those pretty eyes met his. "Can I ask you a favor?"

"Sure, babe. What do you need?"

"Hold me a minute?" He knew how hard it was for Sage to ask.

"Of course." Damn, he should have set Sage up on the couch instead of the recliner. Of course, they could both fit in the chair. He just lifted Sage right up and slid in beneath.

Sage rested down on him, trusting him to hold on. He did, happy he couldn't hurt anything on the top half of Sage's body. Sage rested hard, lips on his throat, breath warm.

Being still, there together, felt good. Peaceful. Like maybe the tide could turn in their direction.

"Promise me tomorrow I don't have to see anyone but you."

"You got it. Chicken soup and movies." Maybe cookies.

"Thank you." Sage sighed softly, the sound exhausted, sad.

He kissed Sage's ear. "You're welcome, babe. We'll get past today."

"I know. I just need this for a while."

"Then you got it." They didn't even turn on the TV. They sat there together, their hearts thumping in rhythm.

They'd made it to here. They'd figure the rest of the stuff out tomorrow.

His Sage had paid his dues—to society, to God, to Win's fucking family. It was time to let that shit go.

It was time to just be them. Together.

CHAPTER THIRTY-THREE

SAGE STARED at his boots, and he felt a hell of a lot like they were staring back.

Two weeks at Adam's house, and he still couldn't quite get them on. He shouldn't complain, he knew, because his knees were healing good. Hell, he had to admit, they both felt better than he could remember, and he even managed to get up on the roof of the barn over at the ranch for about ten seconds before Adam had lost his shit.

He grinned. That had been fucking fun.

The insurance money was in, and he needed to go find him a work truck, a horse trailer for him and for Sister both. He had shit to do.

And those fucking boots sat there, looking at him. Daring him to try again.

A knocking at the door distracted him, and he moved to open it up and came eye to eye with a barrel of a gun.

Well, damn.

"I'm not letting you get away with it, Redding."

Sage met Teddy and his .32 straight up, refusing to panic. He didn't have so much as an ounce of scared left in him. "I ain't never got away with anything, man. Not then, not now. I done paid."

He hadn't killed Angel. Sure, he'd been there. Sure, he'd been stupid, but he hadn't set the fire, he hadn't made Angel use drugs or fuck around or choose to stay. He didn't have nothing left in all the world but Adam Winchester and his pride, and he wasn't giving either one of them away.

"You took my boy!" Teddy Dale's cheeks were crimson, his mouth an ugly line. Adam didn't look a thing like this man, thank the Lord.

"No, sir. That was meth and fire and God. I wasn't in that house that night. I was sleeping in my truck, hoping he'd come home with me in the morning." And even if he was to blame, he'd done his time. Every second.

Teddy went to hit him in the face with the pistol, and Sage lifted his arm, letting the blow glance off. The old man didn't have a lot left in him, and if hitting on Sage helped, it was better than getting shot at. Sage didn't have to worry about his momma this time either.

"I hate you!" Teddy was sobbing, spit flying from his mouth.

"I know." Everybody needed someone to blame. It was the way of shit. Too bad for this old man that Sage wasn't about to be a whipping boy no more. "If you're gonna shoot me, you ought to know Adam is home. He'll hear it."

"You're going to destroy his life too!"

Oh, he doubted it. Shit, if nothing else, Sage was going to save the man thousands in maid service. A neatnik his Adam was not. He actually smiled, which made Teddy Dale take a bead on him again.

"Now, Uncle, that would be a real bad idea." The sound of a rifle cocking shot through the front room.

Sage nodded. "Just go home, man. Angel's gone, been gone a long time. He's probably loving Heaven. God knew the man liked to fly."

"I—you." The gun swung wildly, first pointed at him, then Adam. "No. No. You have to pay." The man wasn't in there. He was gone, his eyes wild and vacant.

"I called Jim, Teddy. He's going to come arrest you. Just go," Adam said.

Sage sighed, stepped forward, and took the pistol, jerking it right out of the old man's hands before handing it to Adam. "I'm not supposed to be in possession of one of them."

It violated his parole.

Adam blinked, then grinned a little. "Good thing I'm an officer of the law." Then Adam carefully took the gun and the rifle to lock them away.

Teddy had crumpled like a ball of newspaper, collapsing on the porch. Sage wondered if the man had ever been scary, or if it had been his own guilt and fear making it so.

Sage stood there for a second, watching. He didn't have nothing to say. Not a thing.

Then he turned around and closed the front door, locked it, and went back to the kitchen and his boots. He needed to pour another cup of coffee.

"You okay, babe?" Adam was right there, hand on his shoulder.

Sage could hear the sirens coming.

"I am. You want a cup of coffee?" He wasn't even being stubborn. He was doing all right.

"I do." Adam sat at the kitchen table, where all the paper in the world had resided until last week.

Sage could hear jabbering outside, and he poured them both a cup before the doorbell rang. "I'm gonna let you get that, love."

"Yeah. We can have some pie after." Wilma had brought some by earlier. Adam left the room, and it was Sage and his boots again.

Maybe he'd just try them tomorrow. He stood up, headed for the fridge, and pulled out the pumpkin pie, then served up two pieces. Smelled good. He had a can of cream to spray on top. He heard the sheriff, but closed it out.

He hadn't done a thing wrong, hadn't hit no one, hadn't hurt a soul. He didn't have anything to be scared of. It did seem like it took a while before Adam came back and slid into a kitchen chair.

"Pie?" He slid the plate over.

"Looks amazing." Adam glanced at him, lashes half shielding his eyes. "I didn't press charges. Jim's taking him in, anyway. Teddy needs help."

"Yeah. You... you pissed at me?" He didn't think so, but he reckoned he ought to ask.

"No." Adam met his eyes head on, smiling huge. "I'm damned proud of you, baby."

He sat and handed over the spray cream. "I just... I did my time. I followed the rules. I paid. Now I get you."

"You do. Every bit of me."

Now, that was promising.

"I can handle that, Officer. I like all the bits of you."

"That's a fine thing." Adam glanced at his boots. "How are your feet, babe?"

"I'm thinking tomorrow. Tomorrow, I'll be a cowboy again."

"Mmm. My pocket cowboy. You can be a schlep today if you want."

"I might at that. I organized your movies. You got a bunch I ain't seen." He offered Adam a smile. "Feel like having a sit on the sofa?"

"You're gonna have us ready to move in no time, huh?" Adam bounced. "I love it. Let's watch movies and eat a whole pie and a big bowl of popcorn."

"Got to be ready to find our land, once you decide where you're gonna be the law." Then he'd let his parole officer know where they were landing. Where they were going to make their home and let the horses run.

"I have two interviews next week. Jim kinda put me on a paid leave of absence. That ought to give us time to look where I might be working."

"I'm all over that." He put the plates in the sink and refilled their coffee. "I'll ride out with you, look at land."

Sage passed Adam, and one of Adam's warm hands cupped his ass, patted. "Sounds perfect."

He nodded. It did.

It sounded like a plan.

For the first time in his life, he had a plan worth fighting for. Something to keep.

Sage was just grateful he'd met the good Lord's terms of release.

BA Tortuga spends her days with her basset hounds, getting tattooed, texting her sisters, and eating Mexican food. When she's not doing that, she's writing. Texan to the bone and an unrepentant Daddy's Girl, she spends her days off watching rodeo, knitting, and surfing porn sites in the name of research. BA's personal saviors include her fiancée, Julia Talbot; her best friend, Sean Michael; and coffee. Lots of coffee. Really good coffee.

Having written everything from fistfighting rednecks to hardcore cowboys to werewolves, BA does her damnedest to tell the stories of her heart, which was raised in Northeast Texas but is madly in love with the stories the high desert mountains tell her. With books ranging from hard-hitting GLBT romance to fiery menages to the most traditional of love stories, BA refuses to be pigeonholed by anyone but the voices in her head.

http://www.batortuga.com

http://batortuga.blogspot.com

https://www.facebook.com/batortuga

@batortuga on Twitter

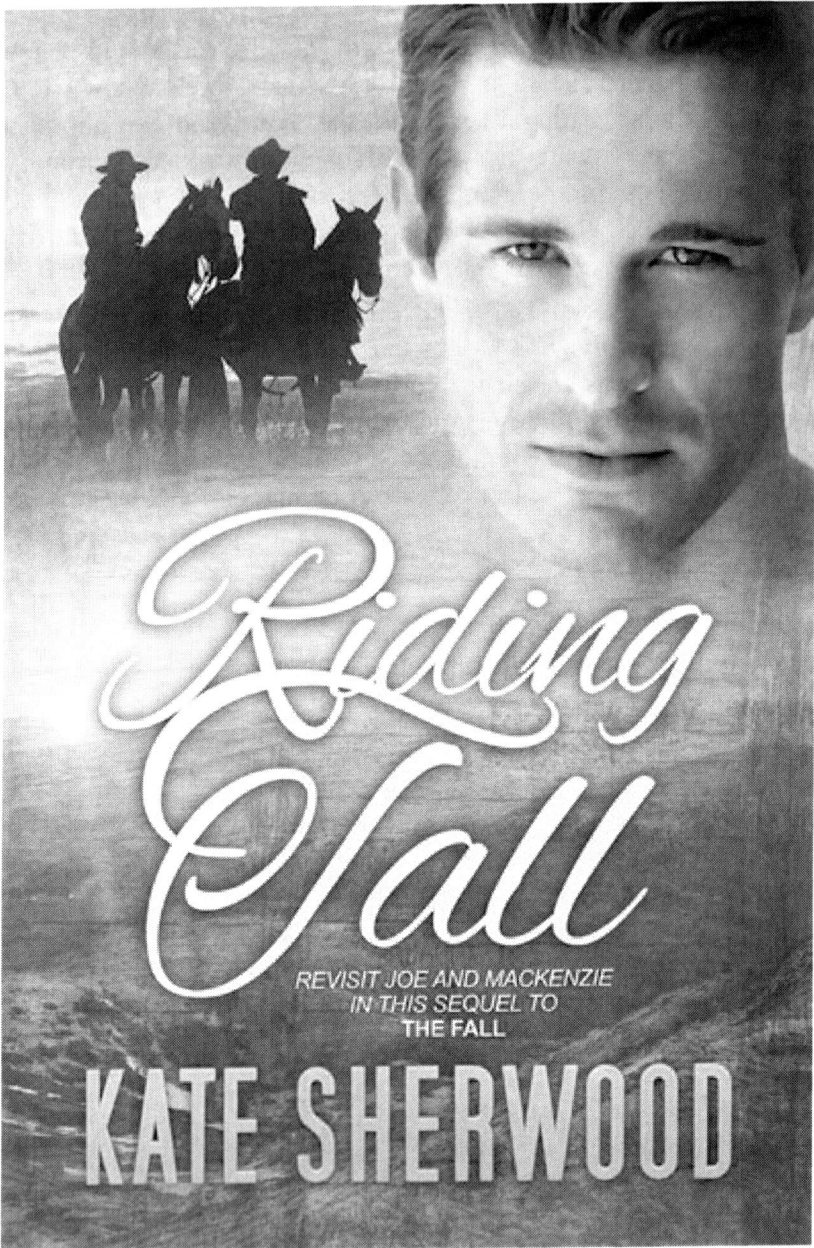

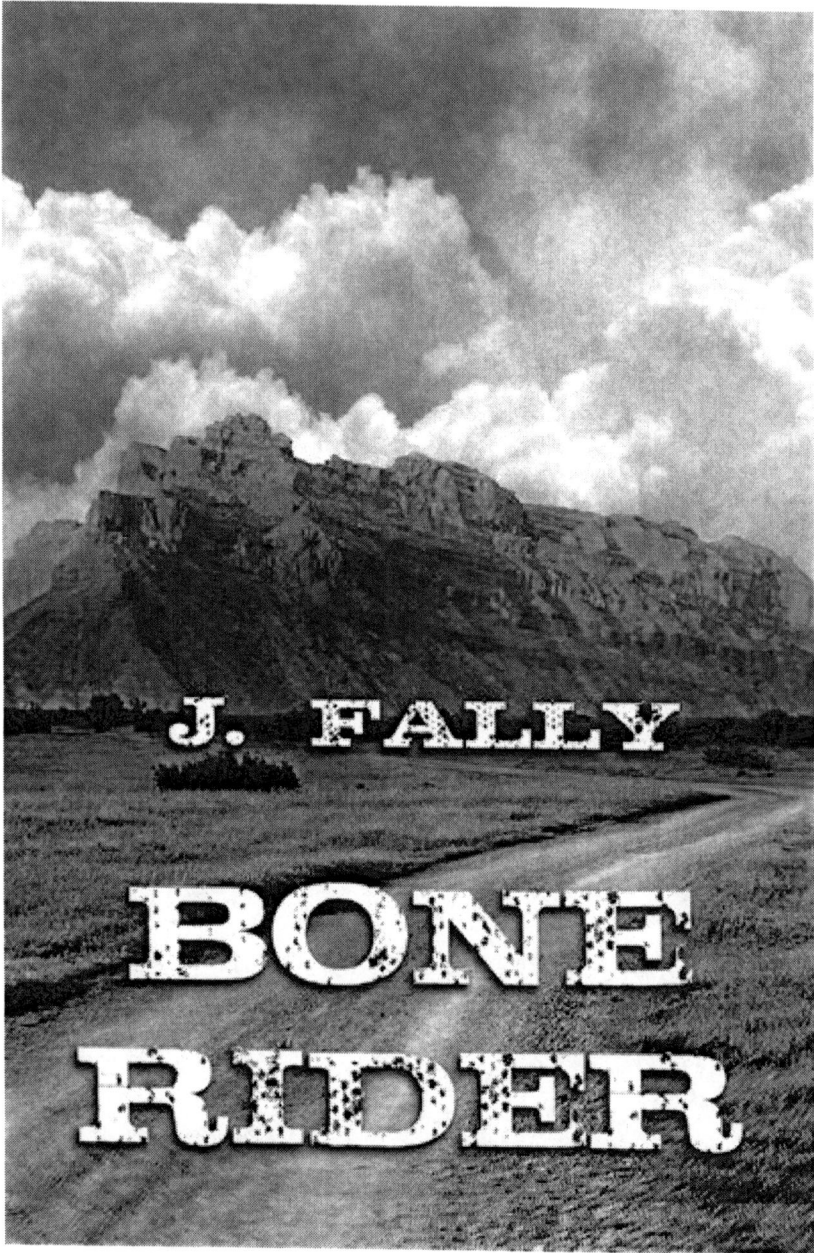

Also from DREAMSPINNER PRESS

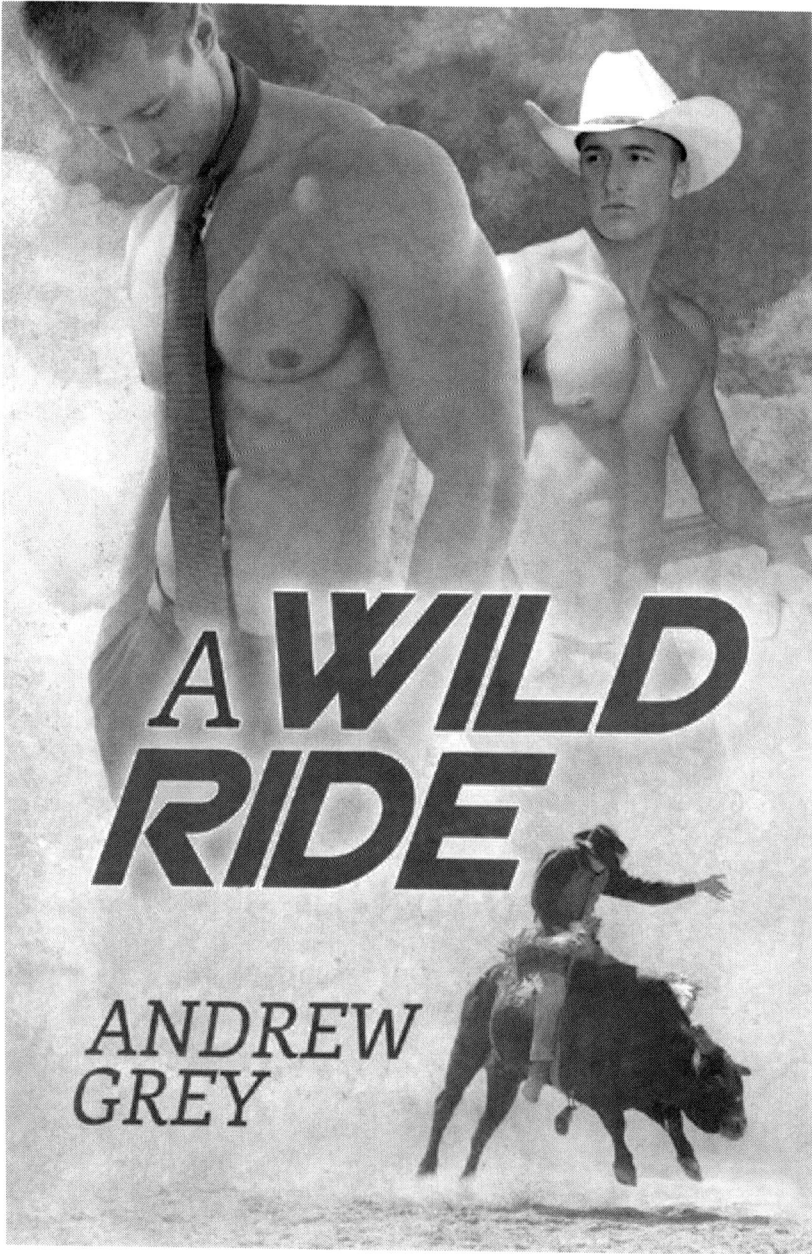

A WILD RIDE

ANDREW GREY

http://www.dreamspinnerpress.com

CPSIA information can be obtained at www.ICGtesting.com
Printed in the USA
LVOW12s0705040514

384258LV00007B/35/P